Secrets of the Gros Ventre

John Hansen

DEDICATION

To my parents, Dale and Joan Hansen. From an early age, they encouraged my ambition to write.

FOREWORD

According to the internet, there are a couple of ways to pronounce Gros Ventre. Having grown up in the West I'd always heard it pronounced as GRO - VANT, which seems to roll of one's tongue fairly easily.

CHAPTER ONE

When it was brand new, the big billboard at the edge of town had clearly read: WELCOME TO FREMONT – FRIENDLIEST LITTLE TOWN UNDER THE BIG SKY. But now its tattered strips of colorful paper were fluttering gently in the wind, causing the person who truly wanted to read the sign to slow way down, probably under the 35 miles per hour speed limit. But, since I had grown up in the area and knew exactly what the sign said, I paid it little attention. Up ahead was the official sign put up by the Montana Highway Department. It made no boast of the inhabitants being friendly, just the facts: Entering Fremont – Pop. 1,204. I had just taken my foot off the gas pedal of my county owned pickup when a somewhat shaky, but authoritative voice, sounded from the metal box bolted to the underside of my dashboard.

"Base to Car 604, come in."

I smiled as I reached for the mic. Grace Brown, our secretary and dispatcher didn't have so many options to call on the radio that we couldn't use our names. At least to my way of thinking there wasn't. There was me and the Sheriff and two city cops. The volunteer fire department didn't have radios and the highway patrol were on another frequency. I seldom ever talked to them. For the first sixteen months of my employment as Deputy Sheriff for Gros Ventre County I had appeased Grace. Lately, however, I had become less formal. I came back, "Grace, this is Andy, go ahead."

For a moment the radio was silent due to, I assumed, Grace collecting herself to say what it was she had to say. In the interim, I shifted my Ford pickup down to third gear and coasted over the railroad tracks causing it to shudder vigorously. And then the radio crackled again.

"Andy, Herman Schultz called a little bit ago. He said Ezra Coggins beat up his son, Bernie, last night. Says he wants Coggins thrown in jail."

Having spent the first fourteen years of my life in the Gros Ventre river valley, I knew, or strongly suspected, that Bernie may have been deserving of a beating. I keyed the mic. "Did Herman say what this was all about?"

"He said Bernie drove past the Coggins place last night on his way home and the Coggins' dog chased his car. He said the next thing his son knew Coggins was chasing after him in his pickup and flashing his lights and honking his horn so his son pulled over and then Coggins supposedly jerked him out of his car and started beating him."

"Why Grace? Why was he beatin' Bernie?"

"He claimed Bernie hit his dog but Mr. Schultz said the dog is just fine. He said too that Coggins won't be just fine if the law doesn't come out there today and arrest him."

"Okay, Grace. I gotta gas up and then I'll head that way."

The radio went quiet, as if Grace had been distracted. Up ahead was the Texaco. I had just turned into it when Grace responded. "Tom says you're to be real careful how you handle these men. He says they're hotheads and –"

In the background Sheriff Tom Woods could be heard shouting, "Dammit, Grace, you can't say that over the radio." The radio went silent again but, in my mind, I could see and hear what was likely going on. The Sheriff was now apologizing to Grace who had probably teared up, but at the same time he was explaining to her why you couldn't say such things on the radio. The reason being, there were people like seventeen year old Jeremy Royer who was standing next to the gas pump and a few feet from my open window. His usual greeting of, *filler up*, was replaced by, "So, who are these hotheads yer after, Andy?"

I looked at Jeremy in his greasy Texaco shirt with his shiny black-billed Texaco cap and was about to tell him that it was police business when Grace threw a little more gas on the fire. "You just be careful, Andy. Tom says situations like this can go south in a hurry. Base clear."

"Alright, Grace, I will. Andy clear."

I was still in the process of trying to fit the mic onto its little slotted holder on the dash when Jeremy's voice penetrated my left ear. "So, who ya after?"

I glanced over at his whiskerless babyface. His blue eyes were expectant, like if only I would divulge the details of my radio call, he would be rescued, at least temporarily, from the monotony of pumping gas and fixing flats. But I did not oblige him. "Can't tell ya Jeremy. Police business."

"Ah, c'mon. I bet if Mitch was here, you'd tell him."

Mitch Royer was Jeremy's older brother. He and I were good friends and in the same class. With no money to go to college, and the job situation being what it was, he had joined the Army about a year after we graduated. Now, he was somewhere in the Pacific fighting the Japs. I, on the other hand, had been lucky enough to spend three summers fighting fire for the forest service and the winters helping a rancher feed and calve out his cows. It pained me to leave both those jobs but when I turned 21 and the deputy sheriff job came open, I applied. Being a lawman was something that I had always wanted to do. With a grin, I said to Jeremy, "Yer right. I probably would tell Mitch what that radio call was about cuz I know he'd keep it to himself."

Jeremy came back quick. "Well, so would I."

I laughed. "How 'bout you just filler up and put it on the county's tab? I got to be goin'."

The narrow highway, which had more than its share of pot holes, ran through rolling hills that were sporadically covered with timber and pasture and crops of hay and grain. It was 20 miles to Cedarville, which was also home to me courtesy of the county. I lived in a one room cabin with a tiny yard surrounded by a woven wire fence stapled to wooden posts that had turned gray a long time ago. Several big ponderosa pine trees, that were probably a lot smaller when the cabin was built, stood to the east of it, just outside the fence. The pavement, or the *oil* as the locals called it, ended at the north end of Cedarville right next to where I lived. Main Street, which was also the beginning of County Road 29, was about a quarter of a mile long. I shifted my black Ford pickup down to third gear and idled along at about 20 mph. To my left was an old gray cinderblock building with dirty fly-specked windows. A solitary gas pump stood out front. The drabness of the building was offset somewhat by several tin signs that had been nailed to the front of it. Among the goods being promoted were Phillip Morris cigarettes, Shasta soda pop and Bardahl. To the left of the normal sized door was a garage door, both stood open. A wooden sign in bold black letters hung above the bigger door, it read:

FLATS FIXED HERE. The building had a flat roof, which made no sense in snow country. I rolled on past the neat and tidy white brick general store on the right side of the street and the less presentable Antler Bar on my left and then, a short way beyond it was a log building that reflected some semblance of care. It housed the Lumberjack Café in one end and in the other, where the American flag was flying out front, was the post office whose lobby was not much bigger than a good-sized double-hole outhouse. And then finally, at the north edge of town was a white clapboard building that served as the Cedarville elementary school. When classes were in session, there were about 35 to 40 kids in attendance but now, it being summer, the swing, teeter-totter and slide were all unoccupied. Across the road from the school was my cabin. A stained wooden board that was six inches high by three feet wide with black lettering hung from the fence in the front yard, it read: GROS VENTRE COUNTY SHERIFF. At first, having that sign out in front of where I lived caused me to have some swagger in my step. But then, in time, I realized it was a guarantee that I would be working all hours of the day. In a valley where there were no phones it meant that if someone needed the law, or thought they did, they would come and knock on my door regardless of the time of day. I suppose it saved them from going to the pay phone in front of the store and calling the Sheriff's office and him calling me. When I analyzed the situation in this way, it was clear to me why the sign was there.

My dog Grady had spied me coming up the street and was waiting by the gate as I stopped my truck nose in towards the sheriff sign and got out. I clapped my hands and shouted, "Hey Grady, you no account hound dog, did you just wake up?"

Grady's sad looking eyes were betrayed by his vigorously wagging tail. I opened the gate and reached down and tousled his floppy ears with both of my hands. "C'mon let's go," I said as I headed towards the passenger door to let him in. Most days, Grady was my patrol partner.

It was a hot August day and I had not seen a single living soul outside on my way through Cedarville. However, a half mile north of town at the Forest Service Ranger Station there was a beehive of activity. There appeared to be about eight or ten men drawing tools from the fire cache and loading into an old pumper truck and a Willy's Jeep. Seeing them made me envious and, had it not been a quarter mile off the road to the ranger station and the fact I needed to settle the dispute between Schultz and Coggins before it got out of hand, I would have gone over to see where the fire was. But duty called, so I drove on up the Gros Ventre valley road another five miles where I turned east towards the river and Ezra Coggins' place. It was about a mile to the Coggins ranch. To either side of the road were grassy meadows that were punctuated in several locations by big stacks of loose hay that resembled a huge loaf of bread. These fields were being flood irrigated. Ditches, for the purpose of transporting water from the river, snaked their way through this lush oasis. Standing near one of these ditches, leaning on a shovel no more than a hundred yards from the road, was Ezra Coggins. His dog, King, was sitting on the ground next to him. I pulled over to the side of the road and parked. I got out and started toward the barbed wire fence with the intent of climbing over it and going to Ezra, but he waved me off just as I was about to push the top wire down. He shouted while walking towards me, "Stay there. You'll get wet as hell comin' out here." What he said made sense. He was wearing hip boots and, while I could not see the water in the knee-high grass, I could hear the sloshing sound Ezra's feet were making. He was still laboring through the tall grass and maybe 30 feet from me when he called out, "That damned Schultz sic you on me?"

Even at this distance I could see the anger in Coggins' eyes. It was partially hidden in the shadow cast by the brim of his dirty straw hat, but there was no mistaking it being there. When I had lived in the valley as a kid, I had never heard of him being a mean man, but back then most of my opinions were those I picked up from my folks. It was just him and his wife. They were quiet, good people. This was the way I recalled him up until I was 14 when my pa was killed in a logging accident and we moved to town. So, for me, Mr. Coggins had a clean slate. I said, so as to be heard over the splashing water and his heavy breathing, "Yes sir, he sure did. He called the Sheriff and told 'im you gave Bernie a whippin'."

Coggins stopped suddenly about ten feet from the fence and laughed sarcastically as he stabbed his shovel into the ground. He looked down for a few seconds, still quietly laughing, and then he faced me. There were little streams of sweat running down his cheeks. The day was hot, but a better justification for the sweat might have been his gray hair and moustache. He was old enough to be my grandpa. Finally, he said, "So, that's what that sorry lard ass kid of his is sayin', huh?"

I looked at Coggins. Fully clothed and with his waders on he'd be lucky to weigh 160 pounds. I nodded. "Yeah, he said you chased Bernie down in your truck."

"That's right, I did. And when I caught up to him, he come boilin' outta the cab of his old man's pickup all full ah piss and vinegar and starts towards me ah hollerin' and swearin', *why in the hell was I chasin' him* when he knew damned good an' well why I was after him. He tried to purposely run over my dog. There was him and another kid. They was takin' turns trying to run him down."

"Yer purty certain on that?"

"Hell yeah, I am. It musta been around midnight. They woke me and the missus up. I had the bedroom window open on account of the heat. At first, I thought it was just somebody going home late. Maybe been in to Fremont to the picture show or something. But then a few minutes later here comes another car from the other direction. And then in a little bit here come another one. Well, this got me suspicious so I got dressed and went outside to fetch King and that's when I could see their car lights down the road and I could hear loud voices and laughing. And that's when I heard one of 'em say, *I almost got 'im that time.* Well, that's when I jumped in my pickup and took off after the next one that came by and that happened to be the Schultz kid."

"So, who threw the first punch?"

"He tried to but I dodged it and popped him a good one right on the end of his nose. That's the one good thing I learned in the Navy, was how to box."

It was an effort to not laugh. I had gone to school with Bernie Schultz. He was a couple of years behind me, but I knew him as the kid who was always running his mouth and picking on kids smaller than him. He was a good head taller than Coggins and probably 40 pounds heavier, closer to my size I suppose. I said, "So, that was it? That was all that happened?"

Coggins turned his head to the side and spit some tobacco juice and then wiped his moustache with the back of his gloved hand. A slight grin had come to his face. "Well yeah, but I suppose to his old man it looked worse than it was. That kid's nose kind of erupted like that geyser they got down in Yellowstone Park. He was wearing a white tee shirt and it got pretty nasty lookin' in a hurry and the kid started to cry and -"

"Bernie was crying?"

"Oh, hell yeah. He was sobbin' and blubberin' like ah two year old that had been pulled off his momma's tit. I actually felt sorry for him or I woulda smacked him again. I suppose if he was still carrying on like that when he got home it would've made all this look real bad."

I looked down at Coggins' dog who was sitting quietly next to him on a small piece of dry ground. I said, "Did your dog get hurt?"

"Well, one of those two peckernecks musta clipped him cuz he was bleedin' from the nose last night, but I ain't noticed it today."

"Ya got any idea who was driving the other car?"

"It was purty dark, but if there was money ridin' on it I'd say it was that Swaggert kid in that Plymouth Coupe his folks drive."

I sighed, causing Coggins to pause. He appeared to be studying my face and the effects of him having told his side of things. I remained quiet as I pondered my options. It was peaceful. Four posts down the fence line a meadowlark landed and called out its melodic song. Off in the distance were two rooster tails of dust coming up from CR29. It was the forest service boys headed north to the fire. At this very instant I wished that I was with them, but then I said, "I believe Mr. Coggins you was justified in punchin' Bernie. He brought this on himself."

The edgy, defensive look in Coggins' eyes suddenly drained away as he absorbed my words. It was like one of the canvas dams he used for irrigating had been abruptly pulled from the ditch and the water behind it just whooshed on its way. He came back in a tone to reinforce the guilt I had already assigned to Bernie, "I know my dog is a car chaser, but that's no excuse for somebody to deliberately try and run him over. Most folks slow down and steer away from him."

I shook my head. "I know, but I don't think Bernie Schultz, or that Swaggert kid, will ever fit in with most folks." I paused briefly as the words that I had just spoken echoed in my mind, disrupting my train of thought. It came to me that I wasn't much older than these *peckerneck kids* and the respect that Coggins was showing me was due only to my badge. This sudden realization made me feel odd, almost embarrassed. For a brief moment, I wrestled with this emotion before breaking free. I allowed my disdain for these wanna be dog killers to come through in my voice, "When God made those two, he was fresh outta decency." Right away I regretted saying this last part and not staying neutral as an officer of the law.

Coggins, on the other hand, snorted and laughed politely. "Maybe we could send 'em back and get that part installed."

I nodded but said, wanting to distance myself from where the conversation was going, "I'll go talk to Herman and Bernie. I'll let 'em know Bernie was in the wrong here and that he needs to stay away from yer place."

"I'd appreciate that." And then he added, "Next time I see the Sheriff, I'll tell him yer doin' a good job."

There was a sudden pulse of feeling good within me. I looked Coggins in the eyes. I hoped to see he was sincere and not just relieved that things had gone his way. I said with a smile, "Always glad to get an atta boy."

"Well, when I heard Zeke Yarnell's boy was the new deputy here I told the missus that you'd be good, that you'd be a straight shooter just like yer pa was. I was sure sorry when he passed on."

It'd been almost nine years since my father had been killed but now, hearing Coggins bring it up made me feel like it was yesterday. I could feel my eyes starting to moisten. I turned and hollered at Grady who was investigating the smells in the grass and weeds a short way down the fence. He came running and jumped in the front of the pickup. I looked back across the fence at Coggins and made eye contact. I said, "Thank you for the kind words." And then I turned and climbed into my pickup. Just before starting it, I hollered out the window, "I'll let you know if anything comes of this business with the Schultz's."

Coggins nodded and waved before he and King started back up the ditch from where they'd come.

It was close to 60 miles from Cedarville to the headwaters of the Gros Ventre river valley. County Road 29 ran up the middle of the valley all the way to where it topped out on the divide with the Willow Creek drainage. If a person kept on going and connected with the right roads, they could eventually end up in Great Falls. The Schultz place, however, was the last ranch on CR29, which was about 15 miles short of the divide. To get there on the gravel, and sometimes rutted road, would take close to an hour. In another ten miles, I would be out of radio coverage. I decided I'd better let Grace know where I was going.

"Base, this is Andy."

There was silence except for the rattling and squeaking of my pickup to the extent that I was about to call again when Grace came on, "This is base, go ahead Andy."

"Grace, I just visited with Ezra Coggins. Tell Tom I believe Coggins was just defending himself, so now I'm headed to the Schultz place and see if we can't just put this to bed. I'll likely be out of touch for a good while."

"Andy, Tom has gone home. He wants you to call him when you get to a phone."

My heartbeat quickened a bit due to the somewhat ominous nature of Grace's request. Why would Tom be going home during the middle of the day and why would he want me to call him? Why couldn't Grace just pass on a message? My curiosity and apprehension caused me to key the mic again, "Did he say what he wants?"

"He'll explain it to you. Base out."

Had I been standing in the office looking Grace in eye, I would have pressed her to tell me what this was all about, but it was pretty obvious by her clearing herself on the radio that she didn't want to tell me. My mind continued to spin with the possibilities of why Grace was being mysterious about all of this. As usual, I went to the worst possible scenario and that was being reprimanded or fired. Two weeks ago, I gave Roy Glover, one of the county commissioners, a ticket for running a stop sign. He'd gotten mad as hell about it and threatened me with my job. For a time, I had considered just giving him a warning, and would have had it not been for the bottle of Lucky Lager between his legs. The beer had spilled, I suspect, when his right front wheel bounced in and out of a hole at the edge of the road as he pulled over for my flashing red light. I didn't know where he was going, but since he now looked like he had pissed his pants I figured his next stop would be home. His parting words to me were, *You know, Deputy Yarnell, not only does your boss answer to me but I'm friends with some of the men on the draft board. A little stint in the Army might teach you respect for authority.* And with that parting shot he defiantly spun the wheels of his car, throwing gravel into the front of my pickup. One of the rocks, about the size of a large marble, shattered the left headlight. True to his word, Glover called the Sheriff and complained about me. He said, according to Tom, *that snot-nosed deputy of yours gave me a ticket for runnin' a stop sign, when in fact I had looked and slowed way down before going past the sign.* He had left out the part about a car coming that had to brake for him. The Sheriff, at least back then, was on my side. Maybe something had changed with him. I tried to put it out of my mind as I drove on, looking at the fields on either side of the road and feigning genuine interest in the quality or quantity of people's second cutting of hay or judging when they should start harvesting their grain. From the cropland, my visual inspection spilled over to the sage covered benches at the edge of the timber covered mountains. The slopes rose up gently at first but then got steeper and steeper until finally the dark green carpet of trees gave way to gray purplish rock. And then it was inevitable that my thoughts were overtaken by recollections of the fires that I had fought in these mountains. I went a good way reliving those times before it occurred to me that maybe the draft board had contacted the Sheriff to see what kind of a bind it would put him in if they were to take me. I considered this possibility for a few more miles, but even in my mild state of paranoia it didn't gel. Mitch Royer's father was on the draft board. So was a neighbor of ours when we lived in the valley. The both of them knew something about me that Roy

13

Glover didn't, and that was, when Mitch had joined up it had been my intent to join at the same time, to go together. The prospect of this, however, had sent my mother into a deep depression, a near emotional collapse. She'd never really recovered from the death of my father and couldn't deal with the possibility of losing me. Because of this I didn't go and stayed home to fight fire which didn't exactly put my mother in a comfortable place either, but it was my life to live.

I had just topped a small rise in the road which allowed me to see the Schultz place about a mile ahead. It was a collection of old log buildings down by the Gros Ventre. The logs were so old they had turned nearly white. Herman Schultz' father had homesteaded the place in the late 1890s or so I'd been told. They were one of the original settlers of the valley, which I supposed was good for them given the animosity people had towards Germans these days.

The road leading off of CR29 that went over to the Schultz place was still, after all these years, not much more than a well worn two-track. As I bounced along over this road, it occurred to me that it had probably not been bladed or graveled due to the rock that was already there. Surprisingly, a strip of scraggily vegetation consisting mostly of stunted sage and grass had somehow survived between the paths of the wheels. Barbed wire fence ran along either side of the road. Beyond the fences, the brush had been removed years ago. Now, a good number of Angus cattle kept the pasture mowed to where it looked like a golf course. Some of them stared back at Grady who was quietly looking out the passenger side window. We rolled on towards the wispy column of blue smoke hanging above the rusty stovepipe protruding from the roof of the Schultz house. It was nearly noon. There was nobody in sight. I sighed. A green '39 Chevy pickup was parked out front. I was a good 50 yards from parking beside it when a black and white dog came at a dead run from the big open door of the barn off to my left. Within seconds, he was barking and snarling at the rear wheels of my truck. I shook my head and said to myself, *they got a car chaser too yet Bernie wants to kill the Coggins' dog for doing the same thing, or maybe that's just his idea of fun.* I had barely come to a stop when Herman came out of the house. He was followed by Bernie, who was still eating from a biscuit in his hand. Herman stood briefly in the shade of the covered porch before descending the three wooden steps into the hot sun. He squinted his eyes against it as he glared at me and then his dog, who was still barking and growling just outside my door.

And then Herman yelled angrily. "Dammit, Gopher, that's enough."

My feet had barely hit the ground when he continued, just short of a yell, "Where's the Sheriff? Where's Tom Woods? That's who I called."

Anger instantly consumed me. I wanted badly to say, *why you dumb shit, I've been the law in the valley for almost a year and a half. Been livin' in Cedarville and what do you do but drive in there to use the phone to call over to Fremont and Tom Woods. Well, I guess the joke's on you.* But I knew better than that. I gently closed the door of my pickup and looking through the open window said in a voice loud enough for Herman to hear, "You wait here, Grady. This won't take long." I then turned to face Schultz. "Tom sent me."

Schultz scowled. "Alright, have you arrested Coggins?"

"No. The way he tells it, this was him defending himself."

"Defending himself! Why that's a load a horseshit if I ever heard it." Schultz turned to his son. "Bernie get out here so the, *DEPUTY*, can see yer face."

Bernie came down from the porch and out into the light beside his father. His nose was swollen and his eyes were not full-blown shiners, but they had a darkness beneath them. It was more damage than what I had expected, but it still fell within the realm of believability as Coggins had described the fight. I came back, "Coggins claims Bernie threw the first punch, he dodged it and landed just one punch on Bernie's nose. Apparently, he was some kind of fighter in the Navy."

I immediately regretted saying the part about the Navy as Schultz got even madder. "Well, there ya go. That old sonovabitch snookered my kid into a fight just so he could use him as a punching bag."

"He didn't snooker anybody. Bernie started all this by him and the Swaggert kid trying to kill Coggins' dog." I paused just briefly as Herman shot Bernie an angry look, but he said nothing. I went on, purposely not addressing Schultz by his name. "This was a one punch fight. According to Mr. Coggins, Bernie started crying after he got hit and the fight ended right there."

"Crying?" said Herman as he glanced over at Bernie.

"Yeah, the way I see it, Bernie is lucky Coggins felt sorry for him and didn't lay into him. Had he done that this might have been the beating you think it was. But, as it stands now, I'd say we ought to drop the whole thing. If not, I guess you can take it to the Sheriff or the District Attorney and we'll have Coggins and Bernie come in and tell their side of things." I paused and then added, "it might not have been so lopsided if Bernie hadn't started crying and had fought back, but that apparently didn't happen. But hey, I'm just a deputy. Maybe the Sheriff or the DA would see things differently."

Bernie, who'd been oddly mute up to this point, suddenly blurted out, "Just drop it Pa. It's like he said."

Anger and then embarrassment flooded Herman Schultz' eyes. "What?"

"Let it go." And with that Bernie went back up the porch steps still clutching the partially eaten biscuit in his right hand.

I knew I should just go but I said, "I'd appreciate it if you'd ask Bernie to tell the Swaggert kid that trying to kill the Coggins' dog, or any dog, will get him in big trouble with the law."

Herman looked at me. His eyes were filled with a helpless hate. He nodded. "Alright." And then he went into the house letting the screen door slam behind him. I was just reaching to open my pickup's door when the yelling started. *That damned kid shamed me out there. It's one thing to get whipped like a man but it's another to break down and cry like a mama's boy.* And then the outline of Mrs. Schultz appeared briefly behind the screen door as she looked out at me before closing the regular door. I started my truck and backed around, fairly confident that the Sheriff wouldn't be getting any more calls about this. True to who he was, Gopher, biting and barking at my wheels, escorted me out of the Schultz' yard.

I turned onto CR29, or the Gros Ventre road as the locals generally called it, and headed south towards Cedarville and the phone call to Tom that I needed to make. It had occurred to me, with money being as tight as it was, that Roy Glover might have convinced the other county commissioners that they couldn't afford a deputy sheriff. Several years ago, it had been just Tom to cover the county with some help from the highway patrol. But then, just before the war with Japan started, they had decided the county needed a deputy, specifically for the Gros Ventre river valley. I remember, at the time, Tom telling me that the decision to hire me had passed by just one vote. He said it was because I was young and had no experience. Regrettably, I had responded with, *Even Wyatt Earp had to start out somewhere.* Tom frowned and shook his head. *Yeah, well Wyatt, just the same you'll be spending three months at the law enforcement academy over in Helena.* And so here I was, headed for town to see if I still had a job.

Because of the war lots of things were being rationed, among them were gas and tires. To save gas, the government had lowered the speed limit throughout the country to 35 miles per hour. On the oiled road between Cedarville and Fremont it seemed unbearably slow, but here on the Gros Ventre it was plenty fast. I had gone about eight or nine miles, my mind being occupied with the call I had to make and how hungry I was, and I suspected Grady too, when off to my right I saw a dark green pickup approaching 29 from the Badger Creek road. I recognized the truck as belonging to Bill Kyle, the local game warden. He was old enough to be my father and had kind of a crusty personality, but I liked him. We had worked together on a couple of poaching cases. I had found him to be pretty much by the book, but fair-minded and friendly. I pulled over near the forest service sign marking the Badger Creek road and got out of my truck to wait. Momentarily, Kyle arrived accompanied by a small cloud of dust that partially enveloped his truck as he got out. He shouted in a cordial tone, "Deputy Yarnell, how the hell are ya?"

"Doing good," I said as I went toward him, "and you?"

We met midway between our trucks and shook hands. His grip was the strongest I'd ever felt. It was like he was trying to impress me with his strength, but I knew he wasn't. It's just how he was if he liked you. He sighed heavily. "I'll tell ya, some days it don't pay to leave the house."

"How's that?"

"Well, I got a call about somebody hearin' gunshots in the night." Kyle paused and frowned and then said sarcastically, "course this was three nights ago." He paused again and shook his head in disgust before going on, "well, anyway I go up here to where this reporting party said they thought the shots was comin' from and sure enough I find gut piles and heads from a cow and bull elk, a dandy six pointer, up in Skinner Meadows. And then, as if that wasn't enough, I find the head, guts and hide of a good-sized steer, so I'm glad that I run into ya as I was gonna toss that little headache yer way." Kyle then laughed in a friendly way and added, "we'll share the pain." And then he laughed some more.

I briefly joined in the laughter so as to be polite and then asked, "Did ya get a brand off that hide?"

"I did. It was the /S, one of ole Sherman Duke's critters if I'm recalling the brand correctly."

I nodded. "I believe ya are. Sherman Duke lived close to where I did when I was a kid growing up out here."

Kyle took a pack of Camels out of his pocket. He shook one out as he extended the pack towards me. "Smokin'?"

"Naw, I can't afford the habits I already got."

Kyle lit a cigarette and took a deep drag off of it before blowing the smoke out into the hot afternoon air. He said, "Ya know, poachin' and butcherin' cattle wasn't this bad before we had all these rationing rules."

"Well, ranchers got all the beef they can eat. So, I suspect yer culprits are likely town people wanting more meat than their ration books will allow. Sometimes rules bring out the worst in people."

A weak smile materialized on Kyle's face. Instantly, I realized why it was there. Here I was a not quite yet 23 old kid telling him, a man who had been chasing bad guys for almost 20 years, about human nature. An awkward moment was beginning to take hold as the embarrassment registered in my eyes, but then Kyle purposely moved on before it became full-blown. "Oh, I believe what you say is likely true but I'm thinkin' anybody who kills three big animals, and takes all of the meat, is wanting more than a few extra steaks. He's out to make money."

I was hesitant to counter what Kyle had just said, so I proceeded as if I were the student seeking guidance. I said, "With the ration boards monitoring everything so close, how would a fella go about gittin' around 'em?"

Kyle immediately laughed before taking another drag from his Camel, holding the smoke in his lungs for a split second, and then forcefully exhaling it from both his mouth and nose. His bushy salt and pepper moustache caused much of the smoke from his nostrils to boil up in front of his face. From behind this blue haze, he said, "Yer probably too young to remember prohibition."

"Oh no, I used to go with my father over to a friend of his place. He'd get it in quart Mason jars. It was clear as water but it packed a punch"

Kyle smiled. "I can tell ya from experience, it did. But my point here is, laws don't mean nuthin' to some folks. The moonshiners didn't just sell to their neighbors, they took their product to the cities. There was no shortage of businesses there who would buy it and sell it illegally. They gave people what they wanted. So, I'm thinkin' it ain't no different with meat."

"So, where ya thinkin' this meat is endin' up?"

"I don't know. It's just my suspicion at this point, but if I was to guess it would be Billings or maybe Denver."

"Denver? That's a long ways."

Kyle laughed. "Well, it ain't like these guys have got a lot of overhead costs. Besides, it's a bigger town."

"Lots of customers there, I suppose."

"More importantly, I think, is the fact there are likely more businesses there that would be willing to run the risk of selling illegal meat."

And then I said, changing the course of the conversation slightly, "You suppose I could get that cowhide from you. I'll run it by Sherm Duke's place just to make sure it's his."

Kyle turned and started towards his truck. He said, over his shoulder, "Suits me, I don't much care for the fella."

I was about to ask why, even though I strongly suspected I already knew, when he moved on, perhaps sensing I was about to revive Gros Ventre valley gossip. He said, kind of quick like, "I got some pictures of some fresh tire tracks in wet ground next to where they gutted the elk. Don't know if it'll help but the tread wasn't just yer standard highway tread. It was more jagged a traction tread, I'd guess you'd call it. I'll drop my film off at the Rexall in town. Probably have the pictures back in a week. You can take a look at 'em when they come in." Kyle stopped at the back of his truck and let the tailgate down. "Well, here it is."

Laying in the bed of his truck were the elk heads, the steer's head because of the distinctive ear marks it had, and the hide of the Hereford calf. A massive cloud of flies was crawling and buzzing over this bloody mess. Kyle laughed. "Well, help yerself." But before I could get to the hide, he reached in and grabbed two fistfuls on the hairy, non-bloody side and drug it out. He said jokingly, "Ya want me to just throw it on yer front seat?"

I played along. "Sure, that'd be fine."

Grady met Kyle, who was holding the smelly hide and its flies out in front of him next to my truck. He hollered, "No Grady dog, this ain't for you." And then he swung the hide up over the edge of my truck's bed and let it drop. "Well, there ya be."

"Thanks, Bill. I'll call the brand inspector up in Great Falls. I'm not sure if he'll come down or just tell me to deal with this and keep him in the loop. I generally don't ever see much of him until fall when ranchers start selling their calves."

Although Kyle had tried to not get blood on his hands, he'd not been totally successful. He said, as he wiped his hands on the legs of his Levis, "Well, I'm gonna git on down the road. I've acquired an appetite this afternoon and I don't want to be late for supper." And then he laughed again.

I waved as Kyle pulled onto 29 and headed south. It was too hot for me and Grady to drive with the windows up, so I purposely waited a couple of minutes before starting out so as to put distance between his dust cloud and me. I killed the time by setting Grady's metal bowl on the ground next to the truck and pouring him a drink from my homemade canteen, a gallon apple cider jug that I'd wrapped in burlap that was held on with baling wire threaded through it and tied around the neck of the bottle. If I started out with cold tap water, stuffed a tray of ice cubes into the bottle, soaked the burlap with water from the faucet at my cabin, and kept the jug out of the direct sun, I usually had good drinking water all day.

It was ten past two, time enough left in the day for me to go over to Sherm Duke's and let him know that he had one less steer. On the way there I tried to not dwell on the rumors about Duke that had surfaced over the years, about him beating his wife. As a kid I'd personally never seen the proof of it, but my father claims to have. I overheard him tell my mother, *somebody needs to give that sonvabitch a dose of his own medicine. If I ever hear of it again, I might just be that person.* But then my pa got killed not long after that and we moved away and I lost touch with the rumor mill until I moved back to the valley about a year and a half ago. And then one day I was at the store when Betty Duke, Sherm's wife, came in. One of her eyes appeared to be recovering from having been a lot blacker than it currently was and her right forearm had a large purple bruise. Although she and my mother had been friends, and she knew darned good and well that I was little Andy Yarnell all grown up, she pretended like she didn't know who I was. I suspect it was because of her injuries and the fact I was wearing my deputy shirt and badge and gun. It occurred to me to just leave things be, to let her wear her shame anonymously, but there was something within me that wouldn't allow it. I thought at the time, if she knew that she had a friend in the Sheriff's office she might just turn Sherm's sorry ass in for beating her up. So, I said, "Hi Mrs. Duke. Do you remember me, Wilma Yarnell's boy, Andy?"

She froze, right in front of the old white, two-sided refrigerator where they kept the dairy stuff. Her face became fearful like she'd been caught shoplifting. She looked at me, pretending at first like she still didn't know me and then she said, "Oh yes, I'd heard you were the deputy sheriff now. How's your mother?"

I sighed. "Other than being lonely, she's ok."

"What does she do to keep busy?"

"Waits tables at the Coffee Cup in Fremont. You should drop in and see her sometime."

She nodded and smiled. "I will, but we don't get to town very often."

"She'd like it if you did," I said knowing full well that Sherm had forbid her from associating with my mother years ago because, as I heard my mother tell my father, *Sherm thinks I fill Betty's head with lots of radical nonsense. He says you need to rein me in.*

The Dukes lived down next to the Gros Ventre in a white clapboard house with a green shingle roof. Huge cottonwood trees that were fed by water that percolated out from the river towered over the house and the grass that surrounded it. A picket fence made from pine boards that had never been painted and were now gray, enclosed it all. The Duke's pickup, a green Ford, was parked near the gate in the fence. Beyond the house, to the right, was a shop, barn and corrals, all made from logs cut in the mountains nearby. In the opening created by two big double doors on the front of the shop was a green and yellow mowing machine with iron cleated wheels and a metal seat. Sherm Duke stood up from where he appeared to be working on the mower's sickle and looked at me. I pulled on down to the shop and got out.

Duke knew exactly who I was. "Deputy Yarnell, what brings you my way?"

"Bad news, I'm afraid."

Duke's eyes widened, curious, then angry. "How's that?"

I started towards the back of my truck. I yelled over my shoulder, "Somebody butchered one of yer steers."

"What?"

I looked up as I pulled the hide from the bed of my pickup. He was walking quickly towards me. "You sure it's mine?"

I spread the hide on the ground like a blanket and pointed to the brand. "Isn't yer brand the slash S?"

"Yeah, it is."

From the corner of my eye, I suddenly caught movement in the garden just to the north of us. It was Betty who was hurrying to the house like she didn't want to be seen. The fact she was walking so fast caused me to turn my full attention towards her. It was only then that I could see she was carrying her far-side arm in a sling. I tried to make eye contact with her, but she quickened her pace and wouldn't look at me. I looked back at Sherm but before I could say a word, he blurted out, "I got me a one-armed weed puller. That silly woman ah mine decided she was gonna ride this rank colt that I been breakin'. Things didn't work out too good for her." And then he laughed.

I wanted right then to just call bullshit on the lie I suspected Duke was telling me, but I figured it would probably get me another phone call to Tom, or worse maybe, one of the county commissioners. I moved on. "Bill Kyle found this along with a coupla gut piles from elk up in Skinner Meadows."

Duke frowned. "I don't suppose he's got any idea who did it, does he?"

"Nope, not yet he don't. He took some pictures of tire tracks next to the gut piles, he –"

"Shit, what's he gonna do, run all over the county checkin' tires?"

For a brief moment I drew back from Duke's sarcasm, while making no attempt to disguise my anger. But then I said, purposely sounding indifferent to him being wronged. "You never know. It might lead to something."

Duke scoffed. "What about you? What are you gonna do about it?"

I may have read too much into it, but Duke's tone of voice suggested to me that, because of my age and inexperience, I'd never catch who butchered his steer. I came back quick. "I'm gonna stop in at the forest service office and see if any of those boys has seen any strange trucks in the vicinity of Skinner Meadows."

Duke snorted and tossed his head back. "Well, good luck with that. Those boys never get too far from the coffee pot." And then he laughed at my idea.

I was now angry to the point that I wanted to challenge the lie he had told me about Betty, but common sense had not deserted me entirely, so I said respectfully, "Well, Mr. Duke, I'll let you know what we come up with."

Duke came back. "Maybe if you and that game warden was to do some night patrols you might catch somebody."

I nodded. "What you say makes sense if we had unlimited gas but, you know as well as me, with the rationing I just don't have the luxury of going out night after night at random hoping to run into these thieves."

"Well, I'll tell ya Deputy, if I run into 'em I may just give 'em a little 30-30 justice."

"You don't want to be shootin' anybody."

Duke pointed angrily at the hide on the ground. "That was a hundred dollar bill. You got one you wanna give me?

Or, maybe you can just stop in to the store in Cedarville and pay my tab. That'd be alright."

Suddenly, from the corner of my eye I saw a teenage girl emerge from the house and start towards us. I suspected she was Duke's daughter, Katie. She had been a baby when we moved away. But now, she was nearly as big as her mother, slender with red hair. She was wearing jeans and a green short-sleeved blouse. And, she appeared to be crying.

Duke shouted his voice filled with an urgent anger. "Dammit, Katie, get back in the house. There's nuthin here that concerns you. Do you hear me? Go back to the house."

Katie was looking directly at me. Her father's hostile outburst had stopped her dead in her tracks. She appeared paralyzed with fear.

I called out to her. "Are you alright?"

But then the front door to the house opened and Betty stepped out. She said, her voice sounding fearful, almost desperate, "Katie, it's alright. Come back to the house."

Katie looked at her mother and then back at me. It was obvious she wanted to talk to me, but then Sherm chimed in. "Do as yer mother says, Katie. Now."

Reluctantly, Katie started back to the house. Beyond her, I made eye contact with Betty. She waved with her good arm and made a feeble attempt to smile. I barely waved back before Sherm jumped in again. "Katie and her ma ain't gittin' along too good these days."

I looked Sherm hard in the eyes so he would know I was suspicious of him. "Anything serious?"

His expression became nervous, but at the same time, cocky, he said, "Boy trouble mostly. Nothing that would warrant the law wasting their precious time on."

I looked over at the house. Katie and her mother had just gone inside and closed the door. From behind me, Sherm said, "Thanks for stopping by, Deputy. You'll let me know what you find out about them tracks?"

Sherm was basically inviting me to leave. His look was smug, like he'd snowed this green kid. I wondered if Tom would have gone after Katie and demanded to talk to her, and to Betty too? But it was them who walked away. I said, ignoring the issue of the butchered beef, "Tell Mrs. Duke that I hope her arm mends ok and that she doesn't have any more riding accidents."

Duke hesitated briefly before nodding. "Alright, I'll tell her."

I left the steer hide where it was and climbed into my truck. As I drove past the house, I could see a hand parting the curtains just far enough to see out. In a way, it made me feel as if I hadn't done my job but I continued on towards 29 and the next stop I had to make before calling Tom to see if I still had a job.

The forest service had its own little community of white buildings with green roofs just outside of Cedarville. There were corrals next to a pasture and a half shed for the horses and pack mules, a shed for tack and grain, bunk houses for the summer help, regular houses for the permanent help and an office building with a sign out front that read, GROS VENTRE RANGER STATION. To the right of this was another brown wooden sign with yellow letters that was much smaller. It was situated at the edge of where the grass ended and the gravel parking lot began, it read, VISITORS.

As I came to a stop in front of the little sign my brakes squealed slightly, due, I suppose, to the dust they'd accumulated on 29. I reached over and gave Grady a pat on the head.

"I won't be long, hound dog." His sad brown eyes seemed to say, *I've heard that before.* I'd no sooner got out of my truck than my attention was drawn to the gentle clanking of the gromets in the American flag against the metal flagpole. As usual, being late afternoon, the wind was coming from the west. At times it would completely unfurl the flag, but mostly it was just gently rippling it so its colors and pattern were all mushed together. My three seasons on the fire crew caused me to render a guess. I said to myself, *5-8 mph, gusting to 10-12.* I missed being on the fire crew, but there was no need for a firefighter in the winter and I still had bills to pay so here I was pursuing my other passion in life. I opened the door of the ranger station and stepped inside.

"Hello, Andy. You come to sign up for the fire crew? We're still needing a few more people."

I looked beyond the counter, seated at a desk with a typewriter on it was Ellen Lujack. I knew she would be here and, truth be told, it was as much my motivation for coming as was looking for the Skinner Meadows people. Ellen, who was half Japanese, had shoulder length black hair and dark eyes. She had been two years behind me in school. I said, "I wish I could sign up but duty calls."

Ellen smiled. "Are you working on a case?"

It was hard to not be distracted by her beauty. It was ordinary, not gaudy like some girls. She was petite but shapely and seldom wore makeup, as was the case today. Her plain white blouse complimented her figure. Before the war started, she always had guys chasing after her but now, with the hatred for the Japanese, things were different. I said, figuring it was no secret, "There's been some poachin' and cattle thievery going on up around Skinner Meadows. Have you guys had anyone workin' up that way lately?"

She did not hesitate but came back quickly, like she knew what the question was beforehand, "Yeah, Russell's been up there doing range use checks."

"I don't suppose he's around, is he?"

"No, he's on the fire. Everyone is except for me and Allan and he's about to head that way with their supper."

I uttered a weak laugh, "C rations?"

Ellen grinned. "Part of fire, I guess."

"Ham and beans was always my favorite and the pound cake is good. I mean it won't edge out yer grandma's baking at the county fair but on a fire, it sure hit the spot." I hadn't even completed saying what I had when I saw the hurt in Ellen's eyes. She herself had told me last year that her grandparents had been locked up at an internment camp down near Cody, Wyoming at a place called Heart Mountain. And now here I was, being the bumbling idiot that I sometimes am, making casual reference to her grandma as if she was free to enter her baked goods at the fair.

And then Ellen said, her face having suddenly become sad, "Maybe someday, after the war is over, my grandma will make a cake for the fair."

I was about to apologize for what I'd said when the door behind me opened. "Well lookie what the cat drug in. Are ya lookin' for a job?" At that very moment it was frustratingly difficult to turn away from Ellen but I did and extended my hand to Allan Grimes, the district packer. He ran a string of mules all summer keeping the trail and fire crews in the back country supplied.

"How ya fairin'?" I said as we shook hands.

Allan, who was in his 50s with graying hair and moustache and a beer belly that partially hid his belt buckle that read, Bareback Riding Champion – 1932 Miles City Rodeo came back in a booming voice, "Well, I'm still on the right side of the dirt so I guess I'm alright." He laughed as did I. He went on, "So, how's being a law dog workin' for ya?"

"Well, so far it agrees with me but then I ain't run into any real desperados yet."

Allan laughed again as he slapped me on the shoulder. "Was you thinkin' you'd find a desperado around here?" He paused and glanced over at Ellen and then back to me, "or was you lookin' to spark the help here?" He laughed again, even louder. I looked at Ellen. Even as darkly complexioned as she was, I could see that she had turned red. When we were in high school, I had danced with her at some of the dances after football and basketball games, but I'd never been confident enough to actually ask her out and then I graduated and didn't see much of her after that. Today, with her being alone in the office, would have been a good time for me to ask her to the show on Saturday night. Had she turned me down nobody would have been the wiser, but now Grimes had revealed my ulterior motive for coming here. And then, out of the blue, Ellen came to my rescue.

"Allan, somebody poached some game and butchered a steer up in Skinner Meadows. Andy was wondering if any of our people have seen any strange vehicles in that area."

I looked over at Ellen as if to express my appreciation when Grimes' deep, gravelly voice penetrated my left ear, "You know, those boys that went out on that little spot fire a few nights ago up in Van Dorn canyon said, when they was comin' in, some damned fool come high-ballin' 'round a curve in the road and nearly hit 'em head-on. I guess they had to go plum off the road to avoid him."

My interest was immediately piqued. "Did they say what kind of a vehicle this guy was driving?"

Grimes snorted a derisive laugh. "Yeah they did, said it looked like a furniture truck."

"A furniture truck?"

"Yeah, one of them van type affairs. One of the boys was pretty certain he saw the words furniture and Custer Street on the side of the box part of the truck."

"They say what color the truck was?"

"As I recall, just something dark, black or blue or green. They said there was lots of dust, headlights bouncing every which way, and the next thing they knew they was sittin out in the brush and the furniture truck was on down the road."

I sighed and shook my head. "Did the fire boys say what time of the night this was?"

"That was the strange part. They said it was about 2:30 in the morning. Kinda makes a fella wonder what the hell a furniture truck is doing in Van Dorn canyon at that time of day. When the boys was telling me this I thought some poor city slickers had come out to make a delivery and took a wrong turn and got themselves totally turned around, but now I wonder if they wasn't up to no good."

I nodded. "A big boxy truck like that would sure be a good way to hide carcasses."

"I 'spect it would. A fella -" Grimes stopped mid-sentence as the radio on the table behind Ellen came to life.

"Gros Ventre Station, this is fire camp."

Ellen slid her chair back and started for the radio. I said to Grimes in a lowered voice, "Where's the fire at?"

He said, not looking at me but the radio, "East side of Weasel Mountain. It ain't much, five-six acres in some Doug Fir but as dry as it is, it has been giving the boys fits."

"Fire Camp, this is Gros Ventre."

"Ellen, make sure Grimes brings plenty a cold drinks. It's hot as hell out here."

Ellen looked over at Grimes to get his response. He said, "I got 40 gallons of water and three cases of soda pop."

She keyed the microphone, "He's bringing lots of water and pop."

The voice, loaded with sarcasm, came back, "Well, has that old turd left yet?"

Grimes blurted out. "Who's he callin' an old turd? He ain't no spring chicken his self."

Ellen looked over and frowned. "Yeah Russell, he left about ten minutes ago."

I hadn't seen much of Russell Jenkins since the last summer I fought fire, but it didn't sound like his personality had changed any. He worked alone most of the time. His job was to ride the various grazing allotments and make sure the ranchers hadn't put more cattle out than they were authorized, and to see how the grass was holding up. It was a lonely, solitary job, as he often took a pack horse with him and stayed out all week. I often wondered if him being gone so much was why his wife frequented the bar in Cedarville like she did. Gertie, short for Gertrude, was there most nights when Russell was gone and even some when he was home, they would sometimes both go. She was part Sioux with black hair and eyes and easy to look at if you were a middle-aged man. I'd hear rumors about her leaving the Antler Bar with other men, but I'd personally never witnessed it and wondered about such rumors as Russell Jenkins was not someone you wanted mad at you.

Allan laughed. "Well hell, if I left ten minutes ago, I guess I oughta be about to Dead Horse springs."

Ellen looked at Grimes, stern for a 20 year old girl in her first season with the forest service, and said, "Yeah, you should."

Grimes smiled and opened the door. "Be seein' ya, Andy," he said as he pulled the door closed behind him.

With all that Grimes had told me in the presence of Ellen about the furniture truck, there was no real tangible reason for me to be standing at the counter in front of her desk. The sudden awkward silence that enveloped the room made that more than obvious. Hanging on the wall beyond her was an old clock encased in dark oak wood. Its brass pendulum swung back and forth and back and forth, ticking loudly, drawing even more attention to the fact that I was still there. And then she said, "Well, Andy, it was good to see you."

My mind immediately went to, *does she want me to leave? Maybe I should and not make a fool out of myself. Just git the hell outa here you half-wit huckleberry before you embarrass yourself.* So, I said, "It was good to see you, too."

She smiled and nodded as she reached for a government form and began inserting it into her typewriter.

I turned and took a step towards the door. Her typewriter began to sing out clickity-clack like she wasn't bothered in the least that I was leaving. Suddenly, another bolder version of me took over. I stopped and looked at her. I heard myself say, "Would you like to go to a picture show sometime?"

She did not seem surprised, amused was probably a better description of her reaction. She said, as she got up from her chair and came to the counter, "That sounds like fun. When were you thinking of going?"

"Well, *For Whom The Bell Tolls* is playing Saturday night."

"Oh, I love Gary Cooper."

"Me too."

"You remember reading that book in senior English?"

"Yes, I guess we'll see if the movie does justice to the book." I paused, uncertain if I should include supper.

"What time should I be ready?"

"Well, if you'd like to eat at the Coffee Cup before the show, 4:30, if not 5:30."

"Supper sounds good, but only if we go Dutch treat."

"We'll see about that."

"Alright, I'll see you at 4:30."

As I walked out to my pickup, I felt almost giddy. It was a good feeling, a happy feeling and, for a brief moment, shoved from my mind the feeling of doom that had been there ever since Grace had told me that Tom wanted to talk to me by phone.

CHAPTER TWO

I unlocked the door to my cabin, or rather the county's cabin, and stepped inside. It was shadowy, almost dark-like on account of I had pulled all of the curtains to keep the sun out and last night's coolness in. Nonetheless, it was warm. Flies, trapped between the dark red fabric and the four pane windows, were buzzing incessantly looking for an escape. For some reason, as it was not usually my habit, I went to the west side of the room and slid the curtains above the sink to the left and the right along the white tin rod that held them up. The sun immediately poured in allowing several big black flies to escape into the room. Now their annoying drone was no longer muffled behind the curtain, it seemed to be everywhere. I sighed. *Shudda had my fly swatter ready for those guys.* In the far corner of the room was my brass bed. Next to it was a small night stand with a wind-up alarm clock sitting on it that read 4:50. I had decided that I was going to wait until after five to call Tom. It may have been faulty logic but, in my mind, calling then would reinforce the fact that I'd put in a full day and was now calling on my own time. I wanted him to know that I was a hard-working, dedicated employee and if Roy Glover had found a way to do away with my position, then this is what he would be losing.

In my preoccupied state, I had failed to notice that Grady had taken up a vigil over his food bowl on the floor near the door. He was looking at me as I sat at the table in the center of the room making notes in my patrol log. "Sorry Grady," I said as I got up and went to the cupboard next to the sink. "Supper's comin' right up." I took a bag of dog food from beneath the counter and filled Grady's bowl. "Alright, hound dog, there you go," I said as he began chomping his way through it. From behind me the phone rang, at 4:52. I set the bag of dog food on the counter and went to the dresser sitting along the wall across from my bed. The phone had just completed its third ring when I picked it up. "Gros Ventre Sheriff's office, Cedarville substation."

"Andy, this is Tom."

My heartbeat immediately surged. It flashed in my mind to call him sir, but I did not. "Yeah, Tom, I was about to call you. I had a busy day. I was just catching up on my field notes."

"Things go ok with Schultz?"

It was faint, but I heard Tom exhale. He was likely smoking a Chesterfield as he talked to me. I'd seen him do it many times before. He'd light up a cigarette just as he got on the phone. I said, "Yeah, his boy Bernie was purposely trying to run over Coggins' dog."

Tom cut in, "Why that sorry shit."

I laughed. "Coggins caught him at it so then Bernie takes a swing at him. But, unbeknownst to Bernie that little old man was some kind of a fighter in the Navy. He dodges Bernie's punch and then pops him a good one right on the end of his nose. I guess then Bernie started to cry like a school girl."

"The hell you say."

"Bernie, pretty much fessed up to it. I don't think either him or his old man want that version of the fight gittin' around."

Tom said, his voice trailing off like he'd suddenly lost interest in what we were talking about, "I spect not."

For a few seconds the phone on his end was quiet and then I heard the gentle clinking of ice cubes against a glass. My mind's eye instantly went to him sitting there with a rum and coke, which I knew was his favorite drink, but hell, it wasn't even five o'clock yet. I said to myself, he *probably needs that so he can work up the courage to tell me I'm through. You'd think he'd be man enough to drive out here and tell me in person.* But then the tinkling of the ice cubes went away, he said, just straight out, "It's your show now, Andy."

I was taken aback, like this chunk of black plastic next to my ear had distorted his words. I said, "What?"

Briefly, there was silence and then the rattling of the ice cubes followed by, "My Ma's dying, Andy.'

I instantly felt like a jerk for thinking what I had been, but at the same time, mixed in with that shame was some relief that I wasn't being fired. I said, "I'm real sorry to hear that, Tom."

"Just like you, my father died when I was a youngster. But not like you, I never stuck around to be there for my mother. As soon as I graduated high school, I was out of there. I'd had enough of that hot desert country. Been up here ever since."

"So, when are you leaving?"

"Tomorrow."

I instantly, but unintentionally, parroted back, "Tomorrow."

"I'm sorry to spring this on you like this. I thought I had more time, that she wasn't this bad, but my uncle called last night. Said I better come now. He said she's been asking for me."

I felt awkward, uneasy, but I said, "Sure, Tom, you need to go. You'll regret it if you don't." And then I played in my mind what I'd just said. I shook my head. *I'm the snot-nosed kid giving advice on life to a man old enough to be my father.* I said into the phone, "Don't worry about things here. Between Grace and I, we'll manage."

I had expected Tom to come right back with, *Oh, I know you will.* But he did not. After a pause that was defined by the shaking of the ice cubes, which caused me to envision him draining his glass, he said, "You should know that Roy Glover isn't real happy that you'll be filling in for me while I'm gone. He wanted me to see if I couldn't get a neighboring county to detail a deputy over here, but I told him no. I told him you were up to the job. You are, aren't you?"

A pulse of anger shot through me. I thought, *well shit, Tom, if you've got to ask me you must not trust me.* Now, he had me doubting myself. Nonetheless, I said into the phone, "I believe I'll be alright."

"I believe ya will too, but just know that he'll be watching you like a hawk for any screwups that he can use to fire ya. And another thing, George Royer said your name came up at the draft board meeting they had a few days ago. George was assigned the job of finding out what kind of a job you were doing with the Sheriff's Department. Seems Glover complained about you to one of the board members."

Glover's vindictiveness caused my heart rate to shoot up again. I said, "Tom, don't worry about the draft board. If they want to take me, I'm ok with that. It's how it'll affect my mother is what worries me."

And then Tom said, "Well, there's that and then too, me and the county would be out a good deputy."

A flood of positive emotion came over me. "Thanks, Tom. I appreciate your confidence,"

"I ain't sure when I'll be back. Might be a coupla weeks or it could be a month. I don't know, but I'll check in from time to time or you can call my wife. Being this close to school starting her and the kids are staying here. Well, I better go."

"Ok, Tom. Good luck."

"You too." And then the line went dead.

I replaced the phone on its cradle and for a time I just stood there next to the dresser watching and listening to Grady crunch through his chow. My mind drifted back to that day when I watched Glover roll past the stop sign, likely knowing but not caring that the oncoming car was going to have to brake for him. I began to replay this and the open bottle of beer and look for some reason, other than him being a county commissioner, to have let him off with a warning, but it didn't come to mind then and it wasn't now either. I shook my head and whispered, "The uppity sonovabitch got what he deserved."

I hadn't eaten since breakfast. My stomach was growling. I had two choices for supper. One of them would involve building a fire in the cook stove that sat along the wall opposite where the sink and cupboards were located. In about an hour, I could be eating chili or beef stew from a can. The other option would be corn flakes. There was cold milk in the cream-colored refrigerator at the end of the counter. In a couple of minutes, I could be eating and listening to music on the radio my mother had given me when I had moved out. I always suspected her motivation for giving it to me was to keep me in at night and out of the bar. But it was, according to the thermometer at the ranger station, 91 degrees in the shade. I looked over at the stove. Firing it up, without leaving the front door open, would turn the inside of the cabin into something that would rival an Indian sweat lodge, but to open the door would allow unlimited access for more flies and some mosquitoes too. I knew from experience that leaving the door open could result in a real buzz fest making sleep next to impossible. I'd asked Tom about getting a screen door but he said the county was too broke. So, here I stood, with a bead of sweat working its way down from my right temple and onto my cheek. I'd not moved from where I stood next to the dresser because way in the back of my mind, I could see the third option and I knew damned good and well that I would surrender to it. But, like so many times before, I had to rationalize to my conscience why it would be ok to go to the Antler Bar, on my meager salary, and have a hamburger and a cold beer when I had chili and Wonder bread or corn flakes and cold milk right here. As I unbuckled my gun belt I was still berating myself for having given in to the lure of the Antler. I rolled the belt with its handcuff pouch around the holster that contained my .38 Caliber Colt and put it under the pillow on my bed. By the time I had changed out of my tan Gros Ventre County deputy shirt and put on a red T-shirt with my Levis and a dark green ball cap with yellow lettering that read, BASIN SUPPLY, I was mostly free of my guilt for eating out.

"C'mon, Grady dog," I said as I stepped outside. "Let's go to supper." It was about 250 yards to the Antler, not far enough in my opinion to warrant driving my truck, a '37 Chevy that was tucked in amongst the big trees by my cabin. With the gas situation being what it was, I left it parked as much as possible. But then, when I was within about 40 or 50 yards of the bar it suddenly occurred to me that in barely three days I would be taking Ellen to supper and a show with sodas and popcorn in Fremont, which was 40 miles roundtrip from Cedarville, plus another five miles on up the valley to where she lived. The naysayer in my mind shouted, *you shudda ate at the cabin.* And then the practical side of me joined in. *You could go to the Lumberjack and not the bar. Have a burger and fries for a quarter and a glass of water instead of beer and not put nickels in the jukebox cuz they don't have one or play pool.* But it was too late for the practical side of me to win out, I kept walking.

A large hill with scattered ponderosa pine trees borders the west side of Cedarville. In the dead of winter, it is high enough that by 3:30 in the afternoon the sun is no longer visible, leaving the town in a deep shadow. It is one of the things I hated about Cedarville. Today, however, sweat stains were already beginning to show under my arms by the time I reached the bar. The Antler, which was located midway through town at the base of this hill, was not much to look at from the outside and maybe not the inside either, depending upon how you viewed things. It was a good sized rectangular shaped log building with a pitched roof that was covered with tarpaper. Maybe when it was first built its sides had been coated with a dark stain, but it appeared that was a long time ago. The narrow side of the structure faced the street. A green wooden door whose upper third was glass, was situated directly below a big white sign with black letters that read, ANTLER BAR. To either side of the door was an undersized window, at least to me they were. Neither was very useful as far as looking out. Each had a neon sign that obscured most of the view. The one on the left read, Pabst

Blue Ribbon, while the one to the right said, OPEN, when it was illuminated.

There was a black Dodge pickup with a homemade stock rack parked in front of the bar. As Grady and I approached, a brown and white Australian Shepard dog came out from beneath the truck where it had been shaded up. It immediately ran over to Grady and they began sniffing noses and butts and anything else of interest. I knew the pickup belonged to a sheep man named Jim Meadows. If it had not been there, or if Jim had gotten a new truck but had the same dog, I would still know that he was inside. I'd come to recognize a lot of people in the valley that way.

Directly in front of the door was a slab of cement about four feet square that served as the porch. I paused and looked down at Grady and his new friend, Buster. I said, "You two behave yerselves." And then I went inside. My eyes had not quite adjusted to the semi-darkness when a voice off to my right boomed, "Hey Andy, is she hot enough for ya today?"

I looked over at the bartender, Oscar Reynolds, a middle-aged plump man who'd become soft and cynical from having stood behind a bar for too many years listening to drunks and pretending to be interested in what they had to say. I came back, trying to sound older than I was, "I wished to hell somebody would find the knob to turn the heat down a notch or two."

Jim Meadows, who was sitting towards the other end of the bar, finished taking a long drink of his Schlitz before pivoting his head towards me, "Ain't you heard, somebody broke the knob."

I played along. "So, that's the problem."

Oscar cut in, "Whaddaya drinkin', Andy?"

43

I glanced to my left across the room to a set of honey colored pine wood bat doors at the entrance to a hallway that led to a rest room, a shower and then opened up into the café part of the bar. Oscar appeared almost desperate for something to break the tedium of drunk talk and the whir of the ceiling fan overhead. Nonetheless, I said, "Well, I'll take a Pabst, but I believe I'm gonna go to the back and have a hamburger. I ain't had a thing to eat since breakfast."

"Ah, sit yer ass down. I'll order yer burger. Whaddaya want on it?"

It wasn't that I disliked Oscar, but at this very moment I was still processing the fact that I was now the main lawman in Gros Ventre county. I kind of wanted some quiet time.

"You want fries?" asked Oscar as he reached into the big upright cooler behind the bar and took out my beer.

I nodded. Seeing that I was still standing he said as he set the beer on the bar, "Sit down, I'll be right back."

Reluctantly, I sat down on the stool across from my beer. The stool appeared relatively new, as did the others to either side of it. They had a square, soft leather cushion top that was supported by four legs. I could see how, after a few drinks, it would be tough to break away from it. It put most men at just the right height to rest their forearms on the slick cherry wood bar top. And the temperature, my fireman's guess put it at a good 15 degrees cooler than outside. *It's no wonder*, I said to myself, *that Jim Meadows spends so much time here.* But then, in the mirror beyond the back bar, just to the left of the brass looking cash register and directly above a bottle of Old Crow, was Jim Meadows reflection. He was looking at me. For a split second I considered pretending that I hadn't seen him but, suddenly, that was no longer an option. He said, as he twisted around on his bar stool, "You know, I sure do miss that old man a yers. He was a good hand."

Memories of my father drinking with Jim came back to me. As a kid I was stranded, left to kill time until my dad would allow himself to break away from Jim. This didn't happen real often, maybe every two or three months when I guess the drudgery of living in the Gros Ventre caught up with him and he would go on a bender. Since Jim didn't miss many days at the Antler, he was usually part of it. I suspected this was his basis for judging my father to be a *good hand,* as I'd never known them to have much association otherwise. Back then I resented Jim. I dreaded seeing his pickup in front of the Antler as he could turn a non-bender day into a full-blown drunken one. I recalled the times when my dad had said, *Well, we better git the hell outta here. I got two streams ah water that needs changing.* But then that damned Jim would tell Oscar, *we need another round here.* And then he would look over at me standing behind my dad's bar stool and ignoring my frown, add, *and ya better give Andy another Coke too and a sack of peanuts.* There had actually been times when my father had said, *naw, I'd better go,* to which Jim had countered, *oh hell, you got time for one more.* And my dad would say, *I'm gonna be in hot water when I get home.* Jim would then come back, half laughing, *hell, another beer 'll put lead in yer pencil.* And then the both of them, along with Oscar who was setting up the drinks, would laugh while glancing over at me to see if I got Jim's intent. Back then, I didn't know what he was talking about so I remained stone faced. Even if I had known, the realization that I was going to be stuck there for another 30 or 40 minutes would likely have suppressed any laughter from me. Finally, I managed to extract myself from the quagmire of bad thoughts in my mind. I said, "Thanks Jim. I miss him too."

Jim looked like he was about to say something when his eyes abruptly shifted away to the window with the steady blue glow of the open sign. Outside, a pickup was just pulling in next to his. Momentarily, the door opened. I'd not quite gotten turned around when a loud voice called out, "You're just the man I was lookin' for."

Elmer Garrett, a rancher from up the valley was coming straight towards me. He appeared to be upset about something. When he was within about three feet of me, he stopped with his hands on his hips. The sour, almost acrid smell of his sweat reached me at about the same time as his words, "Somebody's been stealin' my gas."

Elmer had a look about him that was borderline intimidating, even when he wasn't mad. He was wearing a white Tee shirt and Levis that were stained with mud, grease, and sweat and were torn in several places. His white straw hat was equally as tattered and dirty. And his cowboy boots were so worn and scuffed it was nearly impossible to tell what color they were. On his right bicep he had a tattoo that read, PROPERTY OF USMC. His hair and droopy moustache were coal black. I guessed him to be about 40. Basically, he had the look of a man struggling to make a living. I said, "I don't doubt it with all of the rationing going on."

There were beads of perspiration on his cheeks just below his green bloodshot eyes. It seemed to accentuate his anger and the fact he was an honest working man. He said, "I got a 500 gallon tank at my place. It ain't been all that long ago that I had it filled and I'll be damned if I didn't run out yesterday. So, I called the gas man in Fremont, told him I needed more. So, he says I got all I can have till the first of the month. I told him I was a farmer and they got priority over some damned kids riding around town ogling the girls, but he said he still couldn't do it."

"How much do you figure that you lost?"

Garrett shrugged and then gave a deep sigh. "I don't know. Hunderd gallons maybe."

Jim chimed in, "Holy shit, that's a lotta gas."

"You damned right it is and I got hay to cut," said Garrett as he briefly made eye contact with Jim before coming back to me as if he expected me to fix things. "You heard about anybody else losing gas?"

"From time to time we'll get a call from someone that's had the tank in their car siphoned, but nothing like this." I paused for a second, questioning if I should even say it but then I did, "I take it you ain't got a lock on yer tank."

Garrett scowled at me. "It ain't like I live in town where some stranger is going to rob me. Ever body out here is in the same boat. A man shouldn't have to worry about his neighbors stealing from him, but I guess I was wrong about that."

"Sometimes the worst in a man comes out when you least expect it."

Garrett scoffed and shook his head as he looked at me almost as if I was a joke. "I shudda known better. I drove in here thinkin' you might have a suspicion who did this, maybe even get some of my gas back, but I can see I've wasted my time."

I felt insulted. I wanted to lash out at Garrett, to tell him he'd been a fool to not put a padlock on his tank, but I knew he was angry and hurting and needed someone to blame. I knew also that if some overblown version of this conversion got back to Roy Glover it might just result in my getting fired. I said in a sympathetic tone, "I'm sorry Mr. Garrett. I'll do what I can to find out who did this but, at this point, I'm about gonna need somebody to come forward and tattle on somebody else."

For a moment, Garrett just stared at me like he disapproved of my very existence and then he turned and walked out, slamming the door so hard behind him that it rattled the cue sticks in the wall rack next to it.

It was dead silence save for the ceiling fan overhead until Jim said, "Maybe when he cools off he'll figure out that he could probably borrow 50 or 60 gallons if he was to spread it out over half dozen of his neighbors."

"I hope so. It'd be a shame if he couldn't get his hay put up."

Jim took another drink of his beer and laughed briefly in a sarcastic way. "You know what's a real pisser though, is he's gonna have to burn what little gas he's got galavantin' 'round the country to scrounge up the gas to put in his tractor."

I shook my head. "I know, it ain't right." And then in the lull that followed, I reached for my beer and drank about half of it before setting it down. It tasted so good. I was savoring its coolness when Jim laughed again. "Maybe Garrett should send the Japs a bill. Hell, this is all their fault."

I laughed politely so as to disguise my thoughts, as an image of Ellen popped into my mind. Anyone looking at her would never guess that her father was white. But after Pearl Harbor, to a lot of people, all Japs were the same. Suddenly, I saw Roy Glover among those people.

"Be just a few minutes and yer burger 'll be done," shouted Oscar as he came through the back door from the kitchen at the far end of the bar.

I looked over to acknowledge him.

He went on, "I told Maude that you wanted the works so she carved off a slice of onion big enough to choke a horse." He paused and laughed in his cackling way. "She's grillin' it right next to the burger patty, sizzling and poppin' in that grease. It takes some of the bite out of it, but that's the way I like an onion, don't you?"

I nodded as Oscar stopped behind the bar just across from me. "Oh yeah, nuthin' like a good onion."

"Well yeah, some people 'll eat a burger without an onion or tomato or lettuce, not a damned thing but maybe a little mustard and mayo. I can't see eatin' ah burger that way, can you?"

I said, as I reached into my pants pocket for a silver dollar, "No sir, I can't." Without hesitation, I slid the dollar across the bar towards Oscar. "You suppose I could get some jukebox change."

Oscar picked up the dollar and started towards the cash register. He said over his shoulder, "The jukebox man was just here last week. He put some new songs in there. Some of 'em are alright and some ain't."

"I'll tell ya one that is alright," said Jim, "it's called *Pistol Packin' Mama*."

Oscar laid my change on the bar. "That is a good song but just remember, there's two versions of it."

"Well, which one do you boys favor?"

"I can't recall their name just now," said Jim.

"It's Al Dexter and his troopers," said Oscar. "The other version is by Bing Crosby and the Andrews Sisters. Its kind of a sleeper compared to Dexter."

I grinned and slid off my stool. "Alright then, *Pistol Packin' Mama* it is." As I started across the dark hardwood floor and past the pool table towards the jukebox in the far corner of the room, I heard Jim shout out, "Better give us another round here, Oscar." The ring of it took me back, except now, I was not drinking cokes.

"That Old Black Magic is a good tune," shouted Jim. "Glenn Miller does that one."

For a quarter, I got five songs. Without looking around, I raised my right hand to Jim, "Ok, Old Black Magic." I continued selecting under the watchful gaze of a mountain goat that had been mounted as a wall rug and hung to the left of the jukebox, and a nice mule deer buck to the right. Beyond the buck in that corner of the room was a phone booth. My last pick was a Frank Sinatra song. In a way, it struck me as kind of funny that an old sheep rancher would be knowledgeable on today's music but then, as much time as he spent at the Antler, he'd probably heard everything on the jukebox many times over.

I'd just got back to the bar and sat down when two things happened almost simultaneously to the beat of "Pistol Packin' Mama". Oscar set my hamburger and fries in front of me and Gertie Jenkins came through the front door. Her entrance, as my father would have probably described it, was like a horse turd in a cyclone. She'd barely cleared the door when she shouted out, "Did you boys hear about the big fire on Weasel Mountain?"

I immediately turned around on my stool, wondering if the situation had changed from when I was at the ranger station less than an hour ago. I looked at Gertie. Her dark eyes were glassy like maybe she'd already had a few drinks. She was a skinny woman, shapely by some standards. Her long black hair was braided into a single ponytail. She had on a sleeveless red blouse, faded Levis and moccasins. Clutched between the first two fingers of her right hand was a smoldering cigarette. I asked, thinking the worst if the fire was now big, "Did it blow up?"

"Well, that Jap girl up at the ranger station said it's close to ten acres. Russell 's up there fightin' it. The girl said they got more men coming from town."

"Did she say how long before these men will be here?" asked Oscar.

"I guess any time now." Gertie paused long enough to laugh in a hateful way. She took a drag from her cigarette as she stepped next to the bar. She glanced at me but then looked straight at Oscar, "I guess that chickenshit brother of hers is supposed to lead these men from Fremont out to the fire."

"Melvin Lujack is?" said Jim in a questioning tone.

"What I heard," said Oscar, "is he's all doped up. I guess he goes up to Great Falls once a week to see some military shrink."

"Oh, he's a prize," said Gertie. "If it weren't for his sister working for the forest service, he wouldn't be doing this. I guarantee it. Russell tells me the guy's a real basket case."

I'd heard the stories about Ellen's brother. I'd even talked to him a few times since he'd come home early from the Army. He didn't seem right in the head. He was really quiet and into himself, but nobody here knew the particulars of why that was. I said, "Maybe he's got good reason to be like he is, after all, he was in the war."

"In Alaska?" said Jim, "that's where I heard he was at. Hell, there ain't no war up there. All the fightin' is way to the south."

"I heard he never fired a shot," said Oscar.

"Shit," said Gertie emphatically, "he probably couldn't bring himself to kill his relatives." And then she laughed in

51

a cynical tone. Jim and Oscar joined in, I did not. It caused Gertie to cut short her laughter and look straight at me, she said, "you don't agree?"

At the risk of drawing attention to myself, I said, "You gotta give him credit for at least joining up, him and his brother both. Why I read in the paper that Charlie has been wounded."

Gertie was taken aback. At the same time, a temporary lull came over the room as the jukebox changed records and then it suddenly blared out Glenn Miller's "In The Mood". It was a snappy tune that made a person want to dance. It was a favorite song of a lot of people because, for a short while, it made them feel good. Gertie's hateful expression took away from that and she knew it. Gradually, her stare melted away until she turned to Oscar as if she'd not been speaking badly of the Lujack kids, because they were half Japanese, and said, "Gimme a Schlitz. Make sure you get it from the back of the cooler too. It's hot as hell outside. I ain't been ridin' a bar stool all afternoon like some folks." And then she laughed by herself.

I was at a point that I was wishing I'd stayed at the cabin and had corn flakes for supper. Without explaining myself, I stood and took my burger and beer from the bar and started towards the bat doors and the café. From behind me, Gertie shouted, "Whattsa matter, you too good to eat with us?"

I kept on walking. Glenn Miller's saxophone section kicked in as I pushed through the doors. It was my favorite part of the song. *Damn her*, I said to myself. I went past the rest room and then the shower, which was for Oscar's use mostly as he lived in the loft room above the Antler. After about 20 feet of hallway I entered the café. To my left was a lunch counter with five pedestal type stools that had red leather covers. Beyond the counter was another counter with desserts and dishes and silverware and bottles of mustard and ketchup. To the left of this counter was a cream-colored refrigerator and to the left of that a doorway that lead to a kitchen which was mostly taken up by the grill. To my right was a solitary wooden table whose top was covered with a white oilcloth that had little red flowers on it. I could hear Maude rummaging around in the kitchen which caused me to veer away from the counter, and further unwanted conversation, and sit at the table. It had been a long day and the evening was shaping up to be no different. I'd taken just three bites of my burger and had about a half dozen of my fries when I heard Maude strike a match. From the corner of my eye I could see her lighting what was undoubtedly a Camel from the open pack of cigarettes that had been laying on the counter in front of the end seat closest to the kitchen. She took a drag and blew the smoke out into the room. I did not know Maude very well. She was fifty-ish, frumpy with salt and pepper hair, never been married and was generally known as a grumpy woman. Given this and all that had happened out front and the fact I just wanted to listen to the tunes that I had just spent a quarter on, it did not seem unreasonable to me to eat while pretending to be looking at the tapestry hanging on the knotty pine wall in front of me. It was a picture of a grizzly bear with two cubs being confronted by a buckskin clad hunter. And then it began.

"That crew run ya out?"

I looked over at Maude and with a grin tossed my head to the side, "Gittin' a little rowdy out there."

She took another drag from her cigarette and exhaled the smoke in a lazy manner. "Well, yer the law, put the cuffs on 'em."

I laughed. "Can't, left 'em home."

"Well, what kinda lawman are you?"

For an instant, I envisioned Roy Glover answering that question. I moved on, "This is a good burger."

Maude was about to respond when she sensed a fleck of tobacco on the inside of her lower lip. For a few seconds she maneuvered it with her tongue until she had it captured, whereupon she plucked it off with the index finger and thumb of her left hand, while her right hand held the smoldering Camel. As I took another bite of my burger, I couldn't help but wonder if she had washed her hands before making it, or if we were now spit kin. She said, disclaiming anything to do with the quality of my burger, "you know that's Gros Ventre raised beef."

In between chews, I said, "Oh, well it sure is good."

"The meat man from town said it's mostly from Tim Robert's place."

Maude's words triggered a vision in my mind of Sherm Duke's steer hide and the furniture truck running the fire crew off the road. I swallowed and looked over at her. "So, Maude, with all of the rationing can you still buy all the meat you need?"

She scoffed in disgust. "I can if my meat man has got it to sell, but he has to get in line behind the government. He only gets so much from the packing plant and then he's got other customers besides me to keep happy."

"Do you ever run short?"

"Sometimes, like when they had the rodeo in Fremont a while back. They sold a lot of burgers and steaks in town. I couldn't get my full order that week and I plum ran out of hamburger."

"What about across the street, did they run out?"

"The Lumberjack, not quite, but damned close."

I was about to ask Maude who her meat man was when a customer emerged from the hallway and sat down at the counter. She glanced at me as she took one last drag from her cigarette before stubbing it out in the ashtray on the counter. I went back to eating and thinking as she took the stranger's order. It sounded like to me that a small packing plant could sell all the beef they had, and maybe to the right customer, elk too. The problem, however, was there were a lot of little slaughter houses around the country that could potentially be dealing in illegal meat.

I finished my supper and before going out front to settle up with Oscar, I took a shower as my cabin didn't have one, or a toilet, just a sink for doing dishes. To their credit, the county paid for me to take showers at the Antler. Toilet facilities, on the other hand, consisted of an old gray board outhouse, beyond the big trees next to my cabin. As Grady and I walked home, Cedarville had fallen under the shadow of the big hill next to it. The air was a little cooler but I knew what the inside of the cabin would be like. *I wished the damned county could afford a screen door*, I said to myself. *Maybe with my next check, I'll just buy my own door.* And then I scoffed at my stupidity. *Shit, it'll be fall by then. I won't need it.*

CHAPTER THREE

The bad thing about the middle of August, besides it being hot and there are lots of insects, is the days are long. It doesn't get dark until about 9:30. For a long time Grady and I laid on my bed listening to a couple of flies that I'd missed with my flyswatter and a Billings radio station. According to it, the war seemed to be going our way. There were days when my not joining up with Mitch gnawed at me pretty much non-stop and I wished I was out there on some Pacific island with him. But tonight I laughed at such fantasy, as truth be told, it scared me some to be the law, just me, in Gros Ventre county. There were people like Elmer Garrett and Sherm Duke that were expecting me to right the wrongs that had been done to them. And deep down, I suspected Betty Duke wanted rescued from the wrong being done to her. And Roy Glover, he too wanted justice, but of a different kind.

The last thing I remember before falling asleep was listening to "Moonlight Serenade" and playing in my mind how I hoped my date with Ellen would go on Saturday night. I was nervous, if not apprehensive about it, but apparently not so much to prevent me from being sound asleep when

Grady growled and then began barking loudly. My feet had barely hit the floor when I heard someone pounding on my door and then an unmistakable female voice that, oddly, did not come as a surprise.

"Andy, its Betty Duke. I need your help. Please open up."

Betty sounded excited, but not hysterical as one might imagine. I hollered out over Grady's barking, "Just a minute, Mrs. Duke, while I get dressed. My heart raced as I slipped on my pants and deputy's shirt. I went across the room in my bare feet and flipped the light switch next to the door. Before opening it I glanced back at the alarm clock by my bed, it read 1:40. I frowned and shook my head. I said to myself, *What in the hell could she want at this time of day*? And then I opened the door. Light from inside the cabin poured out and blended with the headlights of their still idling pickup. There she stood, her right arm still in a sling. It was obvious that sometime tonight she had been crying, but not now. Her eyes were red and puffy and determined. But what caught my attention was what appeared to be blood on her hands and faded Levis and brown plaid shirt. It caused my voice to take on even more excitement, "What's wrong, Betty?"

Conversely her expression remained steady, I suspect because she had been rehearsing what she had to say all the way down the Gros Ventre until now, she said in a too calm voice, "Sherm has been accidentally shot."

The emphasis she had put on accidentally was obvious. I came back, "How did this happen? Is he all right?"

"Like I said, it was an accident and yes, I believe he'll be ok."

I sensed the irritation in her voice but said, still trying to be compassionate to her situation, "Betty, somebody getting shot is serious business. I -"

"That's why I stopped here before going on to the hospital in Fremont. I'd like for you to call those people and tell them we're on our way and that this was an accident and they don't need to be calling the city cops."

"I suspect I can do that, but first I need to know exactly what happened," I said in a stern voice.

For a few seconds she just stared at me like I was being unreasonable. Finally, she sighed, "A couple of hours ago, our dog started barking up a storm. Sherm got a flashlight and went outside to see what was the matter. The next thing me and Katie know is he's hollering for Katie to bring the shotgun. He says there's a skunk out there and he's got his light on it. Well, Sherm keeps an old .410 right by the door for just this kind of thing. So, Katie grabs it and starts across the yard in the dark to where Sherm is at." She paused like she couldn't say what came next.

"And then what?" I said.

Betty collected herself like it would be hard to continue. She went on, "Katie stumbled and the gun went off and I heard Sherm make a loud grunt or shriek, I don't know, kind of an animal noise I guess, and then he yells at Katie, *dammit, you shot me.* At that point, I ran out of the house to where Katie was and then we helped Sherm up."

"So, you saw Katie stumble?"

"Yes."

"I thought you said it was dark."

Betty frowned at me like I was calling her a liar. "It wasn't so dark that I couldn't make out her shape. You know how it is when it's about that dark. There's just enough light to make you think you're ok to be walking around but, in reality, you can't see dips in the ground or ruts and that's what tripped Katie up."

I looked beyond Betty into the headlights of their truck. "I need to talk to Katie, and Sherm if you think he's ok with it."

Betty nodded. "Katie's pretty upset, but Sherm's a long-ways from being at death's door."

I followed Betty back to their pickup. Katie was sitting behind the wheel. I looked in the open window. "How are you doing, Katie?"

She gave a deep sigh but kept her focus straight ahead, "This is all so terrible. I tripped and the gun went off."

Knowing that she, like most girls on a ranch, had been raised around guns, I asked, "So, the shotgun was already cocked when you picked it up or is that something you did?"

Before Katie could answer, her mother jumped in, "It was already cocked. It was just like Sherm left it."

"Is that right, Katie? Is that how you found the gun?"

"Yes, that's how it was," she said. "I just picked it up."

During the time I'd been talking to her she had refused to look directly at me. As a consequence, I'd not been able to see the right side of her face. I thought back to earlier in the day when I'd been at their place and she'd tried to approach me, but Sherm wouldn't allow it. And now, as luck would have it, she had accidentally shot her father. I said, "Look at me, Katie."

Even in the poor light, I could see the reluctance in her face but she turned. It was as I suspected. I shook my head and sighed. "Katie, if you would, please get out of the truck and come over to my cabin."

Katie started to comply but Betty objected. "Why Andy? Why make things worse?"

As Katie stepped from the truck, I caught a glimpse of Betty's concern. I said again, "Let's go into the cabin."

From the bed of the truck where he was laying and no doubt listening to what was going on, Sherm hollered, "What the hell are you people doing? It's not bad enough that I get shot, but now you've got to fiddle-fart around getting me to the hospital?"

I looked over the side of the pickup's bed. Sherm was laying face down on a sleeping bag. I said, "How ya fairin' Sherm?"

He raised up on his elbows and looked at me. "Well, I'd be better if that fool kid a mine hadn't a peppered my ass with that .410."

I suppressed a smile as I wanted to say, *I can't think of a more deserving person*, but I said, "Well, look on the bright side, she cudda had a 12 gauge with double 00 buck."

Sherm snorted in the darkness. "Why don't you just hurry up with whatever it is you think you need to git done so we can be on our way."

"I just wanna be sure this is an accident, just like everybody is saying."

"Sure it is. Why wouldn't it be?"

"I don't know. Seems like you got lots a bad luck up to your place with your wife falling off a horse and Katie stumbling and shootin' you."

In the darkness I could tell that Sherm was looking up at me, but I couldn't read his face. For a moment, it was quiet between us save for the raspy idle of his pickup's motor. I imagined him calculating what he thought he could get away with saying to me and then it came, "You don't wanna let that badge go to yer head, *Deputy*. There's some fellas that might just turn you over their knee and give you a paddlin."

My anger instantly took hold of my tongue. I was about 30 pounds heavier and four or five inches taller than Sherm and in no mood for his veiled threats. I said, "Well, I'll tell ya Sherm, if *one* of those fellas was to try that, I'd whip his ass good and take pleasure in doin' it." From the darkness, I heard him scoff and mumble something under his breath before sinking back down onto the sleeping bag. I stared at him for a few seconds before turning to face Betty and Katie. I said, "let's go inside." As we walked, I could hear them whispering behind me. I couldn't make out what they were saying but I suspected they were firming up their story. They were purposely lagging behind so as stay out of earshot. I stepped inside the cabin to wait for them. They had stopped just short of the open door. Their whispers had become more excited, angry even, until Betty's insistence escaped their privacy for a split second, *we've got no choice.* And then they came into the light. It was immediately clear to me how the gun got cocked and Sherm was shot. The right side of Katie's face was purple and swollen. I said, "So, yer dad didn't like the idea of you wanting to talk to me earlier today?"

Katie glanced over at her mother and then back to me, but she remained quiet.

Betty intervened. "Andy, just let it go, please."

I shook my head. "Betty, this reads like an open book. People are gonna know just like they have for years. *Those Duke women, they sure are accident prone.* It needs to stop."

Betty's eyes swelled with tears. She said, her voice beginning to break, "Think about it, Andy. If this isn't an accident, then what is it? Think about where that leaves us."

It came to me then, like I was the one being punched in the face. So long as Sherm played along that this was an accident, Katie couldn't be charged with attempted murder. But, if she and her mother told of the beatings they'd gotten, Sherm's story would likely change.

"Please, Andy, just call the hospital."

The tears had now overflowed Betty's eyes as Katie began to cry too. She put her arm around her mother. They stood before me, sobbing and sniffling quietly. I had no doubt their emotion was real and not manufactured to sway my decision. A sudden awareness came over me of how I might be judged once the particulars of all this got around, as I knew they would. People would laugh. *Yeah, ole Sherm Duke hoodwinked that snot-nosed deputy.* But what was the alternative, charge Sherm with domestic abuse and have him turn around and claim Katie shot him on purpose? There would be sympathy for Katie, but there would be those too that would say she should have just reported him and not shot him in the back. I sighed. "Alright, Betty. I'll make the call."

A look of relief came to her face. "Thank you."

"You know this won't be the end of it, don't you?"

She shook her head and looked away.

The operator connected me with the Gros Ventre County hospital. It was 1:52 a.m., after six rings a woman answered. I identified myself and said, "I've got a person with an accidental gunshot coming your way."

"Do you want us to send the ambulance?"

"No, he's not that bad."

"What's the patient's name?"

"Sherm Duke."

Pause. "Oh, we know him, or at least his wife we do."

"I figured you did."

Sarcastic laughter. "What happened, his wife get tired of the *accidents*?"

I looked at Betty and Katie as I said, "Make note that I've questioned everybody involved and this was a simple accident. Nobody is being charged with anything."

The voice, a husky smoker's voice laughed again. "Do you believe in Santa Claus too?"

The woman was still laughing as I pretended that she was being civil and thanked her before hanging up. And so, it began.

CHAPTER FOUR

There was no going back to sleep after the Duke family left. My mind was endlessly spinning the possibilities of how all of this would play out once it became common knowledge. I wanted it to be a new day so that I could turn the page on last night, but time seemed to have stopped. It was like the sun was never coming back. Finally, when the mountains to the east were silhouetted in the pre-dawn light and the coolness inside my cabin had caused the flies to become silent and when, normally, I would have been asleep waiting for my alarm clock to go off, the phone rang. It was 5:43 a.m.. I said to myself, as I picked up the receiver after two rings, *who in the hell can this be*? And then I answered, "Gros Ventre County Sheriff's office, Deputy Yarnell speaking."

"I thought I might be waking you up, but I guess not."

"No Ma, I been awake for a while. I thought you'd be at work."

"I am. Betty and Katie came to see me. They just left."

"So, you know all about last night?"

"I do, Betty says she's ready to take Katie and leave Sherm."

"Do you think she will?"

"I don't know. She talks a good line. She told me years ago that she wanted to leave him, but here she is. This time it might be different."

"You think so?"

"Yeah, she said a nurse at the hospital hinted this was all her fault because she'd stayed too long. It made Betty feel real bad."

"Well, on the surface it doesn't seem like a fair thing to say but if you stop and think about it, she stayed on knowing how Sherm was and now look at the mess they've got. There's gonna be a lot of hard feelings in that house."

I sensed some hesitation on my mother's part and then she said, "Betty didn't say for sure, but at one point she said she might call you to be there if she moves out. She asked me if I thought this would be ok? I didn't know what else to say but yes."

My first thought was that going to the Duke place while Betty and Katie packed up and left would be like busting open a hornet's nest and waiting for them to come out. But, I said, "That's ok, Ma, it's what I get paid to do."

"Oh, Andy, that Sherm Duke is such a hothead. He's crazy, he's just plain mean. Promise me, if you go out there that you'll take somebody with you."

I figured in time that my mother would find out her boy was here by himself now, that the Sheriff was gone down to Phoenix for a good while, so I said simply, "I will, Ma."

And then in a muffled voice, I heard my mother shout, "I'll be right there." She came back, "I've got to go, but remember, you be careful around that Sherm Duke. Like your father used to say, *he's crazy as ah shithouse rat.* Ok, I love you."

"I love you too."

As I hung up the phone, I had a peculiar feeling that wasn't good. For grades seven through twelve, I had to attend school in Fremont. The kids from over there, at least the Mormon ones, had been warned by their parents that the kids from Cedarville, or the Gros Ventre valley, were wild and not a good influence. I'd laughed at such talk back then, but this morning it was like that side of the valley had been awakened. In the past 24 hours I had dealt with wanna be dog killers, a fistfight, gas theft, poaching, cattle theft, a wife beater and now attempted murder. *Maybe the Mormons were right*, I said to myself, *this is a wicked place.*

I'd finished my corn flakes and was on my third cup of coffee as I sat at the table in the middle of the room putting onto official forms the details of all that had happened yesterday, when the phone rang again. I'd already checked in with Grace so I was a little surprised to hear her voice. "Andy, I got a call from the highway patrol up in Great Falls. Apparently, Roy Glover called them and asked that they give you a hand down here, kind of fly the flag so to speak, so folks know the law is still around even though Tom is gone."

Anger instantly pulsed through my body. *That damned Glover, why can't he just let it go.* I said aloud, "Tom never said anything about actually making a request to the state."

"No, I don't think he knew about it. This is a Glover thing."

"He's still mad about the ticket I gave him and now he's trying to make it look like I need babysitting. That's what it is, pure and simple."

"Well now, Andy, there ain't no need to let this snap yer garters. Having a little extra help might not be a bad thing. They can tend to this side of the mountains and you can focus on the Gros Ventre. From what you told me earlier this morning, I'd say you've got a full plate out there. Heck, if Tom were here, he'd have a full plate, any man would, so just settle yourself down."

I knew Grace was right, but when it came to Glover my ego was like a bad tooth, it didn't take much to get a reaction from me. I took a breath and slowly released it. "Alright Grace, I'll try."

"You gonna be doing reports this morning?"

"Most likely, unless I get a call."

"Ok, I guess if I need ya, I know where to find you."

I laughed. "Grace, do you take dictation? Maybe, I could just tell you over the phone about my cases yesterday."

Grace did not laugh. "Yeah, right after I do your laundry. Goodbye, Andy."

After hanging up the phone I went back to the table and sat down. It was quiet, except for a fly buzzing endlessly around the room and the ticking of my alarm clock. I'd had to build a fire in the stove to make coffee and as a result, the room was now sweltering. My mind began to wander from the task at hand. *That damned Glover is determined to paint a picture of me as being incompetent, a snot-nosed kid that needs somebody to hold his hand.* But then in the next instant, the practical side of me came back, *it will be nice though, having the state police watch over the other side of the county. Maybe I can call their trooper to go with me if the Duke women move out.* Anger suddenly gripped me at the thought Glover might have done something that could benefit me but, at the same time, he would try to use against me.

It had not been pleasant describing on paper all that had happened yesterday but, I stuck with it. My clock read, 11:52. It was lunch time. I knew from having been in the fridge earlier this morning there was a partial jar of raspberry jam that my mother had made and some butter. However, I was craving a baloney sandwich and potato chips. This would require a trip to the store. There were times when I wished that I didn't always have to wear my gun belt but it was part of my uniform and I was on duty so I strapped it on and grabbed my straw cowboy hat on the way out the door. Grady, who had been laying under one of the big pine trees spotted me right off and came running with his tail wagging. I reached down and patted his head. "You wanna go to the store? Huh, do ya, there might be a slice of baloney in it for you."

In a few minutes we arrived at the Cedarville General Store. A red pickup was parked at the gas pump in front of it. I recognized it as belonging to Willy Jones, the valley's ditch rider. It was his job to referee the distribution of the water from the Gros Ventre. He made sure that everybody got water according to what their claim said they were entitled to. In wet years, when there was plenty to go around, his job usually went pretty smooth but in a dry year, like this one, there sometimes were disagreements that got out of hand.

"You wait here, Grady dog. I'll be back in a minute," I said as I stepped into the coolness of the store. Hanging from the high ceiling were two fans. They were turning fast causing them to wobble and whir as they circulated the air. Along the wall to my immediate right were two wood frame glass display cases that stood waist high. Each had a sliding door in the front. The first case contained candy while the second one, closest to the counter where you paid, held ammunition, knives and fishing tackle. To my left were three rows of white wooden shelves stocked with various kinds of food and dry goods in cans, bottles and boxes. I turned left and went down the first aisle towards the back wall where the pop cooler and two old refrigerators that held meat and dairy products were located. Also, on the back wall, in the very corner of the store away from most foot traffic was a small table. Stacked on it were boxes wrapped in plain brown paper. As a kid growing up in the Gros Ventre I'd never known what was in the boxes even though, on a couple of occasions, my mother would send me into the store to get one of them with instructions they put it on our tab. Not until I had graduated high school and was in my first season on the fire crew, did I learn that the boxes contained sanitary napkins. I turned right at the brown packages and went along the back wall towards the meat fridge. I was nearly to it when I heard the wooden floor boards in the aisle to my right squeak, followed by, "I heard ya had a little excitement here last night."

I looked over, "How ya fairin, Willy?"

Willy was a small man, about 70, maybe five-six and a 140 pounds soaking wet. His hair was white and cut short. He was wearing a long-sleeved tan colored shirt, Levis, lace-up black boots and a new cream-colored straw hat with a totally flat brim. He came back, still focused on last night, "I heard Sherm Duke's kid shot 'im in the ass." And then he started to cackle until tears came to his eyes. He took a quick breath and added, "You know, I'd be willin' to give that girl ah his free shootin' lessons. Hell, I'll even supply the bullets." He followed this up with more laughter.

I said, "I take it Sherm's not on yer Christmas card list."

Willy scoffed. "The sonovabitch threatened to throw me in the crik here ah coupla weeks ago if I didn't allow him another two days water."

"So, what'd ya do?"

"Gave it to him. A man doesn't want to piss that fella off. He ain't right in the head, ya know."

"I've been told that. But you know, Willy, if that ever happens again, you let me know and I'll go talk to Sherm."

Willy looked up at me and cackled. "Well, stay away from the crik if you do and if you don't, wear yer swimmin' suit."

I briefly laughed along before saying, "Well Willy, me an' my dog are havin' baloney sandwiches for lunch so I better git going."

Willy reached out and gently touched my forearm. He lowered his voice, "Don't mean to keep ya from eatin' but I been hopin' to run into ya. I heard Elmer Garrett lost some gas." Willy paused and glanced back towards the counter where Niko Lujack, Ellen's mother, was working. He turned back to me and whispered, "Last Sunday I saw that Schultz kid pulling out of Garrett's place. Ever-body knows the Garretts go to church so at the time I thought it was just peculiar he was there, but now with this gas thievery it puts a little more light on it, wouldn't ya think?"

I nodded. "It does seem kind of suspicious. Garrett's live a long ways from the Schultz's."

"That's what I thought and the Garrett's ain't got no kids the age of that Schultz boy."

"I appreciate the information, Willy."

"That boy has got too much time on his hands. A stint in the Army might do him some good."

I smiled. "Maybe so."

Willy turned sideways to me as if to walk away, and then paused, "Stop in if your ever by my place and I'll stand ya to a cold sarsaparilla." He then chuckled, as if to convey the fact he was kidding about what we'd be drinking, and walked away.

I said, mostly to his back, "Good talkin' to ya." I liked Willy. As a kid growing up in the valley my father and I had visited his place several times. They would have a snort while I played outside or just sat and listened to their grownup talk. It irritated me that Sherm would threaten an old man like Willy. On the scale of disgusting behavior, I put it one notch above beating your wife and daughter. I vowed that I would warn Sherm about threatening Willy, or for that matter, anybody. Doing this, I knew, wouldn't help matters if I were to oversee Betty and Katie moving out. Sherm would be mad enough without me issuing my own threat towards him. In my mind I laughed sarcastically, *lawmen get shot all the time when they go putting themselves in the middle of domestic squabbles. And for this I get $100 a month and the right to live in the county's cabin.* But then the naysayer in me brought to bear what Mitch had said in one of his recent letters, *I get $50 a month and all the excitement and C rations I can handle.* As I reached for the handle of the meat fridge, I said to myself, *I'll set Duke straight just as soon as he gets out of the hospital.*

There were two rolls of baloney in red, waxy feeling paper along with a slab of bacon that was close to two feet long in the fridge. My mouth watered for some bacon and eggs in lieu of cornflakes for breakfast tomorrow so I pulled the slab out along with the baloney roll that had already been cut on and started for the front counter. Ellen's mother, Niko, who worked part-time at the store, watched my approach without speaking. I did not know her very well but, in the past, she'd always been pleasant and exchanged the usual greetings. Today, she seemed different. I set the meat on the counter, glanced over at her, and then looked back at the bacon. I said, "I need a pound of bacon and I guess the same for the baloney."

71

Still silent, she ran off a length of brown butcher paper from a roll that was suspended on a black cast-iron holder to the right of where the meat was lying. Taking a butcher knife from beneath the paper roller, she made an educated guess as to how much was a pound and sliced it off the slab and then did the same for the baloney. On the counter behind her was a white scale with a little window to read the weight. She said, "The bacon is about an ounce short of a pound and then she added the baloney to the scale and read the number, "The baloney is slightly over but close to a pound."

"That sounds good," I said.

Her look was indifferent, just short of being rude, "You want them wrapped separately?"

"No, one package is fine."

She positioned the meat on the paper and made the first fold and taped those sides and then she did the other fold. She pushed the meat across the counter towards me. "Do you want me to put this on your tab?"

I nodded as I looked her straight in the eyes. I said, "Did Ellen tell you that I asked her out on Saturday?"

"Why now?"

"What do you mean?"

She smiled wryly. "Before Pearl Harbor, she had lots of dates. Since then, no one wants to take a Jap girl out."

I knew what Niko said was mostly true. There were those in the valley that didn't like the fact she still worked at the store. To his credit, however, the owner told these people there was nothing but common sense to stop them from using their gas ration to go to Fremont and shop. I said, "Ellen's a pretty girl, she always had her pick of guys in school. I never saw myself as part of that crowd."

Niko's expression was still serious, "She likes you. I hope you don't abuse that knowledge."

"I won't. I promise you, I won't."

The phone on the wall to the right of her rang. For a few seconds she hesitated, looking at me as if to gauge my sincerity and then she turned away, not indicating if she believed me or not.

On the walk home from the store I pondered what Willy had told me about Bernie Schultz. Stealing gas in times like these was something that I could easily see Bernie doing, and not just because he tried to kill Ezra Coggins' dog for fun. My opinion of him went back to school when he was caught in the boys' locker room going through wallets. For that, he was suspended for a week and made to give the money back, but it was only what he'd taken in that particular instance when he was caught. The thievery, on the other hand, had been going on for some time before that. So now, here was Bernie, two years out of high school and still up to no good. I knew there was little I could do since Willy hadn't actually seen Bernie pumping Garrett's gas. If I were to drive out to the Schultz place and ask Bernie what he was doing at the Garrett's ranch last Sunday morning, he would deny being there. Ultimately, I figured, I'd have to reveal that Willy saw him, in which case, he'd either deny it or make up some lie as to why he was there. I felt helpless.

After lunch, I made a call to the brand inspector up in Great Falls. It went about like I thought it would. He said that he had far bigger fish to fry and couldn't spare the time, or gas, to drive all the way down to Cedarville for one steer. In his defense he went on, at some length, about how he was investigating the theft of 27 head of yearlings north of Fort Benton somewhere down along the Missouri river. I allowed him to ease his conscience by telling him not to worry, that I was working with the local game warden and that I'd call him if anything developed. However, unlike the gas theft, I had no idea other than the mysterious furniture truck guys, who butchered Sherm's steer and probably the elk too.

At 2:05 p.m. the phone rang. I answered in my deputy sheriff voice.

"Andy, you sound like somebody I don't know when you come on like that."

"Sorry, Ma, but anything else might make Joe Blow think he had the wrong number."

"I don't know about that. Operators are pretty good about making the right connection."

"So, Ma, what did you need?"

"Well, Betty says they're bringing Sherm home tomorrow. They'll probably leave the hospital around ten and be out to the ranch by noon, I suppose."

An uneasiness shot through me at the thought I would have to referee the Duke women leaving Sherm tomorrow. I said, "So, is Betty just going to drop him off and leave?"

My mother laughed as if I'd said something ridiculous. "No, she's not as heartless as Sherm. She's going to wait till he's up and around good. I don't think she's going to leave him until sometime next week."

"You don't know when?"

"Not for sure."

"Has she told Sherm yet?"

"No, she thinks it's best if she doesn't give him time to stew over it and instead just one day up and leaves."

"Where's she going?"

My mother went silent to the point I was about to repeat myself, when she said, "Her and Katie are going to move in with me."

"What? Do you think that's wise getting in the middle of all this? You know Sherm isn't going to just let this go. I suspect when he figures out where they're at he'll be wearing the road out between his place and your front door. Do you want to be a part of that?"

"She's my friend."

I frowned and shook my head. I said into the phone, "Depending on how things go, Betty may want to get a restraining order against Sherm."

"I guess we'll cross that bridge when we come to it but you, have you called the highway patrol and let them know they'll need to come with you when Betty moves out."

"No, Ma, I don't know when she's moving."

"You could at least alert them that you might call back next week."

"Don't worry about it, Ma. I'll take care of things. Just tell Betty to let me know when and I'll be there."

"Ok, but promise me you'll take somebody with you."

I laughed sarcastically. "Who are you gonna call?"

"What?"

"You're gonna be invitin' into your house the very thing you're worried about with me going to the Duke place."

There was a pause and then she said, "It's a long ways to the upper end of the Gros Ventre."

"For your sake, I hope it's too far."

"I've got to go, Andy. I love you."

She did not wait for me to respond.

CHAPTER FIVE

For supper on Friday night I heated up a can of chili and ate it along with some Wonder bread and raspberry jam as I listened to the radio and the flies. It was an overdose of solitude that was ineffective in keeping all of the stressful things in my mind at bay. Earlier, around noon, I happened to be out in front of my cabin when the Duke's pickup went by. Katie was driving and Betty was riding up front as a passenger, Sherm apparently, was laying in the back. I looked straight at Betty and waved. She appeared tired, maybe even sad. From inside the cab, she brought her left arm across her body to wave as her right arm was still in a sling. In that moment, I wished they could stop and we would all talk without anybody being mad and Sherm could see how he was and that there was no other way but for his family to leave him. But then reality dictated they roll on up 29 and the Gros Ventre valley. Soon, they were out of sight.

By 7:21 p.m. I'd had enough peace and quiet for one night. *Just one beer*, I'd told myself. Tomorrow night, when I take Ellen to supper and the show, is when I would splurge. The walk to the Antler went by quick. A new looking blue

Chevy coupe with white wall tires was parked out front. It, and unfortunately Gertie Jenkins' pickup, were the only vehicles there. I had no desire to talk to Gertie, which caused me to come to a dead stop about 50 feet short of the Antler. I was debating whether to go to the Lumberjack and have a Coke when the jukebox started up inside the Antler. It was an Ernest Tubb song, "Walking The Floor Over You". There was no jukebox at the Lumberjack, just more peace and quiet. I walked on, leaving Grady at the front door of the Antler and stepped inside. I'd barely closed the door when Gertie, who was leaning on a cue stick next to the pool table, shouted, "Uh oh, watch out, here comes the law."

A tall cowboy, who I assumed was the owner of the Chevy out front, looked over at me from beyond the pool table where he was standing and smiled. He was wearing fancy clothes, clearly not a working cowboy and not from the valley. After he'd sized me up for a few seconds, he said, still smiling, "Does your mother know where you're at?" And then he and Gertie laughed, him because being a jokester at other people's expense appeared to be the kind of guy he was and Gertie because she was drunk.

I glanced over at the guy and said in a sharp, abrupt voice, "Nope, I snuck outta the house." I then walked over to the bar and sat down without waiting for his response. Gertie's, however, I heard, "See, he ain't a friendly type."

"Whaddaya drinkin', Andy?" asked Oscar with a sour look on his face.

"Pabst."

Oscar took my beer from the cooler, opened it and set it in front of me. He still had a disgusted look as he nodded towards Gertie and her new friend. "A little of those two goes a long way. You know what I mean?"

In a way, it struck me as odd that Oscar would be complaining about them as they had to be good for business. Nonetheless, I said, "How long they been here?"

Oscar sighed. "Gertie since about three o'clock, the big guy maybe about an hour."

I shook my head. "Where in the hell does Gertie get her money? I know Russell ain't gittin' rich workin' for the forest service."

Oscar shrugged. "I don't know. She used to run a tab here, but then one day last year she came in and paid it off and ever since then she's been a cash customer."

I took a drink of my beer, as I did, it caused me to look into the mirror behind the bar. Reflected there I could see Gertie bent over the pool table with her cue stick lining up a shot. The big cowboy moved next to her and placed his left hand on her ass. "Here, let me help you."

Gertie laughed and stabbed at the cue ball. She said, sounding not the least bit offended, "Maybe we should try that again." And then they both laughed.

I set my beer on the bar and began to peel at the label, lest I look into the mirror and get caught watching them play grab ass.

Oscar said, "Russell 'd have a shit fit if he could see how she was carrying on."

"I 'spect he would," I said as I remained focused on peeling back the label on my beer bottle. "Jenkins must still be workin' that Weasel Mountain fire or he'd be here."

"Well, you know what they say, while the cat's away the mice will play."

I laughed politely. "Those two 'd be crappin' their chaps if Russell was to walk in right now."

Oscar closed his eyes and gently bobbed his head in agreement.

I picked up my beer and was just starting to take a drink when I saw in the mirror Maude part the bat doors slightly and call out, "Order up."

Another Ernest Tubb song entitled "Rollin' On" had come on the jukebox. The big cowboy looked over at Maude and said in a jovial tone, "Thank you, Ma'am. We'll be rollin' on yer way directly."

Maude pursed her lips as if she was irritated by his attempt to be funny and turned away. Gertie, on the other hand, was amused as only a drunk would be and laughed while she slurred the words, *we're gonna roll on. Yeseree, we're rollin' on.*

The big cowboy laid his cue stick on the pool table, which still had a good number of balls on it. He said in a loud voice, still trying to be the funny man, "C'mon, let's eat. I'm so hungry I could eat the butt out of a dead skunk."

Gertie laughed again, like somebody who was not only drunk but was about to get a free meal from the joke teller. She then laid her cue stick on the pool table before the two of them started for the bat doors. Just as Gertie started through the doors the cowboy slapped her on the ass and said, "Git along little doggie." And then they both laughed all the way down the hall.

It was at this point that I began to wonder if the rumors I'd heard about Gertie leaving the bar with strange men might be true.

As if he'd read my mind, Oscar said in a disgusted voice, "What a little slut she is. That poor dammed Russell out there fightin' fire and she's in here carrying on like that. I'll tell ya, she's a good lookin' woman but I sure as hell wouldn't want her."

Even though I pretty much agreed with Oscar, I was hesitant to bash Gertie knowing how fast gossip can spread in a small place like the Gros Ventre. And if there was anybody in the valley who could move gossip along it was Oscar, as he had the time and, most importantly, the opportunity. And, if a person was totally honest about it, he had the need. Gossip could be a fix for boredom. There was only so much Ernest Tubb or Glenn Miller or drunk talk or silence that a man could listen to before he resorted to gossip. So, I said, "Yeah, it's a helluva note."

Oscar went on, "Does she think people don't see how she is?"

I mumbled, "I don't know."

"One of these days Russell's gonna catch her at this and then the shit's gonna hit the fan. You can mark my words."

I nodded looking at my beer and wondering if Oscar would take offense if I suddenly downed it and left. It was about a third full.

And then he said, "You know as familiar as that guy has gotten with the curve of her ass, I wouldn't be surprised to see her go outta here with him and take a ride to someplace outta town. Probably go for a roll with that fella in the back seat of that fancy car of his. Don't ya think?"

I shrugged and reached for my beer. Three big gulps and a belch later I was done. I stood up, "Well, Oscar, I better skedaddle. I got some paperwork for the county that needs done."

From the corner of my eye, I could see that Oscar was a little miffed that I was leaving. He came back, "It's Friday night, for hell sakes."

As I headed for the door, I laughed and said over my shoulder, "Well, you know how it is, the criminal element never rests."

And so ended my attempt to escape the boredom of my cabin.

CHAPTER SIX

I had known Ellen since midway through the third grade when her parents, Phil and Niko Lujack, and her two brothers, Charlie and Melvin came to the valley. Her father went to work for a big rancher named Milo Peterson. As a little kid attending the Cedarville Elementary School, Ellen was just another kid that I sometimes played with if the activity at recess happened to be Red Rover, but not if it was dodge ball or basketball as it so often was in the winter. The girls would generally be off skipping rope or playing hop-scotch or roller skating or anything that didn't seem to appeal to boys. And being two grades ahead of her, I didn't see her through most of the day when we were in class. The school at Cedarville had two class rooms. One was termed the little room for grades 1-3, and the other was called the big room for grades 4-6. The whole school had maybe 35 kids. When I went into the seventh grade the separation between us really increased as then I rode the bus into Fremont to attend junior high. And then, in the beginning of my freshman year, my father was killed and my mother and I moved to town, as Fremont was generally referred to. Without my father, and being an only child, life seemed far too complex. Among those complexities were girls.

It was about a ten-minute drive from Cedarville out to the Peterson ranch. I had spent much of the day getting ready for my date with Ellen. I washed my truck and wiped down the inside of it with hot soapy water and then I went down to the Antler and took a shower, shaved, trimmed my moustache and splashed on plenty of good smelling cologne that my mother had given me for Christmas. I may have gotten carried away with the cologne as I had barely come through the bat doors into the bar when Oscar shouted out, *Holy shit, Andy, yer gonna have the place smellin' like a French whorehouse.*

Jim Meadows, who was sitting at the bar sipping a beer, smiled broadly into the mirror but then his face became serious. He said, *You better watch yerself if you take that Lujack girl to town. I imagine there's folks there that have lost kin in the war.*

I glanced over at Oscar and frowned. He was the only one who knew why I was taking a shower. I looked back at Jim and said, knowing that he meant well, *Thanks, for the advice. I'll be careful.*

Up ahead, at the junction with a side road, was a big wooden sign that had been left its natural color. It was about five feet across by a foot high and mounted on two wooden posts. In bold black letters it read, HDQT. - PETERSON LAND & LIVESTOCK COMPANY. About a mile down this road, right next to the Gros Ventre, was the Lujack place. As foreman, Phil Lujack and his family occupied the house Milo Petserson had lived in before he made a lot of money. Peterson now lived a couple of miles further up the Gros Ventre in a big fancy brick house. All of the land, for a mile on either side of the river between the two houses, was his. To get to the Lujack house I had to drive past a series of pole corrals, a shop, barn, parked tractors and machinery, stock trailers, and a bunkhouse where, finally, the hard-packed dirt road entered a stand of ponderosa pines and abruptly ended. The Lujack's lived in a white clapboard house with a green shingle roof that was surrounded by a lawn bordered by a white picket fence. A black pickup was parked in front of it. The ranch logo was printed in bold white letters on the driver's side door. I pulled in beside it and got out. My heart was hammering as I started towards the house. I barely passed through the gate when I began to second guess myself. I was wearing gray cotton pants and a short-sleeve white shirt with black and white oxfords. Besides cologne, I had used a liberal amount of gel which had left my hair, that was parted down the middle, as hard as a rock. It was good, I figured, for at least a 40 miles per hour wind. I had just reached the steps to their front porch when the door opened and Phil Lujack stepped out. He was smaller than me, stoutly built with dark hair and moustache. He could probably pass for one of the Basque that worked on the ranch, but he wasn't, what he was though was intimidating. His expression was business like. Over the years I'd briefly talked to him on several occasions as a kid does to an adult, but never since becoming deputy sheriff. I didn't feel that I knew him. Nonetheless, he started out like none of that mattered, just the welfare of his daughter. He said, "You know, I've got some concerns with you taking Ellen all the way to Fremont for a picture show. Seems like a long-ways to go just to watch a show."

It flashed in my mind, *Well, now's a fine time to hear this.* I said aloud, as if it would make a difference, "We're gonna go to supper too."

He frowned and then cut right to it, "You know how it is since the war started."

I nodded. "I've thought about that, but I still want to take Ellen out."

He scoffed. "What you want ain't gonna change how people are."

"So, are you saying Ellen can't go?"

He laughed briefly, in a derisive way, "We plowed that ground this morning. She's dead set on going. Hell, she may be 20 years old but she's still my little girl."

Over Phil's shoulder and through the open door I could now see Ellen and Niko whispering to one another. My eyes settled on her as I couldn't believe that I was about to go out with this cute girl. Ellen was wearing a knee-length bright red dress with white polka dots and white socks with brown and white oxford shoes. Her shoulder length hair had been gathered into a single ponytail by a red bow. But then I sensed Phil staring at me, he said not quite before I'd made eye contact with him, "Don't think, just because you're the law, that people won't confront you for being out with a *Jap* girl."

"I've got thick skin."

"Maybe you do, but I don't want my daughter to have a need for it."

Ellen suddenly appeared behind her father. She said, "Dad, I'll be ok. I've heard that kind of talk before."

"Why subject yourself to it?"

"What, am I just supposed to hide out here in the Gros Ventre until the war is over? Just put my life on hold?"

Phil was about to respond when he saw that Niko had grimaced. Tears had come to her eyes. His face became sad. He said to me as much as it was to Ellen, "Be careful. You come home if there's trouble."

"I will," said Ellen as she hugged her father and then her mother.

"Ten o'clock," said Phil. "You be home by ten."

I said before I realized that I might be perceived as arguing, "Mr. Lujack, the show doesn't get out until nine. I don't think we can make it back by ten. Remember, the new speed limit is 35."

His voice became gruff. "Alright, ten-thirty. I know you can make that."

"Ten-thirty it is," I said, "I'll have Ellen home by then, no later."

"We'll wait up for her," said Phil.

Niko, who had moved along side of Phil, abruptly reached over and touched her right hand to his chest as if to rein him in, but she said nothing.

As we approached my old pickup the image of the sharp looking roadster that the big cowboy at the Antler had been driving flashed in my mind. And even though I'd gave the cab of my truck the smell test before coming, worry that it would reek like dog descended upon me. But then, in the next instant, it came to me that Ellen knew what I drove before she agreed to go out with me and she might have even considered the fact that tonight she would be sitting in the spot usually occupied by Grady. I opened her door to which she smiled and said, "Thank you, Andy. You have a nice truck."

My fears went away as I knew there was nothing special about my old '37 Chevy, with the exception it had a fairly narrow bench seat which resulted in Ellen sitting about a foot and a half from me. I had turned around and was idling along back through the buildings and corrals when off to our left I spotted Ellen's brother, Melvin, coming across the pasture that was next to the river. He wasn't carrying anything like a shovel or fishing pole which might suggest what he was doing over there, so I said, "Melvin working on something down by the river?"

I knew right away I shouldn't have asked as Ellen immediately looked uncomfortable, she said, "No, since he came home from the war, he goes on lots of walks."

From the rumor mill I'd learned that Melvin had gotten a medical discharge from the Army Air Corps due to psychological reasons but exactly what the circumstances were, I didn't know. I said, "Oh, I suppose he needs some quiet time after the war and all."

Ellen glanced over at me. "I know what people in the valley say about him, that he's crazy, that he's a coward and he's weak. But they don't know what he had to do."

Things between us were on the verge of going in a direction that I'd never imagined. I said, trying to downplay her suspicions, "You know how people are, they like to think the worst about folks."

Ellen did not seem to want to let it go. She said, sounding almost like she agreed with the gossipers, "Melvin didn't get shot at and he didn't shoot at anybody else. He didn't even drop any bombs. He just looked for the enemy."

At this point, I was also wondering why was Melvin home? An awkward silence overtook us. I sped up and shifted the truck into third gear as we cleared the last of the corrals. At last, I said, "I guess a person would have to have been there."

"It was the weather, Andy," said Ellen in an unconvincing voice. And then it was like a dam burst. Like she had been keeping all of this in, just waiting to tell it to someone who would believe her, "Melvin said they would make them fly in fog so thick they could barely see to take off and the wind, at times, was over a hundred miles an hour. It was constantly raining or snowing and cold and they were always wet and bored and wading around in the mud, and then they would die. They would die trying to land or takeoff or just never come back. No word, nothing, just disappear, probably crashed into the sea. Or sometimes, if they were lucky, they might find the remains of a lost plane where it had flown into the side of a mountain because they couldn't see in the fog and rain. No, Andy, nobody ever shot at Melvin but like he said, they lost more men and planes to the weather than they did to the enemy. This is what all of these critics around here need to know."

I could see the anger and frustration and moistness in her eyes. I said, "You could tell 'em, but I don't know that they'd believe you."

"Probably not, I'm just another Jap to them."

My face registered surprise, and I suppose, a helplessness to fix things. Ellen came back quickly, "I'm sorry, Andy. I didn't mean to get into Melvin's problems."

"You're his sister. It's only natural for you to be concerned."

She sighed. "Maybe it will be different when Charlie comes home. We got word today that he'll be home next Tuesday. He's getting two weeks convalescent leave. He was wounded by a grenade, you know."

"Yes, I read that in the paper."

And then she said, reaching towards the radio in my dash, "Maybe we should listen to some music."

"That sounds swell. See what you can find."

For the remainder of the ride we both did our best to avoid subjects with the potential for controversy. We talked about high school and the forest service mostly. It was almost exactly 5:30 when we pulled into the parking lot of the Coffee Cup café. It wasn't a fancy place but it had good food. I suppose Ellen sensed that I was trying to be the gentleman and not some country bumpkin with no fetchin' up. She waited for me to open her door, whereupon she pivoted around to slide off the seat. In that brief second, when her legs were pointing towards me, it was hard not to stare at the exposed part of them between the tops of her socks and the bottom of her skirt. They were smooth and firm and conjured up other visions that caused me to suddenly look away, as I was certain my face was turning red. With her being a ranch girl I wasn't sure if I should offer her my hand in helping her out like they do in the movies, so I didn't. We started towards the café, a log building that had been stained a dark red with a black shingle roof. It had good sized windows on the front side of it that allowed those people sitting next them to see out. Halfway to the door Ellen took hold of my hand, which I readily accepted. However, no sooner had she done this than I saw a middle-aged woman through the picture window directly in front of us point with her fork. It was hard not to look back at her. She appeared to chew a couple more times, and then, it may have been my paranoia, but I could swear that she said the word *Jap*. I glanced over at Ellen. She had seen it too. I gave her hand a gentle squeeze. "We can go somewhere else if you like."

"Is that what you want to do?"

"I'm just saying we can go where you'll be most comfortable."

We came to a stop just short of the door. From the corner of my eye I could see the woman, and her husband too, staring at us, waiting apparently, to see if we had the moxie to come inside. They did not, however, let their curiosity deter them from eating their dessert, which looked like lemon merengue pie.

Ellen paused for a few seconds and glared at the woman. Turning to me, she said, "This will give her something to tell her friends." And then she mimicked the woman. *Why if looks could kill that Jap girl would've killed me. I tell you, they're a Godless people, they are. They're wicked.*

As the sarcasm faded away, a smile came to Ellen's face. Seeing it, I laughed briefly. "I'm in the mood for a steak, how about you?"

Her smile grew bigger. "That sounds grand."

We went inside, still holding hands. A waitress, who knew me from the times that I'd gone there to eat and see my mother, approached us with a couple of menus. It was obvious that she was giving Ellen the once over. She stopped in front of us and said, as if she didn't recognize me, "Table or booth."

I glanced at Ellen, "Booth?"

"That's fine."

The waitress, whose name was Cynthia or Cindy for those who knew her well, started towards an empty booth along the back wall of the room beneath a nice buck deer head and next to a big stone fireplace with gray ashes in it from the last time it was used. She set the menus on the table, still acting like she didn't know who I was, and said to me, "What would you like to drink?"

I looked across the table at Ellen.

"A coke would be fine."

I said, purposely using her name, "Well, Cindy, I guess you can make that two Cokes." I had decided to engage her in conversation to force her to admit that she knew me but, before I could say anything else, she spun around and was going away allowing her hostility to bleed through.

"I'm sorry," said Ellen.

"For what?"

She smiled. "You are truly a nice guy, Andy. You don't deserve this."

"It's alright."

"No, it isn't. This may have been a mistake. Things are different out in the Gros Ventre than here."

My mind flashed to the Antler and Gertie and Jim. Their words echoed in my mind. Nonetheless I nodded, knowing that even in the valley where people had known the Lujacks for years, there were those who now disliked them. I said, "Let's not let it ruin our night out."

Ellen smiled again as she extended her hand across the table to mine. "Ok, but I guess you know what you're getting into."

I laughed. "A steak dinner and a good movie, I hope."

When Cindy returned, I did not force the issue of her refusing to recognize me. If it meant that much to her to be this way simply because I was here with Ellen then I thought, *to hell with her*. Besides, it had the potential to just embarrass Ellen so I vowed to let it go until when I was there by myself, and then I'd call her on it. We ordered T-bone steaks. Sometime later, after we were done with our salads, they arrived. About half-way through them I brought up the Weasel Mountain fire, which had been contained last night. I said, "So, did they ever figure out what started the fire?"

My question seemed to catch Ellen off guard. "Not that I know of," she said in a tentative voice.

"Well, there hasn't been any lightning in several weeks so that would tend to make me think it was man caused."

Ellen's uneasiness seemed to persist. "Yeah, that would make sense, I suppose."

"Where 'bouts did it start?"

Ellen laughed. "Boy, once a fire dog always a fire dog, huh?"

"Just makin' conversation."

Ellen's expression became serious. She leaned towards me and looked around before speaking in a low voice. "The fire started just off the road to Camas Springs. The fire crew said there's no doubt that it was set deliberately."

"Maybe a rancher thinking he's gonna grow more grass for his cows?"

Ellen looked at me like she was afraid to say what she obviously wanted to.

I said, hoping to give her the nudge she needed, "So the forest service has a suspicion of who it was?"

She nodded and leaned again toward me, she whispered, "Russell."

Mild shock overtook my face. "What?" I said loud enough to cause her to put a finger to her lips.

"That's Allan's take on it. He says the last three fires we've had have all been in areas where Russell has been working. It makes some sense. I do the time sheets and I can tell you Russell gets more overtime and hazard pay than anybody on the district. I even looked up his records from last year and it was the same way."

It now came to me how Gertie could afford to be drinking at the Antler so much and, just out of the blue last year, walk in and settle her bar tab. I was undecided as to whether I should share this with Ellen when she added, "With Russell living in forest service housing and him making all of this fire money you'd think he'd be pretty flush, but he's always complaining about being broke."

I said, caving in somewhat to the temptation to gossip, "I believe his wife gives him plenty of help spending that fire money."

Ellen nodded like she already knew this. "My mom says on those days she works at the store, Gertie's pickup is parked most every afternoon in front of the Antler. It's sad a woman being like that, don't you think?"

"It is, but what's even sadder is Russell feeling like he's got no choice but to let her do it."

"Well, I know the guys at work are fearful of Russell. So, maybe he just needs to put his foot down with Gertie."

I smiled and shook my head. "She's pretty and ten years younger than him."

"You think she'd leave him if he tried to rein in her drinking."

"I don't know, but just the threat of being left alone can be a powerful tool."

"Well, maybe he needs to stay home more. Right now, him and a couple of the seasonals are up there babysitting the fire. He could've come back. It was his choice not to."

"Fightin' fire gets in your blood. It could be that or maybe he's got bills to pay. Remember, he only works eight months out of the year and when he's not working, he's lined up beside Gertie down at the Antler."

"Maybe they're just not good for one another."

I nodded. "Like I said, loneliness is a powerful thing."

A clock encased in black metal with a white face and black numbers hung on the wall across the room. It was to the left and slightly above a painting of a cowboy roping a wild longhorn steer. The time was 6:35. We had finished our steaks and Ellen had declined dessert. I said, "you suppose we better make tracks for the show?"

"Yes, I guess we should," she said as she reached for her small red purse.

"My treat," I said.

"No, I said we'd go Dutch."

"And I said, we'd see." I paused and grinned, "and now we are."

She smiled back at me. "Oh, alright, have it your way."

We stood, took one another's hand, and started toward the cash register up front. As we neared a sign to our right above a hallway that read: REST ROOMS, Ellen whispered to me, "I'll meet you outside."

"Ok, I'll wait by the truck."

After paying the bill, I went outside. I'd not had a lot of experience with girls in my life so I didn't really have much to compare with, but how I felt about Ellen was the best I'd ever felt. It was close to being euphoric, I guess. My thoughts were elsewhere when I suddenly heard my name. I looked several cars over to my right. A couple of guys had just gotten out of an old green Ford sedan that I recognized as belonging to Billy Edwards, a guy who I had gone to school with. He shouted, "Hey, Andy, did ya hear about Mitch?"

A sick, fearful feeling came over me. I'd received a letter from Mitch just yesterday saying he was in the thick of it, but he couldn't tell me anything more than that. I stood beside my pickup and watched Billy and his friend coming towards me. My fear growing with each step they took. When they were about ten feet away, from the corner of my eye, I saw Ellen come out of the Coffee Cup, Billy said in a loud voice, "The damned Japs got Mitch. They killed him. Killed in action is what the telegram said."

A paralysis gripped my tongue. I could see that Billy's words had stopped Ellen dead in her tracks. The playful smile that had been on her face only minutes ago had been replaced by anguish. She looked as if she was about to cry. And, at the same time, my mind was flooded with images of Mitch. It was like a rapid-fire kaleidoscope of things we'd done together, hunting, fishing, playing football and then, in the next instant, there he was lying dead on a beach with the waves pulsing back and forth over his body as if to gently wake him.

"Andy, did you hear me? I said Mitch is dead."

"I heard ya, Billy. I just can't believe it."

"Well, it's true. My Ma was at their place when they got the telegram. She said Mitch's mother collapsed on the kitchen floor. Hit her head on the table going down. Got a helluva gash, I guess. Those slant-eyed bastards got 'im. I can't believe it myself."

I was torn as to what to do. Ellen had begun to cry. She stood there looking at me, frozen, as if she were in a mine field and unable to move. And then I saw it, Billy's friend had made the connection between her and me. He said, loud enough so Ellen could hear, "is that Jap bitch with you?"

Anger suddenly triumphed over my grief, I said, "Yes, and she's no bitch."

"She's a Jap."

"She's an American. Her brothers are both in the service which is more than any of us here can say."

Billy shook his head. "It's pretty sad, Yarnell, your best friend gets killed by the Japs and here you are datin' one of 'em. It must be pretty good stuff, huh?"

I took a step towards Billy. "Shut yer mouth. One more insult from you and I'm gonna whip your ass real good, so just say it, Billy."

A smirk came over Billy's face. "Hell, it might be worth it. You being mister big shot deputy sheriff and all, I bet you'd be in all kinds a trouble for punchin' a law abidin' citizen."

I laughed. "I think they got a special rule that allows for punching assholes."

To my right, I could see Ellen start walking toward me. She said, in a pleading tone, "No Andy, no more trouble. Let's just go home."

Billy snorted, "Maybe you should just take her down to Heart Mountain with the rest of her kind. The little whore won't cause no trouble there."

I've never been one to look for trouble or pick fights, but my right fist fired out and smacked Billy in the jaw as if it was gun going off. Billy stumbled backwards a few steps. Touching his chin where I'd hit him, he said, "We'll see who get's the last laugh here, mister lawman." And with that, he and his friend got back in their car and spun the wheels shooting gravel behind them as they left the parking lot and took off down the street.

Ellen was crying and walking slowly towards me. Beyond her, the windows of the Coffee Cup had become crowded with faces. They were hateful, disgusted faces, none of them good that I could see. Ellen stopped a few feet from me. I took a step towards her.

She sobbed, "No, Andy. I just want to go home." And with that she started for her side of the pickup.

With so many eyes upon us, I could not resist looking back at the Coffee Cup one last time. There appeared to be no shame among them as they continued to stare, waiting to see how we, or I suppose mostly Ellen, would react to this humiliation. We were free entertainment. I wanted to shout at them, *well, get an eyeful you sonsabitches*. But their collective indifference was more than I could bear. I turned my back on them and went to my truck. Ellen barely looked at me as I got in and started it up. I pulled onto the highway that headed out of town and back to the Gros Ventre. Saying nothing, I methodically accelerated and shifted until we reached the allowed 35 miles per hour. It seemed like a long time that we just rode, each of us alone in our thoughts, listening to the whine of the tires on the pavement while letting the wind rush through the cab of the truck. I'd begun the night with optimism of what the future might hold for us, but not now. And then, in the midst of my sadness and anger and frustration, just bobbing along like a lone stick in a raging flood, was Mitch being killed. *How could a night go so wrong*? Finally, I said, "I'm sorry about tonight."

Ellen looked over, right at me. It was the first time she had since leaving the Coffee Cup. She was no longer crying but her eyes were red and there were signs of where her nose had run onto her upper lip. She said, "For us, I don't think it will ever be different."

My first impulse was to tell her that she was wrong, that it was just town people who were like this and it would be different in the Gros Ventre, and then that day at the Antler popped into my mind. I couldn't bring myself to disagree with her.

She said into the silence between us, "I'm sorry about Mitch. I didn't really know him, but he seemed like a nice guy."

"He was, and the thing Billy Edwards doesn't get is if Mitch had been there tonight, he would've probably punched Billy before I got the chance."

Ellen sighed as she shook her head in exasperation. "I don't know what my family has to do to prove we're as American as any white people."

"You'd think with both Melvin and Charlie having gone into the service that people would see your family for the patriots that they are."

Ellen came back in a sharp tone, like the words had escaped her, "Melvin coming home like he has hasn't helped in that regard."

There was a hint of regret in her eyes, but it wasn't enough to cause her to take back what she'd said. Instead, more spite came to her voice, "Charlie will be home next week. He'll be wearing his uniform and medals and I'm hoping after we pick him up at the train station, the folks will want to go to the Coffee Cup and eat."

"You'd go back there?"

"With Charlie in his uniform, I would."

I was seeing a side of Ellen that a short while ago in the parking lot of the Coffee Cup café, I would swear did not exist. It gave me hope that she might go out with me again but, truth be told, if there were many more incidents like tonight, I didn't know if I would want to. We drove on listening to the radio and talking fluff mostly, except for when we went through Cedarville. The Jenkins' pickup was parked in front of the Antler. I laughed and said while looking at it, "Looks like Russell will be working for free today."

Ellen laughed, her first since when we were eating, she said, "Looks that way."

It was about a quarter till eight when we turned off 29 and started down the lane to the Peterson Land & Livestock Company Headquarters. I knew the minute we pulled up in front of Ellen's house her folks would know something was wrong, as it was still plenty daylight. Ellen said, like she had just read my mind, "There's no need for you to go inside and try to explain what happened tonight to my father."

"Are you sure? I don't mind."

"I'm sure. There's no point in both of us having to rehash this, so just drop me off and go."

I could see in her eyes that she meant it, and not just because she was trying to spare me, but maybe because if I wasn't there, her father would get less worked up. I said simply, "Ok."

All too soon, we were by the corrals and out buildings and passing under the branches of the huge ponderosa pines in front of her house. Lights were on in the house but no one was visible. Ellen looked over at me. She took my hand and squeezed it gently. "Thank you, Andy. I'm sorry about tonight."

"Maybe we could try it again sometime?"

She said, her eyes not suggesting anything more, "Maybe."

Within seconds she was through the gate in the white picket fence and walking quickly over the flat rocks that defined the path to her front door. I was backing around slowly, watching to see if she would pause and wave before she went inside, but she did not. Disappointed, I started back towards 29, idling in second gear through the congestion that comprised the Peterson Land & Cattle Headquarters. I had just made the bend in the road that would clear me of all of it when I spotted Melvin off to my right. He was sitting on the ground leaning against the barn wall staring off to the west, watching I supposed, what remained of the setting sun. He seemed, or maybe he really was, oblivious to my presence.

CHAPTER SEVEN

Sunday morning came real early for me. I was awake even before the birds started to sing or the rooster in the flock of chickens that the Lumberjack kept out back of their place, crowed. During the night the events at the Coffee Cup had played over and over in my mind until I was second guessing my decision to take Ellen out, especially in light of the way our date ended. She'd given me little encouragement to think we'd ever go out again. Even if she had, I suspected her father would not be in favor of it. So, here I was at 5:34 a.m. sitting at the table in my underwear, eating corn flakes and listening to the flies' futile attempts to escape through a glass window. It occurred to me that my breakfast was as boring as my life and that Ellen could have been the thing to change all that, but not now. By 5:41 I was done with my cereal and just sitting at the table trying to fend off the images of last night in the Coffee Cup parking lot and that damned Billy Edwards and his friend and Cindy being the way she was and then, it was more of a thought than an image, that Mitch would never be able to do something as simple as eat a bowl of corn flakes, not ever again. For a moment, I hated the Japs too. At 5:45 I got up from the table and went to the window. I parted the curtains and swung at the fly who had the poor judgement to land on the window sill. The blow was so hard it slightly bent the wire handle of my swatter, but the fly was dead. His friends, however, across the room in that window were already taunting me. I tossed the swatter on the table and looked down at Grady who was laying on the floor with his head resting on his paws. I said, "Hound dog, it's time to go fishin'."

After getting dressed and collecting my gear, Grady and I headed north of town, up the Gros Ventre valley about ten miles to the turnoff for Rock Creek. We turned onto the bare dirt road going east through gently rolling terrain covered with scattered sage and grass that was beginning to cure and wildflowers that were mostly purple and white. In about a half mile we went over the Gros Ventre River on an old wooden bridge that made me feel lucky every time I crossed it and it didn't cave in. We were not quite yet to the forest boundary so I assumed the bridge was the county's responsibility which meant, as broke as they were, it probably wasn't going to be replaced anytime soon. But I'd purposely come up here knowing full well how the bridge was because it tended to thin out the competition. As my mother would say, if she knew I was going fishing on Rock Creek, *You know, Andy, people with even a lick of sense don't go there.* To which I would respond, *but they don't catch the fish that I do.* About a quarter of a mile past the rickety bridge I came to a small brown wooden sign with white letters that read, Entering National Forest Lands. The sign was located at the mouth of a fairly wide canyon that was populated with aspen, willows and alder in the very bottom along Rock Creek and ponderosa pine on the slopes above. The good fishing, however, was another couple of miles up the canyon where the beavers had partially damned the creek creating some deep ponds. From the sign, the road got rocky and was a steady climb. It was slow going as the road wound its way through the brush and trees. We'd gone almost a mile when we came to a trickle of water called Mink Creek coming from a side canyon to the north. Over the years, hunters had created an even rougher two-track road that ran up this drainage. I stopped my pickup and allowed my eyes to follow the stringer of aspen that crowded both sides of the little creek to a point where, as a kid, my father and I had camped. It held fond memories for me as it was the last time we hunted together. Not long after that he was killed. I suppose if I had told my mother about this trip it might have helped her understand my lack of common sense in crossing the bridge below. I sighed, try-ing to shake off the sadness that had come over me. I said, as I eased through the shallow water, "Let's go catch us some fish, Grady dog."

We slowly bounced and jostled along for another ten or fifteen minutes when we suddenly emerged from the aspen into a relative clearing, courtesy of the beavers, and a deep blue water pond that was being held back by a mud and stick dam close to a hundred yards wide. Just the sight of it and knowing the fish that it contained boosted my spirits. The water had crowded the road out of the bottom slightly up the side of the canyon, leaving few good places to park. I drove past where the beavers had tied their dam into the edge of the canyon and was about to pull up onto the side slope where it was mostly grass and park, when I laughed at myself. I said to Grady, "Hells bells, hound dog, it ain't likely there's gonna be anybody else come out here. We'll just park right where we are."

I grabbed my fishing pole and tackle box out of the back and started along the edge of the pond. The fish were rising, taking insects off the surface, but I was not equipped for that. I was an old school bait fisherman, it's all my father knew, and I suppose his father too. I had a wooden bobber on my line about two feet above my hook, which I had loaded with bright red fish eggs. In the past, this combination had fooled plenty of trout. After last night, I was counting on it not letting me down today. The line came off my reel effortlessly for about 40 feet before gravity pulled my breakfast offering down. The bobber splashed gently onto the surface of the water while my hook continued on, hopefully, to eye level of the fish. Within seconds a bug eating cutthroat cleared the water less than five feet from where my bobber was innocently rocking from side to side. I said to Grady, who was sitting just behind me on the road, "Any time now, hound dog, I'm gonna catch a fish as these ain't fish at all, they're pigs disguised as fish. They can't help but take what I've put out there." Grady looked on, waiting for me to make good on my boast. Suddenly, it was as if the fishing gods gave in as my bobber disappeared. I lifted my rod tip and began to reel. A pulse of, *feel good*, surged within me but at the same time, off to the side, in the background, I caught glimpses of Mitch catching a fish not far from where I was standing. He was happy, excited, laughing even. That had been a good day. And then, like it could be no other way on this day, the tension abruptly left my line. And just like that, the *feel good* was gone. And there was that damned Billy Edwards and Ellen not waving goodbye and Mitch too dead to lift himself from the surf.

By 11:30 my corn flakes had worn off. I cast out and then stuck the butt of my rod between two good-sized rocks and went to the pickup for my lunch. The fishing gods had turned on me as I'd caught only two trout. I'd put them in my canvas creel that was submerged in the water at the edge of the pond. The fishing was slow. Even the bug eaters had stopped coming to the top. There was plenty of time, too much time, to rehash the night before. I sat down near my pole and took out a baloney sandwich for me and just a slice of baloney that I'd wrapped in wax paper, for Grady. We began to eat this along with some chips while staring at my bobber. Halfway through, I reached into the brown paper bag for the root beer that I'd brought. Just as I touched the can, which was barely cool, it dawned on me that I hadn't brought an opener. "Ah dammit," I said aloud. Instinctively, I reached for my pocket knife which was laying next to my tackle box. The blade was stained with blood and particles of fish guts. After splashing it in the pond and wiping it on my pants leg I cut two V's in the top of the can. Doing this always made me cringe. It was like somebody running their nails over a blackboard while ruining the edge on a knife. But today, it had an added effect. I said to Grady, "Hound dog, as soon as I finish this soda pop, we're gonna skedaddle. There's too damned much peace and quiet here." Right away the naysayer in my mind followed up with, *like you won't have quiet time on your hands back at the cabin*? This was a convincing argument up until about two o'clock. By then I'd caught one more fish, but it was now miserably hot. The grasshoppers, big greenish yellow ones, were constantly snapping here and there in the grass on the hillside above me. I stood up. "That's it, hound dog. Time to go home."

After having thought about life while staring at my bobber for a half day, I was convinced there was no easy fix to the things currently troubling me. It was this thought, and a *woe is me* perception of myself, that was on my mind when I came to Mink Creek. As I eased through the water, I looked up the canyon and was surprised to see Phil Lujack's black truck coming to a stop not far from where my father and I had camped years ago. It was probably 400 yards but I could see that the person getting out wasn't Phil, it was Melvin. He paused close to the truck and appeared to be looking directly at me. I stopped just clear of the creek and looked back at him, debating if I should drive up there and talk. I felt sorry for him and all that he had gone through and how people talked about him but, at the same time, I thought he might be able to tell me what went on between Ellen and her dad last night. And more importantly, he might be able to tell me where I stood with Ellen and her father too. I started my turn up the two-track along the creek, when, almost immediately, Melvin began walking away from his pickup and started climbing up the ridge. I stopped as it was clear he didn't want to talk to me. His pace was beyond a casual hike, it was like he was trying to escape. I sat there for about 30 seconds, watching him go higher and higher on the ridge, not once did he look back. Finally, he disappeared into the pine trees and I continued on down the canyon.

It was late afternoon by the time I got back to my cabin. I'd just rinsed the fish off and put them in a pan of cold water in the fridge when the phone rang. Even though it was my day off I answered as if it weren't, on account of that's who a stranger would be expecting. "Sheriff's Department, Deputy Yarnell speaking."

"Where have you been?"

"Fishin', Mom. I just got back."

"Well, I've been trying to call you since about noon."

Her tone caused an uneasy feeling to come over me. I played dumb, even though last night's spectators at the Coffee Cup were staring at me again, I said, "Why's that?"

"Why's that, well, I'll tell you it's because of the spectacle you made of yourself in front of the place where I work and where I have to make my living. Just about every table I walked by today was talking about the fight that the sheriff's deputy was in. They say it looked like it had something to do with that Lujack girl, is that right?"

Reluctantly, I tossed gas on the fire. "Yeah, Ma, I suppose that's what set it off."

"Well, you know I like the Lujack women and I certainly have nothing against them for being Japanese, but there's a lot of people in this town that don't agree with me. I guess I should've warned you too that Cindy's nephew was killed in the war about a month ago. It's just not a good time to be courting a Japanese girl."

"After last night, I don't think I'll have to worry about that."

My mother was briefly silent and then she said, "I'm sorry, Andy, but it's probably for the best."

"I suppose so."

"I don't know if I should even bring it up. I don't know if it's worth mentioning, really."

"What, Ma?"

"Roy Glover came in this morning after church."

"He goes to church?"

"His wife makes him."

"And?"

"Well, Cindy was twisting his ear, or vice versa, for a good while. At one point, when I was close enough to hear, I heard your name and Billy's."

I sighed. "I imagine Glover was eatin' that up."

"Are you and him still on the outs?"

I laughed in a derisive tone. "Yeah, I guess that'd be a good way to put it."

"Maybe nothing will come of it."

"Yeah, and maybe the sun won't come up tomorrow either."

"When will the Sheriff be back?"

"I don't know, it could be a while."

"He seems to be a good buffer between you and Glover, it's too bad he's not here now."

"Well, Ma, I gotta build a fire so I can fry up these fish I caught."

"The county still won't get you an electric stove?"

I laughed. "I gotta go, Ma."

"Alright, Andy, just remember if you get fired you can always come home."

It flashed in my mind to say something sarcastic like, *Gee, Ma, thanks for the vote of confidence,* but I said simply, "Thanks, Ma."

The heat from my supper fire caused me to eat my fish and fried spuds while sitting on a stump in front of the cabin. It was almost pleasant there. The big mountain to the west of Cedarville had shaded the town, and a gentle breeze that wasn't quite enough to unfurl the flag outside the post office, but almost enough to dry the sweat on my temples, had come up. It made me not want to go back inside my cabin anytime soon but if I didn't do that what was I going to do, sit on this stump and stew over what Roy Glover might do to me? Or pine over a girl that I'd had about a half a date with? Or, I could go down to the Antler and have a cold beer and listen to Oscar, who seldom went outside except to empty the garbage, bitch about how hot and dry it was. Within a few minutes, Grady and I were walking towards town. We'd not gone far when I saw Niko Lujack, in their black Chevy sedan, pull out from the side of the store and start up the road towards me. It was a little past six o'clock. She had likely just closed the store and was going home. As she neared me I could tell she was undecided if she should stop, nonetheless, I held out my hand for her to do so. The car had barely come to a halt when she said out the window, as if she had dispensed with any pleasantries and jumped ahead to the tense part of the conversation, "I knew this was a bad idea."

Niko appeared angry, I said to her, "Is that the way Ellen sees it?"

She came back curtly, "Yes, it is. Please leave her alone." And then before I could respond, as if there was anything that I could say that would make a difference, she was gone, picking up speed on the oiled part of the road before dropping onto the gravel part at the edge of town and soon she was invisible in a cloud of dust that I suspected was the result of something more than 35 miles per hour. I stood where I was and watched her trail of dust roll off towards the river, like there was something to be gained from it. I felt hurt and angry. She was probably a good mile away before I turned and went on to the Antler.

As I closed the door behind me, Oscar called out, "Hello, Andy, how the hell are ya?"

"Doing alright," I said while taking a seat at the bar directly across from him.

"Whatcha drinkin?"

"Pabst, I guess."

He turned to the cooler to get my beer. "She hot enough for you today?"

I smiled and said to myself, *bartenders and barbers probably talk about the weather, when they could care less, more than anybody in civilization.* I said, "It damned sure is."

Oscar set the beer down in front of me. I was the only customer in the bar on a Sunday evening, which struck a chord with my conscience. I was momentarily pondering the significance of this when Oscar interrupted, "So, whatcha been up to today?"

"Ah, me an' Grady went fishin'."

"You take that dog with you everywhere you go?"

"Pretty much."

"Years ago, I used to have a dog like that. He went everywhere with me." Oscar paused as if he was remembering the dog and laughed. "And I'll tell ya what, not everybody wudda done that, not with that dog they wouldn't."

"Why's that?"

Oscar made a sour face and shook his head. "That damned mutt had more gas than any dog I ever saw. He could clear a room real quick cuz the odor would just about peel the paint off the walls. And God help you if you was driving down the road with the windows up."

I laughed and then asked, "Well, what were you feeding him?"

Oscar was about to respond when the sound of a vehicle pulling up outside diverted his attention to the window. He snorted, "Holy shit, here's a train wreck comin'"

I was about to ask who it was when I heard Gertie shout, "Dammit Russell, I don't see why we can't go to town. It'd give me a chance to try out my new dancin' shoes. C'mon, I been cooped up here while you been on the fire."

"It's Sunday, Gertie. There ain't gonna be no dances."

Gertie laughed just as the door opened. "All ya need is a nickel for the jukebox and the Lariat's got one."

Oscar hollered out. "Well, you finally got that fire put out, did ya?"

Russell was stocky, maybe five-ten with dark hair, green eyes and a bushy salt and pepper moustache that covered most of his upper lip. He was wearing a white straw cowboy hat, red-checkered short-sleeved shirt with a white T shirt underneath that showed at the base of his neck, Levis and lace up boots with a pointed toe and tall heels so they would fit a stirrup. His boots smelled strongly of ash and smoke. He said, emphatically, "Yes sir, we did." And then glancing in my direction, he said, "How ya fairin', Andy?"

"Can't complain," I said.

"Buy ya a beer?"

It may have been a foolish thought, or not, but it suddenly struck me that I would be benefitting from Russell having deliberately set the woods on fire, if the gossip Ellen had passed on to me was true. Regardless, my excuse appeared solid, I said, "Appreciate it, Russell, but I got almost a full one in front of me."

Gertie cut in. "Well, I ain't bashful. I'll take a Schlitz, draft."

"Make that two," said Russell.

Oscar began drawing their beers, as he did, he asked, "So, how big did the fire get?"

Russell came back, "I drew it on a topo map. My calculations, using this little dot counter thing the forest service has got, put it at 11.2 acres."

"Oh, the hell you say," said Oscar as if he were impressed.

Russell laughed and slapped me on the back. "We cudda used yer help, Andy. Them boys they drug outta the bars in town were draggin' ass right from the git-go. Purty damned sad examples of mankind if you was to ask me."

Before Ellen had told me of the suspicions about Russell, I had respected him as a firefighter. Now, my opinion of him was a whole lot less. It caused me to want to make him squirm, I said, "So, Russell, how'd the fire start?"

For just a second or two, or about the amount of time it takes for a bolt of lightning to hit the ground, I thought I saw a panic look in his face, but then it was gone and he came back all cocky like, "Oh, I figure some simple ass dude from town threw a cigarette out. It's bone dry, you know."

And then, as if she knew to divert attention from the cause of the fire, Gertie stepped out to where I could see her and raised the pant leg on her right boot to show it off, she said, "How do you like the new dancin' shoes that Russell got me."

Russell threw in but not too strongly, "That damned Monkey Wards catalog is not a good thing for a lonely woman to possess. It can break a man."

Just as Russell had started to speak a Frank Sinatra song on the juke box ended and, in its place, Ernest Tubb's "Rollin' On" started to play. Gertie looked over at me wondering, I supposed, if I recalled that the big cowboy had been mimicking this song on the day he was massaging her ass. I guess it was the side of me that wanted to get back at her smart mouth on that day, so I said to Russell, "I'd say when it gets to that point, a fella ought to be *rollin' on* to greener pastures." I glanced over at Gertie causing the anger in her eyes to melt quickly away to puddles of fear.

Gertie turned to the bar and took up her beer. She said, "Russell, honey, why don't we take our drinks to the back and have a good home cooked meal." And then she laughed, apparently making light of herself.

Russell scoffed. "I guess if I wanna eat that's probably the best choice."

It was almost like a replay of a few days ago as they went through the bat doors to the sounds of Rollin' On, except this time Gertie didn't get a slap on the ass.

CHAPTER EIGHT

I was mid-way through my breakfast when the phone rang. My clock read 7:20. I grinned and shook my head as I mumbled, "Probably Ma callin' to get me lined out for the day." I answered the phone expecting that's who it would be, "Hello."

"Andy?"

Instantly, I recognized the voice, "Hello Sheriff, you caught me with a mouth full of corn flakes."

"Oh, I thought for a second the operator had hooked me up wrong."

I knew there was a hidden intent in his words as he'd told me when I first came to work how I should answer the phone in the county's cabin. It was akin to the formality that Grace had tried to get me to follow on the radio. I mentally kicked myself and moved on, sensing that this was no routine call, I said, "So, how's your mother doing?"

"Not good."

"I'm sorry to hear that."

"Well, she's old. I guess it's just her time."

Tom's end of the phone went silent leaving me in an awkward spot as to what to say. And then I heard him slurp a drink, probably his morning coffee. He came back, "I got a call from yer buddy last night."

Instantly, I said to myself, *Oh shit*, to the Sheriff I said, "Glover?"

"Yup, and I suppose you know what it was about."

"These fellas were insulting my date. They called her a bitch and a whore and-"

"Andy, that don't matter to Glover and probably the tax payers that saw all this."

"Tom, it was a one punch fight. I just had to put this guy in his place."

"So, you were at the Coffee Cup with that Lujack girl?"

"Yeah, I was."

"Probably not a smart thing to do. You know there's been a number of people in Fremont that's lost relatives in the war."

"I never thought it would come to this. Maybe some ugly stares, but not this."

"Well, Glover says your behavior is unbecoming an officer of the law. He wants me to fire you."

It was all there, kind of a collective or panoramic view of my life in the county's cabin, my half-eaten bowl of corn flakes, that damned wood stove and the seemingly endless drone of the flies pestering the window. It was a lot to absorb in a second or two, but I did, and in the process mustered more courage than may have been prudent as I said, kind of in a flippant way too, "Alright, Tom, it probably won't take me more than about 15 minutes to pack my crap and be on my way. You want me to drop the keys to the truck off at the office in town?"

Tom came back quick, there was surprise in his voice. "Well now, hold yer horses. I said he wants to fire you. I didn't say that I agreed with him."

"So, where do I stand?"

"They wanna hear yer side of things."

"They?"

"The commissioners are meeting today at 2:00 at the courthouse. They're adding you to the agenda."

I snorted into the phone. "Kinda like a school boy getting called to the principal's office."

Tom sucked up some more coffee before responding, "You should know that I've acquainted those other men on the commission with the history you and Glover have. This may not be the execution you've got it conjured up to be."

"You think so?"

"I told Glover I was opposed to firing you but he said, well, we'll just see how the commission votes."

"So, basically I go in there today and beg for my job?"

"If you want to stay on with the Sheriff's office you don't have a choice."

I went quiet to the point Tom asked, "Are you gonna go?"

I sighed heavily into the phone, hoping that he could hear it, "I guess I have to if I wanna keep my job."

He came back, kind of high and mighty like, "Don't be surprised if they want to suspend you without pay for a few days."

"What, that's bullshit Tom. You think that if somebody was to call one of those guys' wives a whore they'd just stand there and take it?"

And then Tom, his voice softening a little, said, "Ain't none of them married to a Japanese woman. So, if they wanna slap yer hands by suspending you, you agree to it. I'll try to make it up to you on down the line, maybe get you a screen door or an electric stove."

"I thought the county was broke."

"I didn't say it would be tomorrow." He paused and then added, "Listen, Andy, don't let this derail you. Two o'clock today you be there, and a word of advice, it'll go a long-ways with these boys if you was to tell them you're sorry for how you conducted yourself, alright?"

Reluctant to answer I stood there, listening to the distant static of the phone. It didn't sit well with me having to apologize for defending Ellen's reputation.

Tom came back, his tone arbitrary, "I gotta go, Andy, but you be there, two o'clock." And then the line went dead.

The Sheriff's call left me in an angry, defiant state of mind. I wanted so bad to ignore Glover and Tom's demand that I show up today and explain myself. To me, I had done what any other man in my position would have and here I was being told to apologize. The naysayer in my mind screamed at me, *if Ellen was white, things would be different. You can bet yer ass on that.* I left my bowl of cereal sitting on the table and went outside. I sat down on the stump in front of the cabin to ponder what I should do with the roughly four hours I had before leaving for town, assuming I didn't cave in to my radical side and quit. At about nine o'clock I was still in this state of limbo when the phone rang. On the third ring, I answered, Sheriff's Office, Deputy Yarnell speaking."

"Andy, this is Ellen."

"Ellen, what –"

"My father may need your help. Melvin didn't come home last night."

A sick feeling instantly overwhelmed me as I recalled Melvin climbing the ridge yesterday. "Where's your father?"

"He's here, at the ranger station."

"Tell him to stay there. I'll be right out."

"Thank you, Andy. I appreciate it."

I was anxious, hungry almost, to talk to Ellen about our botched date but now was obviously not the time. I said in a friendly tone, "It's not a problem."

As I hung up the phone, my mind went to what I was about to get into. Through no fault of his own, Melvin had become a strange duck. He knew, I suspected, that people talked about him being crazy. I wondered, had he gone to Mink Creek to watch the sun set or had Ellen's humiliation at the Coffee Cup overloaded his plate of emotions? I suddenly felt like the snot-nosed kid that Roy Glover thought I was.

After making sure Grady's water bowl on the north side of the cabin was full, I gave him a pat on the head. "No hound dog, today is not a good day for you to go." Reluctantly, he laid down in the coolness of the grass and watched as I drove out of the yard.

Being just up the road, it took only a couple of minutes to get to the ranger station. Ellen and her father were standing out front, both had worried looks on their faces. I'd barely gotten out of my truck when Phil said, in a loud voice, "Sorry to call you, Andy, but we looked in his usual places about dusk yesterday. I don't know where in the hell he could have gone to."

I said, like it was a reflex, "I do, or at least I know where he was at around two o'clock yesterday."

Relief suddenly came to their eyes. Ellen was first to cash in on it, "Where, Andy, where's he at?"

"Mink Creek, he was parked at the end of that little two-track that runs up there."

"Did you talk to 'im?" asked Phil.

"No, I didn't."

"Well, why not?" said Phil, like I was one of those in the valley that shunned his boy on account of his peculiar ways.

"I was going to but he took off up the ridge. He didn't want anything to do with me."

Ellen cut in, "It's how Melvin is, Dad. He doesn't want to talk to people anymore."

"Maybe we should go," I said, "we can take my truck."

Phil shook his head, "Damned kid just needs to put the war behind him. Get on with his life."

"He's trying, Dad," said Ellen, "but life isn't easy for him here."

"And it will be someplace else?"

Ellen frowned, "Just go, Dad."

Phil started towards my truck. "Alright, let's get out of here.' And then he added, "I sure hope he hasn't busted an axle or some such on Milo's pickup. I can't afford it."

I could hear the fear in his voice suggesting that this wasn't his real concern. I played along, ignoring the white elephant that stood amongst us, I said, "I've got a pretty hefty chain that we can use to tow it if it's road worthy."

"That'd be good," said Phil as he got in my truck.

Behind me, Ellen shouted, "Thanks, Andy."

I glanced over my shoulder and waved but said nothing, and then we were going down the road, just me and her father. We'd barely turned onto 29 when Phil said, "Damned kid is just trying to upstage his brother. You know he's comin' home tomorrow?"

"Yeah, Ellen told me."

"I guess you heard he got a purple heart. He's been right in the thick of the fightin' you know."

"Yeah, I read that in the paper."

"I think that story in the paper didn't help Melvin any. Made him feel worse about who he is."

"I can see how that might be, but I sure don't think any less of Melvin."

Phil paused like he knew he shouldn't say what he was about to but then he did it anyway, like he needed to get it off his chest, he said, "I told him he needed to man up. I didn't know what else to say with him moping around like he is. I'm kinda wishin' now I hadn't."

It felt awkward, counseling, so to speak, a man old enough to be my father, but I said, "Did you ever tell him you were sorry?"

Phil shook his head. "No, I guess I've never been very good with giving out sorrys."

I was glad, given the way the conversation was going, that my radio went off, "604 this is Base."

I glanced over at Phil as I reached for the mic hanging on the dash. "Excuse me, but I'm 604." After wrestling the mic out of its metal bracket, I pressed the button, "Good morning, Grace."

"Hi Andy, I got a call this morning from Roy Glover. He wanted me to remind you to be at the commission meeting at two o'clock today."

Phil said, real quick like, "Hell, Andy, we'll go up and roust that daydreaming kid a mine and I'll ride back with him and you can be on yer way in plenty a time to make that meeting."

I could hear the hopefulness in Phil's voice and see it in his eyes and I knew he wanted, in the worst way, to believe that things would turn out like he'd just said, but I couldn't shake the bad feeling I had, so I said, "I don't think I'll be able to make that meeting, Grace."

"Why 's that?"

"Melvin Lujack didn't come home last night and I've been asked to help look for him. I'm not sure how long I'll be."

"From what I hear that might not be totally out of character for him."

From the corner of my eye I could see a ripple of anger in Phil's face. It caused me to say, "You heard wrong, Grace. So, you tell Glover I'll be there if I can, but that he shouldn't hold his breath."

"Ok, but if you're not there I have a feeling the fur is gonna fly."

"I'm just doing my job, Grace. 604 clear."

"Sounds like this Glover guy wants you at this meeting pretty bad," said Phil.

I nodded, "Yeah, he's trying to get me fired."

"Fired, why's that?"

I sighed, not sure if now was the time to air out the Coffee Cup incident.

Phil broke the ice. "It's over you punching that Edwards kid, ain't it?"

"There was bad blood between me and Glover before that, but I guess it's the straw that broke the camel's back."

Phil snorted, "That Glover is such an asshole, he's another one that needs a poke in the nose."

I laughed, "I couldn't agree more but right now he seems to be the one holding the better hand."

"Well, I'll tell ya," said Phil purposely catching my eye, "I'd be glad to stand up for ya at this meetin'. We get Melvin on his way home and we'll just head for town."

Phil's offer gave me a feel-good moment but I knew better than to take him with me and, truth be told, I didn't figure I was going to the meeting, not this one anyway. I said, "I appreciate it, Phil, but the Sheriff is in my corner so I'm hopin' that'll be enough to save my job."

Phil fished a sack of Bull Durham and papers out of his pocket, as he did he said, "well, you keep me in the know on this deal, or I suppose Ellen can, but if that sonovabitch cans you I'm gonna raise hell with that whole bunch of commissioners."

The fact that he'd thrown in the part about Ellen suggested to me that all was not lost with her. I said, "Well, I guess we'll just see how things play out."

Phil began to shake out some tobacco into the paper trough he had formed, as he did he said, "Yeah, I reckon so, but I'm serious as a hangover about twistin' these fellas' tails if they try to rough you up over this deal."

It was apparent to me that Phil wasn't oblivious to the white elephant, his hands had the beginnings of a nervous, fearful tremble. It was even creeping into his voice. I said, trying to put distance between us and it, "I'll tell ya where these boys need their tails twisted is puttin' a new bridge up here where the Rock Creek road crosses the Gros Ventre."

Phil tore a match from a book with a red cover that I knew came from the Sawtooth Club in Fremont, struck it, and cupping his hands around the flame so the breeze from the open window wouldn't extinguish it, lit his cigarette. He said, as he spewed smoke out in front of himself, "I plum forgot about havin' to cross that thing. The last time I went over it my pucker factor was kinda high."

I laughed. "You can walk across if ya want."

"No, hell, if yer gonna risk getting wet I may as well too."

Up ahead was the line of aspens and willows coming out of the mountains that told exactly where Rock Creek ran. Shortly, we turned off of 29 and headed for the bridge. Within a minute or so, we were there. I stopped at the edge of the bridge, mostly for Phil's benefit. There was a good-sized hole in the middle of the wooden planks that had been created years ago by someone trying to trailer heavy mining equipment over them that had fell through. So now, for about six feet, the bridge was a two-track with open water in between the tracks.

Phil took a drag from his cigarette while leaning forward in the seat so as to get a better look. He exhaled the smoke into the windshield and snorted, "I guess we ain't got a choice."

The confidence that I'd had yesterday in crossing the bridge to go fishing had mysteriously deserted me. Common sense was telling me that this wasn't a smart thing to do, but then it came to me that maybe my hesitation was due to my knowing, fearing, that the white elephant was real. I sighed heavily and put the truck in gear. We idled across and started on up the canyon. Phil became strangely silent, just smoking his cigarette and staring ahead. Each of us was imagining what we would find when got there, but neither of us was able to put a good spin on it. And then, all too soon, we were at the turn to go up Mink Creek. Phil's truck was still there at the end of the road.

He said, his voice cracking slightly, "I don't see anybody around, do you?"

I suddenly wished that I was somewhere else, anywhere but here. The naysayer in my mind shouted out again, *maybe Glover is right, you're just a snot-nosed kid*, a *kid in a man's job*. I subtly took a deep breath to steady my voice and said, "No I don't, but the last I saw of Melvin he was going up that ridge to the west."

"Probably gonna go watch the sun set. Ever since he came back from the Aleutians, it's like he can't get enough of the sun. It's almost like he's afraid it's gonna go away and never come back."

I recalled all that Ellen had told me about the terrible weather and how it had caused so many airmen to die and how this could have affected Melvin, but I said only, "That's too bad."

Even though I was going slow, the truck bounced and rocked from side to side on our way to where Melvin had parked. Still, I was in no hurry to get there, but then we were. Phil got out, paused and dropped what little was left of his cigarette onto some bare dirt and crushed it into the ground with the heel of his boot. He walked over to his truck and looked in the open window. "Keys are in it," he said without turning around.

I shifted my eyes to the hillside and followed, as best I could recall, the route that Melvin had taken yesterday. The lower half of the slope was dominated mostly by sagebrush and grass with a sprinkling of Douglas fir trees. The top half, however, the part that Melvin had disappeared into was fairly thick timber, as mother nature had created a shallow bowl here with just enough northern exposure to cause the snow to linger in the spring. I said, knowing full well that it might strip away Phil's hope, "Maybe he never came down from this ridge."

Phil stared at the hillside. He appeared to be as reluctant as I was to go up it and discover, what we were both afraid to admit, that the white elephant was real. For a time, he was silent and then, mostly to himself, he said while shaking his head, "Damned fool kid."

I began walking, going past Phil's pickup to where the ground pitched upward. I stopped, nestled amongst the brush and grass was a game trail. It wasn't real well defined but it would be better than blazing our own way. And then I saw it, about ten feet in front of me where the dirt was soft, I called out, "He went this way, got a fresh boot track here."

Phil walked quickly to where I was standing and on to the track. He knelt down and gently touched it, tracing its shape with his fingers until my presence invaded the moment. Abruptly, he said, "If he stays to the trail, we can track him."

I nodded, "Alright, you lead the way."

And then, just as we were about to start, high above the very top of the ridge we saw them, two vultures, their black shapes silhouetted perfectly against the blue sky. They were circling. For a few seconds, neither of us spoke until Phil acknowledged what we'd been trying to keep at bay all morning, he seethed the words, barely above a whisper, "Those sons-a-bitches. Ain't they got no respect."

I thought to give him another helping of false hope, but couldn't bring myself to do it. Instead, I said to myself, *Dammit, Melvin, this ain't right.*

He started off at a brisk pace such that I was struggling to stay with him. The day was heating up. I could hear him breathing hard. The trail got continually steeper as we approached the trees. My lungs and legs were screaming for a break, but on we went. His steps had become unsteady.

They were punctuated by even heavier breathing and cottonmouth, causing him to expel stringy spit. But he pushed on, stumbling once, twice and finally going to his knees on the third time, his fall being broken only by planting his bare hands in the rocks before him. I could see that his palms were cut and bleeding, I took a deep breath and expelled it so as to be able to speak calmly and said, "Phil, what's done is done."

His look was more hurt than anger, he said, "We just need to find him."

Before I could respond, he was off again. Into the trees we went. It was better here. The coolness of the shade felt good. Even the trail with its thick layer of pine needles was easier to walk on than the rocky soil below. There were Steller's jays crying out in their screechy voice and the staccato chatter of pine squirrels announcing our arrival. In a way, it was almost calming in spite of the sweat that was running into my eyes and the burning in my legs and lungs and even my gut. But we were nearing the top where Melvin could have seen the sun set and there would be no more kidding ourselves. And then the slope started to flatten and our hearts should have slowed and our breathing should have become easier, but they didn't in anticipation of what we would find. It was time to take on the white elephant. I suddenly had no stomach for it all, not for a hundred dollars a month and a cabin without an electric stove or even a screen door. But then the naysayer in my mind shouted out, *Hell, it wouldn't matter if you were getting a thousand dollars a month and lived in some fancy upscale place, it wouldn't be enough for today*. Suddenly, up ahead and down the backside of the ridge, I heard ravens quarreling. I looked at Phil and nodded towards the noise,

I said in a humble, somber voice, "I suspect that's where we need to go."

Tears had come to his eyes. For a moment he just stood there staring at me, like to not go over there would prolong Melvin's life.

I said, drawing upon courage that I somehow willed myself to have, "Why don't you wait here, Phil, and I'll check it out."

The temptation to accept my offer briefly surfaced in his face but then he said, "No, he's my boy."

I nodded, "Alright," and fell in behind him as we went off the trail towards the ravens. The further we progressed toward the influence of the western exposure the more scattered the pine trees became until, finally, they gave way to the sage and grass. At this divide, however, was a big ponderosa pine. It was bigger than all the other trees. Beneath it was a mob of ravens and several turkey vultures, and barely visible, in their midst, was Melvin.

Phil instantly charged towards the irreverent birds, screaming, "Get out of here you filthy sons-a-bitches. Go on, git." Some of the more defiant ones merely hopped off a short way as if they had been insulted by having their lunch interrupted. Their arrogance caused Phil to suddenly stop and pick up a stick and throw it at them, and then a rock, and then he went on ranting his profanity laced tirade until he reached Melvin and abruptly stopped. He appeared to be paralyzed by what was before him. And then, just as I came along side of Phil, I saw why. Within seconds, I felt my breakfast coming up. Quickly, I turned and ran a few steps before vomiting. Behind me, Phil had dropped to his knees, sobbing uncontrollably. I stood, bent over with my hands on my knees, hoping that I would not throw up again but then the image of Melvin's bloody eye sockets and the gaping hole in the back of his head that oozed gray cottage cheese and dried blood, lots of blood that had turned black, overwhelmed my senses and I retched painfully. My stomach felt as if it was being turned inside out. I had nothing left to surrender but a smattering of green bile. Behind me, Phil continued to cry and wail, "Dammit, Melvin, why? Why? Why?" I turned, totally uncertain of what to say. At the moment, I was unappreciative of Melvin's pain. I was mad at him for the hurt he had caused Phil and no doubt the rest of his family. And deep down, I was mad too for my being subjected to the image of him slumped over at the base of that tree with that .38 still loosely clutched in his right hand and his mouth still slightly agape. I knew there'd be no erasing that memory from my mind, not ever. Finally, the deputy sheriff within me kicked in. I went to Phil, stopping a few feet short of where he was kneeled on the ground beside Melvin. I said, "There's nothing we can do here now, Phil. We need to go."

He looked up at me, like I was being indifferent to his pain, he said in an angry tone, "*Go*, we can't just, *go*. We've got to take Melvin with us."

I glanced at Melvin, trying to not look at his head, and then back to Phil, I said, "My guess is Melvin is a little over 200 pounds, Phil. I don't know that we can carry him down that steep ridge we climbed getting up here. We might end up dropping him or one of us twist an ankle or knee and then we'd be in an even worse fix. We need a pack horse."

"That'll take time. These damned birds will peck him clean before we get back."

My first thought was, *he's right, look at what they've already done*, but then an idea came to me, I said, "We'll

127

cover him with pine boughs. That should keep them off him until I come back with a pack horse. I'm thinkin' maybe two or three hours."

"What's this, *I stuff*? I'm coming with you, ya know?"

"Phil, I'm thinkin' Ellen and Niko is probably gonna need you more than either me or Melvin. I'll see to it that he gets into town."

He looked at me as if he wanted to argue, but then he closed his eyes and turned away allowing his chin to drop almost onto his chest. Tears began to seep from the corners of his eyes and run down along the sides of his nose. I felt like an intruder. It was quiet except for a couple of ravens down the slope and the gentle moan of the wind in the trees behind us. I said nothing as I went into the woods and began breaking off green branches. It was good to be away from Phil's grief and the helpless feeling that it caused me. And it felt good too, to be surrounded by the smell of the pines and away from the odor of death. But more than anything, I was feeling anger at Melvin for the pain and sadness he was causing people. And I was mad at him for ruining a boyhood memory as I would never look at Mink Creek in the same way ever again.

CHAPTER NINE

After finding out that Melvin had shot himself, Ellen could not drive in the mental state she was in. It pretty much left Phil with no choice but to take her home and leave to me the retrieval of Melvin's body. I was relieved that it worked out this way as I had absorbed a lot of Phil's sadness on the way back to the ranger station and then Ellen's once we got there. They had gone outside, just the two of them, so Phil could tell her. Even from inside, we heard her scream. She never came back, going instead, with her father's help, to the pickup that Melvin had driven to Mink Creek. And then they went home.

I debated going to my cabin and using the phone there to call Grace, or just using the radio in my truck and giving the city cops first crack at what was sure to be juicy gossip in town, or doing what I finally decided upon, using the forest service phone.

Grace answered, "Gros Ventre County Sheriff's Office."

"Grace, this is Andy. I -"

"Where in blazes are you? Do you know it's 2:15? Roy Glover just called here. He's hoppin' mad you aren't at his meeting."

"I already told you I didn't think I could make it and I can't."

"Well, did you find that Lujack kid?"

"I did. He's dead."

"Oh, no."

"Yeah, he shot himself way hell and gone up on Mink Creek. I'm about to head out with the forest service packer to get 'im. I was wondering if you could call the coroner and ask him to meet me at my cabin around six o'clock and pick up the body."

"You know, he'll want all the particulars on this."

"There ain't no doubt it was a suicide. Phil Lujack will testify to it."

"Alright, I'll let him know and I'll let Roy Glover know why you're not at the meeting."

I laughed. "Ok, Grace, you do that."

"So, how are you doing? Do you think I should call Tom?"

A pulse of anger shot through me, like she didn't trust me to handle this. I said, "For what, Grace? He's a thousand miles away."

"Well, well, just in case you missed something."

I shook my head as I sighed into the phone, "Call him if you like, Grace, but I gotta go."

We, Allan Grimes and I, repeated the trip to Mink Creek that I had just made, except this time Gussie, a big white forest service mule went along. It took some convincing on my part to get Allan to leave behind horses for us to ride. To quote him, *God did not intend for man to walk everywhere, especially uphill. That's why he made horses*. But I countered with the possibility that the weight of two horses, a mule, and the forest service truck might get us all a bath in the Gros Ventre if we tried to cross the rickety Rock Creek bridge. He was still grumbling up until we actually went over the bridge and it creaked and moaned and gave a little. I could see the concern in his eyes. He said, "I guess you weren't joshin' 'bout this."

I grinned, "Nope, and we gotta go back across it."

He laughed briefly and then took a drag off his Lucky Strike cigarette with his left hand while steering the truck with his right. Turning his head, he blew the smoke out the window before glancing back at me. I sensed he had something more important to say than banter about the bridge so I kept quiet. He said, "It's a helluva deal, that Lujack boy shootin' his self."

I nodded, "Yeah, it is."

"The sad part of it is, there's people that's gonna think he did it cuz he went nuts in a war that didn't exist."

"I suppose so, but if you talk to Ellen, she'll tell you that Alaska was no picnic for Melvin."

"I know, I talked to him just last week. He told me how it was."

"He told you? I didn't think he talked to many people."

"He didn't, but it was in the evening, I was fishing down along the river and ran into him. He was just sittin' there on the river bank tossin' rocks in the water. I've been where he was at, so I knew he was hurting."

"You were in the service?"

"Yeah, the Army in World War I over in France."

At first, I was hesitant to say it but then I eased the words out, "So, did you get one of those mental discharges like Melvin?"

Allan looked away and took another drag from his cigarette, held it briefly, knowing that I was waiting for his response, and then exhaled into the steering wheel, he said, staring straight ahead, "No, but if the war had gone on much longer I don't know if I could have stood it." He paused and then looked right at me, "Some of the things a man sees in war just never go away. When I came home I was probably as messed up as Melvin. There were times, plenty of times, that I thought about doing just what he did."

I suddenly felt like I was a boy in the presence of a man. My experiences in life were pretty milk toast compared to Allan and Melvin's. I didn't know what to say to Allan. It occurred to me that maybe that was why Melvin had killed himself, nobody knew what to say to him. We drove on in silence.

I was relieved when we finally parked the truck and unloaded the mule. It was another step closer to ending this nightmare. In a way, hearing Allan's confession, so to speak, lessened my resentment of Melvin for what he'd done. Nonetheless, climbing the ridge in the peak heat of the day was no easier. The stench of death seemed to have grown in the short time I'd been gone. If the smell or the vigil the ravens and vultures had taken up bothered Allan, he didn't let on. He seemed mechanical in his actions as he unfolded the canvas tarp he'd brought. It was like this was nothing new to him, and maybe it wasn't. Following his direction, I took hold of Melvin's feet leaving Allan to grasp his arms and be closest to the gore that represented his head. And then I saw it, kind of a far-away look in his eyes.

I wondered if Allan was envisioning himself where Melvin was now. But then it was gone almost as quick as it'd come. We placed Melvin on the tarp and rolled him over twice so as to get a tighter wrap and then tied ropes around the body in three different places. Melvin was, as I had expected, very heavy and not easy to lay across the pack saddle. After Allan tied the body to the wooden cross-ties of the saddle, so as to prevent it from sliding off either side of the mule, we set off down the mountain. Neither of us said much, not all the way back to the ranger station. It was like the somberness of death required it. We transferred Melvin to my pickup. I thanked Allan for his help, knowing that this might have dug up a past he had probably worked hard to bury. It was a little past six when I got to my cabin. The coroner, who was also the undertaker in Fremont, had brought the hearse. As we loaded Melvin into it there were two cars, on a road that often goes a couple of hours without any going by, that stopped and gawked at what we were doing. Finally, the big black death wagon rolled out onto the road and back through Cedarville before who knows how many sets of eyes. I was hungry and tired and needed a beer, maybe several beers to rid my mind of all that I'd seen today. But then I recalled what Allan had said, that *some of the things a man sees in war just never go away*. I suspected today would be like that and going to the Antler for a burger and a beer would come at a price, I would be expected to provide all the details of Melvin sticking the barrel of that pistol in his mouth and pulling the trigger. I shook my head and started toward my cabin with Grady trotting along beside me.

The night had gone about like I'd expected it would. After a supper of a baloney sandwich, chips and an orange soda I tried to occupy my mind with something other than what had happened. I tuned in to a Billings radio station that played lots of music and dug out a book by Ernest Hemingway that my mother had given me. The book was entitled, *For Whom The Bell Tolls*. *You need to read this*, she'd said. *It'll be good for you*, like it was medicine that I needed to take. I tried reading it but it was about war and dying which, in my mind, took me right back to Melvin's slumped over body and his father kneeling in the dirt beside him, crying, pleading for an explanation, and Allan, good old jovial Allan whose dark side came out, and Mitch lying dead on a beach. It occurred to me that, had I not been required to go to Mink Creek, I probably could have read the book and maybe even enjoyed it.

It was a little after ten in the morning. I had stepped outside my cabin to take a break from the paperwork that yesterday had generated and to fill Grady's water bowl when I heard a car slow down and turn off the road. It was the Lujack family. They were most likely on their way to town to pick up Charlie from the train station and, I supposed, to begin preparation for Melvin's funeral. *What a homecoming this will be*, I said to myself as I started towards their car. Phil parked next to my deputy sheriff's pickup. He left his motor running, burning rationed gas waiting for me to come along side his car. For some reason, I thought he would get out and talk to me privately about whatever it was he wanted, which I assumed had to do with Melvin. The car windows, all of them, were down. Ellen was in the back seat. Niko was sitting up front. Their eyes looked tired and as if they hurt, except for Phil, who was hiding behind wire rimmed dark glasses beneath his, go to town, gray felt Stetson. I stopped a few feet short of their car. The crook of Phil's left arm, which was encased in a white, long-sleeved shirt, was resting partway out the window. He said, pretty much business like, "I talked to Grimes a little bit ago. I asked him to go easy on the details of Melvin's situation. Said he would. I'd appreciate it if you'd do the same. How Melvin died ain't nobody's concern but ours."

Ellen was looking straight at me, waiting for my response probably as much as her father. I said, "I've got to put every thing in my report. Where it goes from there, I don't have a lot of control over."

Disappointment came to Ellen's face, Phil on the other hand looked angry. He said, "Just because it's in your report doesn't mean that little pecker neck coroner has got to share it with the paper."

I could see Niko's hand reach over and squeeze Phil's arm. He ignored her and went on, "It'll be a helluva note if this week's edition of the Fremont rag has got two stories about the Lujack brothers, one about the wounded hero home on leave and the other about his crazy brother that shot himself. That otta sell some papers, don't you think?"

Across the seat from Phil I could hear Niko whisper his name. He turned to her, "Don't you shush me."

Almost at the same time, Ellen leaned forward and took hold of her father's right shoulder. "Dad, let's just go. Andy can't do anything different. He can't hide what's happened."

Abruptly, Phil turned toward me, he said sarcastically, "You have a nice day."

I was in the process of saying, "I'm sorry," when he backed up fast, changed gears and spun his wheels leaving my yard. I was standing there wondering if I deserved that when I noticed, from the corner of my eye, a blood smear on the tail gate of my truck. It was dark and blended in to where it was hardly noticeable unless the sun hit it just right.

Nonetheless, I went looking for something to wipe it off with, something that I could throw away.

It was late afternoon, I was on my way back from the privy when the Lujack's came through. I glanced over in their direction. My attention was immediately drawn to Ellen. She was sitting in the back seat directly behind Charlie who was sitting up front with his father. She appeared sad, as one might expect. Her hand barely cleared the open window and the movement was brief, but there was no mistaking it, she waved. I did not smile out of respect for her situation, as I waved back. Charlie, who had been looking in my direction but acting as if he didn't know me, suddenly twisted around in his seat. They were about 30 or 40 yards away and just starting to pick up speed when I caught the words, ...*wave at him*? It looked like Ellen had become angry and then there were several voices all jumbled together and then they were on up the road. I continued on to the cabin, wondering if I'd misread things. Charlie and I had never been friends as he was a little too cocky for me, but at the same time, I hadn't disliked him. So, it puzzled me now why he appeared to be questioning his sister's friendliness towards me. Or, I said to myself, *maybe he thinks like his father, that I can do more to keep how Melvin died from the public.*

I was still processing in my mind the Lujack's driving by and doing my best to give Charlie the benefit of the doubt and not be mad at him, when I heard the phone ring. I hurried inside and picked it up just after the third ring. It was Tom. There were no idle pleasantries, no how's it going, he went right to it, he said, "Sounds like the shit has hit the fan up there."

I frowned at the phone, "Did Grace call you?"

There was a brief silence on his end that was interrupted by the tinkling of ice cubes in a glass. I looked over at the clock, it was 4:13. He came back, "No, I called Glover to see how the meeting that you didn't go to went."

"Well, did he tell you why I wasn't there?"

"Yeah, he said that Lujack kid that washed out of the Army on a Section 8 shot himself. That's a helluva deal. You have any problems with it."

I wanted to say, *problems, why no except for this picture in my mind of Melvin's brains hanging out the back of his head and bloody holes where his eyes used to be before the ravens and vultures got to them,* but I said aloud, "No, turned the body over to the coroner last night and finished up the paperwork today."

"Well, you make sure the coroner and the district attorney get a copy of your report. Have Grace type it up and give the carbons to them."

I already knew to do this but I said only, "Alright, Tom, I'll run my report into town tomorrow."

There was another pause and more ice cubes rattling before Tom came back on, he said, "I'm thinkin' of makin' a change, Andy."

My mind instantly went to a bad place, I blurted out, "Glover convince you to fire me?"

Tom's voice sounded surprised as he said, "Oh that, I talked him into just putting a letter of reprimand into your file."

"Reprimand," I said angrily.

"Well, he was pushin' for a three-day suspension without pay so you ought to consider yourself lucky, at least as far as that goes."

"Whaddaya mean, as far as that goes?"

There was another pause as I listened to ice cubes clinking together, and then he said, "I'm thinkin' a changing my line of work and relocating down here, go into the construction business with my brother."

"You'd be happy doing that?"

"I don't know, but what I do know is you can't eat happiness and the way I see it Gros Ventre County is always gonna be a penny pinching outfit."

"So, where will this leave me?"

"I don't know, for now, right where you're at, but Glover wants to see if the commission can't appoint Cecil Burns to fill out the rest of my term. He came out second best to me in the last election so it makes some sense to do that."

I scoffed into the phone. "Well, I suspect if that was to happen and Glover has his own man in as sheriff, I'd be walking a thin line between being employed and not."

"Hard to say, Andy, I think if you was to keep your nose clean you'd be alright."

"So, when do you think you will actually resign."

"I'm not certain, a month or two I suppose, but I'll let you know."

"So, this is a sure thing, it's just a matter of when?"

"Yeah, I believe you can count on it."

CHAPTER TEN

It did not take Grace long to type up my report nor did it require a lot of time to answer what few questions the coroner and district attorney had about the crime scene. In their minds it was all pretty straight forward, Melvin Lujack committed suicide. Unfortunately, the editor for the Fremont Beacon had interviewed the coroner yesterday and he had spared few details, including the fact, since he was also the undertaker, that it would be a closed casket service and there would be no viewing of the body prior to the service, which was to be private and graveside only. The article in the paper didn't spell out the reason for the closed casket, but it did state that Melvin likely shot himself on Sunday and wasn't found until Monday. It was exactly the kind of article Phil Lujack didn't want. And just like he said they would, the Beacon printed an article using a press release the Army had sent them about Charlie Lujack being wounded in action during fighting in the Solomon Islands and that he was being given two weeks convalescent leave.

It was shortly before noon, and since I was hungry and it'd been a while since I'd talked to my mother face to face,

I decided to go to the Coffee Cup for lunch. I'd just stepped inside when I spotted her towards the back of the room, not far from where Ellen and I had sat. She motioned towards a small table near the wall. I started toward it. To get there, I would have to go right past Cindy who was facing me while taking an order from the table next to the window. As I went by her, she focused on her order pad like her life depended on it. My mother was staring at Cindy's back. She frowned and shook her head slightly. When I was nearly to her she whispered, "I hope being this way is worth it to her." And then she gave me a loose hug before I sat down.

I thought to plead Ellen's case to my mother so as to make the loss of her friend more palatable, but I figured I would be preaching to the choir as she had told me more than once that she didn't think it was right to lock up all the Japanese down at Heart Mountain. So, I let it go and said, "What's the special?"

"Meatloaf, comes with mashed spuds and gravy, green beans, rolls and apple cobbler for dessert."

I laughed, "Seems like somewhere in all that you guys ought to be breakin' a rationing rule."

My mother rolled her eyes and walked away. I watched as she clipped my order to a metal cylinder suspended above the half-wall that separated the kitchen from the counter. Sitting on the shelf beneath the orders were several steaming specials. It struck me as being a lot of meat and that took me to the image of Sherm Duke's steer being butchered and, for a fleeting second, the possibility that my meatloaf could have come from Skinner Meadows. But then my mind moved on to the fact I hadn't heard much from Bill Kyle since that day out on 29 when he gave me that bloody hide. I said to myself, *it appears that both him and the brand inspector are leaving this up to me to figure out.*

From my left, I could see Ma coming with a glass of ice water and my silverware wrapped in a white paper napkin. She set them on the table and then, after glancing over her shoulder towards the cash register up front, she sat down. Leaning toward me she said in a low voice, "The Lujack's came in yesterday. It was sad. Not a single person said anything to them. Not how sorry they were about Melvin or glad to see you're home Charlie, just nothing, and I know some of them had to know Phil."

I recalled how Ellen had vowed to come back here when Charlie came home in his uniform with his medals and that things would be different than they were that night in the parking lot out front. I said, "Did you say something to them?"

For a second Ma appeared insulted, and then she said, "Well, certainly. I told them I was sorry about Melvin and I said, welcome home Charlie."

How'd they take it. "They were kinda quiet. Charlie did say thanks and so did Ellen. Niko nodded and Phil just kind of looked at me like he didn't know what to say."

"Ellen said thanks?"

"Yes, in fact she said, thank-you, Mrs. Yarnell. Does that surprise you?"

"I don't know, a little I guess, or I wouldn't have asked."

My mother sighed, "That poor family, they must feel shunned. I see in the paper where Melvin's service is going to be private."

"That's sad," I said, "but they've got to know it's just the war." And then I added, "At least they have Melvin's body to bury. Mitch's mother told me that he was killed in a beach landing and that his body was washed back out to sea and lost. She has nothing."

Ma was silent for a time before adding, "She has memories, look at what the Lujack's have."

From the opening above the half-wall came a shout, "Wilma, order up."

My mother glanced over at the cook who was staring back at her. She instantly got to her feet. "That's your order."

After lunch, I swung by the office and told Grace in person what my plans were. It occurred to me, while I was eating my meatloaf, that I could patrol about 15 miles north out of Fremont to the Pass Creek road which would take me through the mountains into the Gros Ventre valley. I had decided that somewhere along the way I would find a high spot with good cover and just watch and listen for gunshots or vehicles that didn't belong there. I knew the chances were good that I'd be up there by myself, but what else could I do? I had nothing to go on but the suspicion that a mysterious furniture truck that ran the fire crew off the road might be involved in this poaching of elk and beef.

As a kid living in the Gros Ventre, I had always envisioned these mountains as where the sun hid itself at the end of each day but now, sitting on top of the pass, I could see that where it really went to was another range of mountains even farther to the west. It was a quarter to eight. I had driven down a faint two-track towards Bell Mountain, so named because it was shaped like a bell, and purposely stopped in thick trees before I would be visible by the fire lookout on top of the mountain, which was, as the crow flies, about two miles away. I didn't know who the lookout was other than he was just some guy, middle aged, Ellen had said. But it had occurred to me that, unless this fella napped a lot, he would have been in a prime location to see any vehicle that might have been on the Weasel Mountain road when the fire started. According to Ellen, the guy, whose name was Frank, hadn't seen a thing prior to his reporting the fire. And the more I thought about it the more I became suspicious of the fact he hadn't heard any gunshots or seen any headlights in the night. Grady and I had been hunkered down in a patch of trees on the end of a high ridge overlooking a huge basin with lots of grassy areas filled with cows since about three o'clock. It was now 7:55. The only evidence of the sun was a faint orange glow on the backside of the peaks behind us. It caused the landscape to be engulfed in one big shadow. In a little while it would be too dark to shoot and too dark to gut out an animal unless a man had a spotlight and in five minutes the lookout would be going off duty but, since he lived where he worked, I questioned if he was ever totally off-duty. And then I saw movement that seemed more delib-erate than that of the cattle. Way off below me, close to a mile I suppose, a dark shape had come out of some quaking aspen and was moving across a meadow towards a small bunch of Hereford cows and calves. My heart went into a higher gear as I raised my binoculars to see exactly what I was looking at. Right away, I could see it was a man. He was wearing a wide brimmed white straw cowboy hat that shaded his face, which, in the poor light, made it almost impossible to make out his features. I could see too, he had what looked like a pistol on his right hip. The man slowed his pace to where he was hardly moving, but still appeared headed towards the cows. When he was about fifteen or twenty yards from the cattle he stopped. There were three cows and two calves in the bunch. One of the cows became nervous and trotted off a short distance, the others, as they so often do, just stood there and waited to see what this human was up to. With his right hand, the man went to his hip and came away with the pistol. He held it weakly out in front of him, but not in a position of aiming, until finally he casually raised it and fired once and then again. The report of the gun was not loud, its echoes died away almost immediately. *Probably a .22*, I said to myself. All the cattle, but two, bolted and ran off to the far side of the meadow. The man holstered his pistol and went over to the calves, which appeared to be good-sized. He paused next to them and began casually rolling up the sleeves of his blue denim shirt. It was hard for me to believe that the man was unaware of the lookout, even as far away as it was. And then he dropped down on his knees next to the first calf. He leaned over, as if to begin dressing the animal, but then abruptly rocked back and removed his hat. He twisted to his left and tossed it on the ground several feet behind him. When he came back around, he paused and looked up as if to stretch the muscles in his back before starting. I whispered aloud, "Russell, you damned old fool." He seemed to be going about his work with more urgency now. As I watched, I couldn't help but feel kind of sorry for him. Deep down, I suspected I knew why he was here. By some standards, he had a good job and didn't need to do this but then my conversation with Oscar came to mind and images of the big cowboy crowded in as well, probably 20 years younger than Russell, patting Gertie down. And her having money to drink and order stuff willy-nilly from the Monkey Wards catalog and Russell not wanting to go to bed alone at night. If a man was that desperate to avoid loneliness, then what I was seeing through my binoculars made some sense. However, the person that wouldn't be convinced by this logic was who ever owned those calves. Come November, they represented a couple of hundred dollar bills.

I turned over on to my hands and knees and crawled further back into the woods before standing up to walk to my pickup. I knew from having hunted in this area, and my time on the fire crew, that I could take the Pass Creek road on down through the trees for about two miles to a side road that went close to the meadow where Russell was at. The road dead ended at an old timber sale that had been cut years ago. So, unless Russell was going to use his pack horse to transport the meat to some other place, I was bound to run into him on this logging road. As soon as I reached my truck, I called the night dispatch and told the woman as best I could describe it, where I was at and what was going on. She asked if I didn't want some help to which I replied it would be nice, but I suspected I needed to make the arrest before anyone could get clear out here. She said she would contact the highway patrol to see if they couldn't send someone my way via Cedarville and County Road 29. I thanked her and started down the mountain. I would have, under normal circumstances, been driving with my headlights on but this was obviously not a normal situation. I had an awkward, nervous feeling about having to arrest Russell. He was more an acquaintance than friend, even though I worked with him for three seasons when I was on the fire crew. That was the awkward part, what I was nervous about was the fact that I'd only had to handcuff somebody twice in my short career as a lawman. One was a drunk who'd started a minor fight in a bar in Fremont, and the other was a guy who had a bunch of traffic tickets that he failed to pay. With the drunk I had help from one of the city cops and, the other guy, as soon as I walked into his job at the grain elevator, he knew why I was there. He held out his hands and said, *I figured one of you guys would come looking for me someday.*

As I came to the junction where the logging road took off it occurred to me that I had no real plan on how I was going to handle this other than just confront Russell. He undoubtedly knew that livestock theft was a serious offense, something that could possibly earn him a stay at the prison over in Deerlodge. The question in my mind was, what would he do to keep from going there? He had a pistol, would he use it? But, so did I, which prompted an even tougher question for me, would I use mine? I heaved a big sigh and started down the old road. Since it no longer received regular use, it was being crowded hard by brush and trees from the sides while the actual roadbed was disguised beneath a carpet of needles and cones, and grass and wildflowers that had sprung up at random. The trees towered above me. I felt as if I was in a high-sided chute as the only decent natural light was straight up beyond the tops of the pines. It was a situation that caused me to just quietly idle along with my windows down, straining to listen should Russell be greedy or foolish enough to shoot more cattle. But it was quiet, except for a Steller's jay that began screeching as we rolled by. I looked over at Grady. He seemed content to look out the window hoping, I suppose, that we would stop soon and there would be some squirrels for him to chase. He trusted me to look out for him. I wondered if maybe I should have left him at the cabin today.

We went on, farther and farther down the deteriorating road until I began to doubt myself, had I made a wrong turn? And then, in almost the same instant, I saw the broken outline of what appeared to be a van type truck backed off the road to my left. I immediately stopped and cut my engine.

I glanced over at Grady and gave him a pet. "You stay here, hound dog. I'll be back in a little while." No sooner had I said this than the worry surfaced in my mind, *what will happen to him if I don't come back.*

I eased out of my pickup and gently pushed the door shut behind me so that it barely made a click. Where I stood it was quiet, but beyond the truck I could hear ravens and more Steller's jays. I went into the trees at the edge of the two-track and started towards the truck, which was about 40 to 50 yards from me. After a couple of minutes of taking steps, as if I was going through a mine field, I arrived at the mystery vehicle. It was a black Dodge with a large drab green metal box behind the cab. Printed on the side of the box in badly faded red letters was the business name, OLSON FURNITURE – 321 CUSTER STREET – BILLINGS. My first impulse was that I had accomplished something, like I had tracked down or outwitted a bull elk or some other animal equally as smart. But this feeling was short-lived as I heard a pine cone crunch in the trees to my left. It may have been because I knew Russell had a gun, or maybe it was because I knew of his reputation as somebody you didn't want to mess with, but I pulled my pistol out. No sooner had I done this than he brushed through the branches of two jack pine about 20 feet away, straight out from me. In his arms was the bloody hind quarter of one of the calves. At first his face showed surprise bordering on shock, but then he smiled as if we'd just bumped into one another on a fire and said, "Ain't it past yer bedtime?"

It was the voice in which he'd said it as much as it was his words that rubbed me wrong. However, given the situation and not wanting to upset him anymore than need be before I had to arrest him, I laughed and played along like I was the kid he was making me out to be, I said, "It is, Russell, and I've missed having my warm glass of milk and bedtime story to boot."

He laughed in a sad way, "So, you've caught me, now what?"

I said, still holding my pistol in my hand but not pointing it at him, "I suspect you know the answer to that being the cowboy that you are."

An angry, but strangely confident, look came to his face, "I can't abide spending time in the state's gray bar hotel."

I said, knowing that I doubted it myself, "You never know, it might not come to that."

He snorted, "Do you believe in the tooth fairy too? Hell, in the old days they'd hang a man for this."

"Then why do it, Russell? You've got a good job."

He looked at me like I was purposely trying to embarrass him. He said, "you've spent enough time at the Antler to be able to answer that yerself."

From behind me a hateful voice shouted, "Freeze right where you're at mister law man."

Fearful impulse caused me to turn around.

A mustachioed man wearing a flat cap and pointing a .45 automatic pistol at me was standing there, he said, "How damned stupid are you? I said freeze and drop that pistol on the ground. Now."

I let the pistol fall from my hand. My heart was hammering like it never had in all my life before now. I said, the fear in my voice obvious, "You're just making things worse for yourself."

The man laughed in an evil sarcastic tone, he said, "The way I see it, if I don't shoot you, I'm definitely going to prison, but if I do shoot you, there's a good chance I'll remain a free man."

I looked at the guy. He was wearing a white tee shirt that was smeared with blood, and Levis. My father would have called him a *worldly type*, on account of the large tattoos on his forearms. I recalled when I was a kid there was a man in the valley who went by the name of Frenchy, that kind of looked like this guy. One night when my father came home long after Ma and I had eaten, he said it was due to Frenchy having gone berserk in the Antler and cutting Luther Higgins' throat. He said if he hadn't hit Frenchy in the head with the fat end of a cue stick, he might have got cut himself. Desperate for some common sense to prevail, I glanced over at Russell. I said, "You need to tell your friend here that if he shoots me it'll get the both of ya hanged."

Russell, who was still holding the hind quarter of beef, said nothing but started toward the open end of the van. He walked up a short gangplank into the darkness and dropped the meat. Moments later he came back out and walked over to me, he said, "I always thought you were a good kid, Andy, but I wished you hadn't come up here."

I'd barely processed the meaning of what he'd said when I suddenly felt weak, like I was going to be sick. My heart was beating so fast it was painful and my eyes had become watery. I said, "You're better than this, Russell. This 'll haunt you the rest of your life."

The man with the .45 laughed. "It won't haunt you nearly as much as it will if you don't do it and you go to Deerlodge. You'll wish you had of then. Besides, it'll be me pulling the trigger."

I came back quick, lest this *worldly guy* just take it upon himself to end the debate and shoot me, I said to Russell, "You'll be an accomplice to killing a peace officer, in Montana that'll get you hung."

Before Russell could respond, his friend jumped in, "Hell, you ain't no peace officer, at best you're a boy scout masquerading as a cop." And then he laughed.

I glared hatefully at the man, who probably was as old as Russell, it caused him to strike back at me, "Why you pecker neck kid, give me a dirty look will ya?"

Russell said, like he was out of patience with all the talk, "Alright, Sam, let's just be done with it."

My knees instantly felt like they were going to buckle, I shouted, "Wait, Russell, do me one favor, please."

Russell scowled at me, "What?"

I said, my eyes filled with tears, "Grady's waiting for me in my truck. See to it that he gets to my mother, please, he's not gonna understand when I don't come back, but he knows you."

Sam blurted out, "We ain't takin no damned dog to yer mother. That 'd be as good as admitting we killed you."

"I didn't ask you."

Russell looked hard at Sam, "Let it go, it's my problem."

Sam sneered at Russell, "Alright, let's get on with it. We've still got beef to load."

Russell acted as if I wasn't there, he said, "We need to walk him farther back into the trees."

Sam came towards me and motioned with the barrel of his pistol. "Move."

The reality that I was about to die was mind boggling. I wanted desperately to believe that I was asleep back at my cabin and this was a bad dream that I couldn't wake up from and that if I just tried harder, I could break free of it. But then I heard Russell, "This is far enough, Andy." I turned around to face them. We were in a small clearing. I thought, *just run,*

run like hell, but I was paralyzed by the gaping barrel of the .45 and the fact that Sam was taking aim at me.

Suddenly, Russell said, "hold on Sam."

Sam turned to Russell who was standing to the side and slightly behind him, he said in an angry voice, "what in the hell is it now?"

"That cannon of yours makes a lot of racket. You never know who's around that might hear it. Might make more sense to use my .22."

Sam frowned and sighed, "Ok, let me have it."

"Well, give me your .45 so I can hold that on him while I give you my gun."

And then just like that my nightmare ended and my silent prayer was answered as Russell took the .45 in his left hand while pretending to remove his .22 from its holster. He stepped back from Sam, and said, "we can't go this route. The kid's right. They'll hang us."

Sam became enraged. "Why you dumb sonovabitch, they gotta catch us first."

"Well, maybe you can run off to some sandy beach in Mexico, but this is home for me."

"Maybe you shudda thought about that before you shit in yer nest."

"You go on, Sam. I'll allow you a head start. I at least owe you that."

"Gimme my gun back."

Russell laughed and shook his head. "That, I don't owe you. Now you better skedaddle."

Sam scoffed, "You're a fool, Russell, a damned fool." He then started towards the truck but suddenly stopped and looked at me in a hateful way, he said, "Kid, you better hope our paths never cross again, cuz if they do, I'll kill ya and you can take that to the bank."

My anger briefly caused me to consider saying something smart-alecky like, *I've never had a hankering to go to any sandy beaches in Mexico*, but then common sense caught hold of my tongue and I stayed quiet, allowing Sam to salvage some of his ego. I watched, being careful to not let what was in my mind bleed through to my face, as he went to the back of the truck and closed it up. When he was done, he turned to Russell and sneered, "I'll send you a post card. I suppose, Russell Jenkins – Montana State Prison – Deerlodge, ought to get it to you, don't you reckon?" And then he laughed and continued to laugh as he went up along the far side of the truck and got in and drove away.

We stood there in the dark, neither of us saying anything until the sound of the truck had become so faint, we could barely hear it. Russell said, still holding the .22 in his right hand and the .45 in his left, "Now what?"

"I appreciate your saving my hide. That'll count for a lot with the district attorney."

"The state will still want their pound of flesh. Ole Milo Peterson will see to that."

"These calves you got tonight belong to him?"

Russell nodded, "Just his bad luck, I guess."

At the risk of rubbing salt in his wound, I asked, "Why did you do it?"

He snorted, "Stupid, I guess. Gittin' old didn't seem to work for me. It made me dumber, not smarter."

I knew he was talking about Gertie's sway on his judgement, but I did not go there. I said, "Well, just know that I'll put in a good word for you."

"Appreciate it," he said as he holstered the .22, and then he cleared the chamber of the .45 before holding it out to me. "I suppose you want this."

I took the pistol. Having it in my hand confirmed to me that this was no trick and, like a switch being pulled, a good deal of the tension suddenly left my body. But, before I could speak, Russell came back, "Can I have tonight? I promise I'll show up to your cabin tomorrow morning if I can just have the night."

His request took me by surprise as up until a few minutes ago I assumed that I'd be dead by now. I was still gathering my thoughts on the matter when he added, "Hell, Andy, I ain't got no place to run to. I got my horse tied off in the trees just over behind us. My camp is about a mile north of here. I need to go break it down and go home." He sighed heavily, "Gertie ain't gonna be happy."

My feelings toward Russell when I had been driving up here this afternoon were far different than now. But, back then, I didn't owe him my life. I said, "Alright, Russell, how 'bout you be at my place at nine o'clock tomorrow morning?"

He nodded, "I'll be there."

And then, for some reason, I recalled what Sam had said about needing to load more beef, I said, "Is there more meat over yonder?"

"Yeah, there's a coupla hind quarters. Did ya wanna take 'em?"

"I'll catch hell if I don't."

"Well, follow me, I'll lend you a hand."

I fell in behind Russell as we set off at a good pace through the brush and trees. It reminded me of times when he and I had hiked at night after a lightning storm in search of a spot fire that one of the lookouts had radioed in. I wished that was what we were doing now. It did not take long to retrieve the beef and load it in the back of my pickup. Grady was prancing up and down and wagging his tail. I said, jokingly, "I don't know if he's happy to see me or the meat." We both laughed.

But then Russell said in a serious voice, "You know why he's happy."

I nodded and extended my hand to Russell, "Thank you."

Russell shook my hand firmly, "See you in the morning."

After I had got turned around and was on my way out, I radioed the dispatch. The reception was poor but, eventually I conveyed to her what had happened and that the highway patrol should be on the lookout for the furniture truck. I told her too, that I would be stopping by the Peterson Land & Livestock headquarters to drop off the beef.

It was a little past eleven o'clock when I stopped my truck in front of the Lujack house. A dull yellow light was visible through the living room window but beyond that, and their dog barking up a storm, there were no signs of life. I felt real awkward coming at this time of day but I had about a 150 pounds of beef that needed to be taken care of. I'd just started up the walk when, from the darkness to the left of where the light was visible, a voice called out, "Who goes there?"

It'd been some time since I'd last talked to him but I was fairly certain of who it was, I said, "It's me Charlie, Andy Yarnell."

The voice came back, cold and indifferent, "So, why is it you're here in the middle of the night?"

Charlie's tone caused me to stop halfway to the house, I said, "I caught the men that's been butchering cattle out on the range earlier tonight and I confiscated a coupla quarters of beef that belong to Mr. Peterson."

"Well, I'll be go to hell, they do have law around here." And then he laughed in a lazy, slurred way before adding, "I heard since the sheriff left town the ole Gros Ventre had become a wild and wooly place." He laughed some more followed by, "So, who was these boys you caught?"

I was about to answer Charlie when the porch light came on and the screen door opened and Phil came outside. He was barefoot in his Levis and a white tee shirt. Through the screen I could see Ellen in a white bath robe. My eyes settled on her causing Phil to frown and glance over his shoulder. "Go back to bed, Ellen, this ain't yer concern."

"Yeah, don't you be gawkin' at my sister you pervert," slurred Charlie.

Ellen shouted, "Shut up, Charlie, you're drunk."

Phil turned towards Ellen, his voice now loud and angry, "I told you to go to bed."

"I'm not a little girl, dad."

"You are until I say otherwise."

Charlie reared back on his wooden chair and laughed, as he did his foot kicked over some of the empty beer cans in front of him. Phil scowled at him and shook his head. He then turned to me, "You've got Peterson beef?"

"Yeah, it needs to be put some place cool."

"So, you caught who was doing this?"

I said, loud enough so Ellen would be sure to hear inside, "It was Russell Jenkins and some other guy I'd never seen before."

It was almost instantaneous, the screen door behind Phil opening and Ellen shouting, "Russell's been the one stealing cattle?"

I nodded and said, not in a gloating way out of respect for the fact that I'd be dead if it hadn't been for Russell, "Yeah, I caught 'em with a couple of calves up near Bell Mountain."

Phil looked at me in a curious way like he'd missed something, he said, "You caught these boys, *tonight*?"

I sensed where he was going and said, "I let Russell go home to settle up his affairs. He's gonna report to me tomorrow morning."

"And the other guy?"

"Russell let him go, but I'm hoping the highway patrol picked him up."

Ellen cut in, "Russell let him go?"

"The guy was going to kill me, Russell stopped him. I guess he felt he owed the guy for betraying him so he let him go."

Charlie slapped his leg and laughed. "Yessiree, we got a real Wyatt Earp here. Let the crooks call the shots."

I could see in Ellen's face that she might be regretting having defended me earlier to Charlie. I wished that it was just her and I standing there so I could explain, but there was no chance of that happening.

Phil said, his tone condescending, "Well, Deputy, you can hang that meat in the root cellar. There's a light switch just inside the door."

I had barely made eye contact with Ellen when her father put his arm around her and herded her toward the door. He hollered over his shoulder, "Maybe you should call it a night, Charlie."

The sound of the screen door banging shut had barely died away when Charlie got up from his chair and said in a voice, not so loud as to draw his father or Ellen back, but loud enough that I would hear, "Hold on there, *Deputy Yarnell*." I watched as he started across the porch towards me. There was no doubt he was drunk, but he'd purposely slurred my name. He came down from the porch, stumbling at one point but catching himself. Finally, when he was whisper close to me, he stopped and stared into my face, he said, "You know, I've killed men, plenty of 'em."

I could smell the beer on Charlie's breath. When he wobbled just right, so that the porch light reflected in his eyes, I could see they were painfully bloodshot. I said to him, "I don't doubt that you have, being a Marine and all."

And then he drew his face up into a hateful sneer and poked me in the chest with his finger. He said, "I don't like you, *you being a 4-effer and all.*"

I shot back at him, no longer having the patience for his drunkenness, "I ain't 4F. The draft board can take me whenever they see fit."

"Oh, that's right, you're needed here to protect the cows."

"Go to bed, Charlie, yer drunk."

Charlie scoffed. "4-effers don't give orders, *Deputy Yarnell.* And I'll tell you another thing they don't do." He paused, waiting for me to ask. I was tempted to not take the bait and just walk off, but I suspected this had to play out his way or it would end in a fight. I said, "What's that, Charlie?"

He scrunched his face into an even more hateful look and said, "They don't screw my sister. You hear me, that ain't gonna happen."

I gave him a disgusted look and shook my head. "I'm done talking to ya, Charlie."

"You'll be done when I say."

I turned and started to walk away when I felt his hand on my shoulder. I spun around, ready to fight when suddenly the screen door banged again and Phil shouted, "Charlie, get your ass in the house. I've had enough of your bullshit for one night."

157

The sound of his father's voice froze Charlie where he stood. Nonetheless, he continued to stare at me with his fists clenched at his sides. He appeared to be weighing the consequences of disobeying his father when Phil shouted again, "You know, you ain't the only Marine in this household."

I looked back at Charlie, wondering how he could have conjured up so much hate for me. Regardless of why that was, his little grandstand production tonight would likely sour any chance I had of ever taking Ellen out again.

Phil said, in a calmer voice, "C 'mon, Charlie. Your brother has gave this family enough grief already. Now come on inside."

I could see the anger gradually subsiding in Charlie's face until finally he scoffed, "Damned 4-effer," and then he started back to the house. Phil waited for him to actually climb the steps to the porch and open the screen door before glancing back at me, "You'll unload that meat?"

I nodded.

He hesitated for a second like he was about to apologize for what had just happened, but then he said, "Peterson will appreciate it." And then he went inside and turned off the porch light.

CHAPTER ELEVEN

It was about a quarter till one in the morning when I got back to my cabin. Grady and I were both hungry. I gave him an extra helping of dog chow for all that he'd had to put up with and I made myself a sandwich with the last of the baloney. With all that was on my mind sleep was hard to come by, especially since every time I started to doze off I imagined Sam bursting into the room and making good on his threat to kill me. Added to this was the nagging thought that Russell may have gone home, packed up Gertie and skipped the country. How stupid would I look? Finally, however, around five o'clock I was so exhausted, I fell asleep. It was one of those mouth open, drool on your chin sleeps which is probably why the knock on my door had progressed to a loud pounding and Grady barking. My alarm clock read 6:05. I shouted, "Just a second." *Holy shit, I shudda been up by now*, I said to myself as I put my legs over the side of the bed and reached for my pants. The pounding continued. I hollered, "Hold on, I'll be right there." I was barefoot and still buttoning my shirt as I opened the door to, "Some sonovabitch stole my pickup last night."

Standing before me was Victor Hodgson, an old gray-haired man who lived about 30 miles up the valley and his neighbor, Ernie Groves. I said, "So, did they just take it from in front of your house?"

"No, it was parked over by the barn. I went to town yesterday and got a bunch of salt blocks and baling twine and unloaded it in the barn. I just left my pickup sit there rather than drive to the house. Hell, it ain't but a healthy rock throw away."

"I take it the keys were in it?"

Victor became irritated. "They were but dammit, a man ought to be able to do that out here. It ain't like we're in some crime ridden big city."

"Well, tell him about the truck," said Ernie impatiently.

"Truck?"

"Yeah, 'bout a quarter mile down the road from my place was a furniture truck with fresh beef in the back of it. It looked like to me those fellas were up to no good and, for whatever reason, decided to ditch their truck and steal mine. Their keys were gone or I would've drove that thing in here instead of rolling Ernie out in the middle of the night."

My mind was spinning as to what I should say to Victor. To tell him everything that happened with Sam and Russell last night might cause him to judge my actions after Sam took off. I had assumed that, rather than trying to catch up to Sam on those narrow forest roads and get him to stop for me I would just let the highway patrol snatch him up at a roadblock down on 29, obviously that didn't happen. It was just human nature for people to tell you what you should've done once they see what you did do didn't work out. I said, "I bumped into the fella driving that truck last night near Bell Mountain, but he got away from me."

Victor shot me a disgusted look but didn't press me for details. He shook his head. "Well, I reckon he's probably long gone now and so's my pickup. That leaves me afoot."

Ernie chimed in. "I got that old hoopee I use for irrigatin' and feedin'. Yer welcome to use that if ya want. Course the plates on it is expired."

Both of them looked at me with an expectation of common sense. I said, "I reckon if you don't leave the valley in that thing, you'll be alright."

Victor came back, kind of huffy like, "Well, I'm hopin' you find my pickup in the next day or so."

"Why don't you give me the plate number and description of your truck and I'll get the state boys working on it."

"It's a dark blue '39 Chevy, plate number is 143."

"Alright, I'll call that in."

Victor looked less than satisfied. "How long do you think this 'll take?"

I don't know if I thought Russell could tell me where Sam likely went to or if I just wanted to give Victor something good to take home with him, but I said, "I wouldn't be surprised if we find it pretty soon."

"I hope yer right. I need my pickup."

I felt bad for Victor. I watched him and Ernie leave out the window of my cabin as I placed the call to the office in town. Grace pumped me for all the details concerning last night even though I was certain it was all there in the dispatch log. But, more importantly, she sounded genuinely concerned that I barely avoided being killed. And, she tried hard to not question my turning Russell loose to come in on his own. At 9:15 when he still hadn't shown up, I began to kick myself, but not too hard, as he had saved my life. Nonetheless, I got up from the table where I had been doing paperwork and started for the door, intent on driving out to the ranger station to see if he was there. I'd just stepped outside when here they came, him and Gertie, in their pickup. A minor dust cloud accompanied them as they rolled to a stop next to the county's truck. Through the windshield I could see Russell look at Gertie and tell her something that appeared not to her liking. He then got out, as did she. Russell appeared nervous while Gertie seemed hateful. Russell forced a laugh, "Going somewhere?"

I thought to lie and say that I'd just came out to put fresh water in Grady's pan, but I didn't. "Well, it is a quarter past nine."

A weak grin came to his face. "I guess letting go of my freedom is a little tougher than I thought it would be."

"Maybe you can help yourself."

"How's that?"

"Sam stole Victor Hodgson's pickup last night. You got any idea where he might be headed?"

"You sure it was Sam?"

"I'd bet my paycheck on it."

Gertie scoffed. "Wow, that much, huh?"

Russell shot her an angry glance. "Don't start, Gertie." She went quiet, like a dog whose feelings had been hurt. Russell turned to me. "I don't know that I can help you there. The truth and Sam were generally strangers. I can tell you though, he made mention on several occasions of working up around Chinook in the oil field. My gut tells me he's more likely to go there than Mexico."

"What is Sam's last name?"

Russell laughed. "Smith."

I snorted and tossed my head slightly. "Oh." I then paused as the sudden awareness that it was time to go had made it awkward between us.

To my relief, Russell stepped forward. "I guess you need to go on home now, Gertie."

Gertie's eyes had taken on a watery, but angry look. She scoffed, "Home, for how long? You heard the ranger, if you're found guilty of doing this you'll be fired and the forest service will kick us out of the house."

"I guess we'll cross that bridge when we come to it." Russell pulled Gertie in close to him and hugged her for what seemed like a long time before stepping back. "Maybe I can call you tonight." He looked at me. "You suppose they'll allow that, Andy?"

"They might, I'll ask 'em if they will."

"Maybe we can bail you out," said Gertie hopefully.

I said, "He'll have to go before a judge first, that might not happen until tomorrow."

Gertie scowled at me like this was all my fault. It didn't appear that she was accepting any of the blame for Russell being where he was. There was a smugness, an arrogance, about her that made me want to point out her behavior at the Antler and, had Russell not been standing there, I might have, instead, I said to her, "The judge will set the bail. Once he has, if you've got the money, Russell can come home."

Russell said, with some finality in his voice, "Go home, Gertie." Turning to me, he said, "Let's git on down the road."

CHAPTER TWELVE

It was about three o'clock the next day when I saw Russell and Gertie come back through Cedarville. Grace had called and told me that Russell had made bail. Since he had a job, at least for now he did, he had to hire his own lawyer. Next week, he was to go to court for sentencing. I was told by the district attorney that I needed to be there to testify as to the mitigating circumstances that Russell was hoping would keep him from going to prison. On the ride to town he told me that he'd spent too much of his life in the openness of the mountains and sleeping under the stars to be confined to a cage over in Deerlodge. And, although it seemed like it, I suppose it wasn't begging, him reminding me, *you'll tel 'em won't ya, Andy, how I stopped Sam from shootin' ya, you'll be sure to tell the judge, won't ya*? I assured him that I would.

On Friday, the same day that Russell came home, so did Melvin. I happened to be driving by the cemetery, just outside of Cedarville. when they were putting him in the ground. It was a small gathering. There were a handful of strangers, Lujack relations from elsewhere I supposed, that had been welcome to come. And, as one might expect, Milo

Peterson and his wife were there, but no one else from the valley. Of this I was fairly certain, as it didn't take that long, even at 20 miles per hour, to sort through the small gathering. Nonetheless, I didn't make eye contact with Ellen as I'd hoped I would. In a way, I thought it would say to her, *I would've come.* Charlie, on the other hand, did spot me and frowned. I drove on home.

As I approached my cabin, I could see a green ford pickup backing away from it. I recognized it as belonging to Harold Crawford, the mailman. He stopped and waited for me to pull next to him. In a voice, loud enough to be heard over the idling of our vehicles, he said, "Hey, Andy, I put a letter under a rock on your doorstep."

Harold delivered the mail all around the valley except to those people living in Cedarville, as they had post office boxes. I was among this group so I was immediately suspicious of why he would be bringing me a letter. The thought suddenly popped into my mind, *Maybe its from the draft board.* I said aloud, like having a letter delivered to me was nothing unusual, "Thanks, Harold, I appreciate it."

I could see in his green eyes that he was as curious about what was in the letter as I was. He offered up, hoping I supposed, that I would provide some details if I knew who the letter was from, "Betty Duke met me at her mail box and asked me to hand carry this to you."

Instantly, a ripple of concern, coated with dread of what was probably coming, shot through me. "Was she alright?"

Harold snorted, "You mean, has Sherm beat her again? No, it didn't look like it." And then he laughed. "Maybe since his girl shot 'im in the ass he's learned his lesson." He laughed some more.

Harold continued to look expectantly at me. I threw him a bone, "Well, I reckon Betty is just wantin' to let me know she's ok. Be nice if folks up the valley had phones."

Harold's curiosity seemed satisfied, he said, "Yeah, well when hell freezes over that might happen." He nodded, "Alright, Andy, we'll see ya later."

I pulled up to where I normally parked in front of my cabin and went quickly to the letter. It was one of those powdery blue, stationary kind of envelopes. It didn't have a return address, or stamp, not even my address, just; To Be Opened By, Deputy Andy Yarnell. I went inside the cabin to open the letter as if it warranted some privacy, it read;

August 28, 1943

Dear Andy,

It is with considerable regret that I find myself having to make this request of you. As you know, it has been about a week since Sherm's accident. Had he been able to move on from it, to forgive Katie or more importantly recognize why it happened, I wouldn't be writing this now. But that is not the case. Several times a day he launches off into verbal tirades that can be justified only in his mind, with his logic. I fear there will come a point when one of these episodes will, once again, go beyond words. It is for this reason I have decided to leave Sherm. Katie and I will be moving out, taking only our clothes and the family car. Our desire is to leave three days from now on Monday at 10:00 a.m.

If you can be there, I would be truly grateful, if not, I understand.

Sincerely Yours,
Mrs. Betty Duke

After reading the letter a second time, I folded it and stuffed it in my shirt pocket. In spite of the fact I'd told Betty I'd be there, I had mixed feelings about showing up to oversee her moving out. In thinking about it since then, it occurred to me that my presence might be pouring gas on a smoldering fire. I tried to put myself in Sherm's position, when I did, I could see how he might think Betty was just ramming this down his throat. Almost like she was gloating over ruining his life. But then images of her with her arm in a sling and Katie's bruised face came to mind and the gossip that had swirled around their family over the years due to her, *accidents*, and I said to myself, *what in the hell are you thinking? You've got to be there.*

Even though it was almost September, it was still hot. The seemingly never-ending supply of flies in my cabin worked late into the night trying to compete with the big band music I had on the radio. This, coupled with the worry demons at work in my mind, caused me to get up Saturday morning feeling like I had dug fire line all night. Although Grady had no complaints about his dog chow I, on the other hand, was not in the mood for corn flakes. As a consequence, I waited until shortly after nine o'clock when I knew the Antler would be open before setting out on foot with the intent of taking a shower and having some hotcakes and bacon and eggs. A couple of minutes of brisk walking put Grady and me across from the Lumberjack Café. There were several pickups parked in front of it belonging to coffee drinkers who, I supposed, were giving themselves a break from work that likely needed to be done. The Lumberjack and the Antler were the social hubs of the valley. Between them, they accounted for originating much of the community's gossip, and with all that had been going on in my life recently, it was a good place to avoid.

I left Grady shaded up near the Antler's front door and went inside. Oscar, who was sipping a cup of coffee behind the bar, spotted right off the fact that I'd brought my own towel and hair shampoo. "Shower day is it, Andy?"

I looked over and smiled, but kept on walking towards the bat doors as I said, "Yeah, gonna wash some of the Gros Ventre grime off."

Oscar uttered a cackle-like laugh. "She's a hot sonvabitch, ain't she?"

I kept on through the bat doors, shouting over my shoulder, "She sure is."

The shower felt good. It was relaxing and, in a way, made up somewhat for how the night had been. It being Saturday and my day off, I got dressed. My appearance wasn't very deputy like. I had on Levis, white Converse tennis shoes, an army surplus green tee shirt and my green Basin Supply ball cap. If Roy Glover had seen me dressed like this, he likely would have said, *see, I told you he ain't nothing but a snot-nosed kid.*

There was no one in the café part of the Antler but Maude. She was sitting at the counter, in her usual spot, on the stool closest to the kitchen. The ash tray in front of her appeared that she was well on her way to finishing the pack of Camels lying near it. I called out, "Mornin', Maude," as I purposely took a seat at one of the tables across the room.

Maude took a drag from her cigarette and slid off her stool. "You need a menu?"

"Nope, just coffee and a stack of hotcakes and a coupla eggs over easy and bacon."

Maude remained standing where she was looking at me, uncertain, it appeared, if she should ask me something, finally she did, "You sure you want a stack? My hotcakes are plate size, you know."

"Yes Ma'am, I'm hungry enough to wrestle a grizzly bear for leftovers."

Maude seemed unphased at my feeble attempt to be funny and disappeared into the kitchen. Moments later she came out with my coffee. "You take cream?"

"Oh, yeah, I do."

A slight frown instantly appeared on her face, followed by a sigh as she turned to go back for the cream.

On impulse, I slid my chair back and started after her. "I'll come get it."

Maude said nothing but went to the fridge behind the counter and took out a small metal pitcher. She set it on the counter, still acting as if she'd been inconvenienced, and then went into the kitchen. I started toward my table when I heard the bat doors swing open, instinctively, I looked to see who was coming down the hall. "Ellen, what are you doing here?"

She continued toward me, her expression somber and then when she was only a few steps away she stopped, "I saw you go by yesterday."

"The cemetery?"

"Yes, I'm sorry you couldn't-"

"It's alright, I understand."

"I think a lot of people don't."

From the corner of my eye I could see that Maude had edged to the open doorway of the kitchen, seemingly without purpose and then, when she saw that I was on to her, she asked, "Does your friend want coffee?"

Ellen nodded. "That would be nice."

Maude poured a cup and handed it to Ellen. "Thank-you."

I gestured towards my table. "I'm sitting over there."

"I can't stay long."

"That's ok, maybe we could call it a mini-date."

Ellen smiled weakly and started toward the table. I pulled a chair out for her.

I said, "How did you know I was here?"

She grinned again. "I was at the store and I saw Grady laying out front of the Antler."

I laughed. "Yeah, I don't go many places without him."

"I think it's a good sign of a man's character if he likes animals."

"I wish your brother felt that way."

"I'm sorry how he was with you the other night. He's bitter, really bitter how we're being treated."

"So, it's just me being white?"

Ellen became quiet. Before she could respond, I added, "He resents me for not being in the service, doesn't he? He told me that he does. Does your father, him being an ex-Marine and all, does he resent me too?"

"What they think doesn't matter."

I shook my head and sighed. "I don't know, Ellen, between the two of them they could make it almost impossible for us to see one another again. In fact, they'll likely be hopping mad if they find out you're here now."

Tears had come to Ellen's dark eyes. "In a week, Charlie will be gone. He fuels my father's anger. As much as I don't

170

want to see Charlie go back to the war, I know things at home will be better once he leaves."

Thinking it wise to not go deeper into Ellen's family issues, I didn't weigh in on the prospect of Charlie's departure, instead, I took a drink of my coffee. I said, "Will you be going back to work on Monday?"

Ellen nodded and then took a sip of her coffee. "There's no point in staying home. I can't rehash any more why Melvin did what he did. It won't change anything."

"Like they say, time heals all."

"It's been a long time already."

A look of mild surprise came to my face.

She added, "I started grieving for Melvin right after he came home from Alaska and I saw how he was. I was afraid then that the old Melvin would never come back."

I felt unqualified to console her. Recalling my conversation with Grimes, I said, "War is a nasty thing. It changes some people forever."

Ellen shook her head and sighed. "And some people, like Melvin, just can't accept those changes."

I didn't know what else to say but, "I'm sorry, Melvin was a good guy." And then, from the corner of my eye I saw Maude, uncharacteristically, headed our way with the coffee pot. I'd seen her peek out of the kitchen several times since Ellen and I had sat down. In a way, I was glad she was coming. She looked at Ellen. "More coffee?"

Ellen glanced up and then quickly looked away before Maude could see the tears in her eyes, but it was too late, Ellen said, "No, thank-you. I've got to be going."

I know Maude knew who Ellen was. I thought she might offer her condolences, but she did not. Instead, she gestured with the coffee pot towards my cup. "More?"

"Yeah, you can top it off."

She poured the coffee with her usual annoyed or, *you're bothering me*, look and walked away.

Ellen pushed her chair back. "I really do need to go, Andy. Mother is canning today. She sent me in to get supplies."

"What would you say if I stopped by the ranger station one day next week at lunch time and we ate at the picnic table out back?"

She was hesitant to answer. I could see that my proposal had caught her off guard. I added, "I understand if you don't want to with Charlie being like he is."

A faint smile came to her face. "How about Wednesday?"

"That sounds good. I'll get burgers and fries to go from the Lumberjack, if that's ok?"

"How about I make us some roast beef sandwiches and bring some chips and oatmeal raisin cookies and apples?"

"Well, that sounds even better, but I'll bring a couple of cans of Coke."

Ellen's look became more serious. "If Charlie hears about this, I'll tell him you came by the ranger station on business and you ate your lunch there so you could visit with the fire people. He may not believe it, but I'll swear to it."

The doubts that I'd previously had about Ellen liking me suddenly evaporated. I reached across the table and took hold of her hand. She reciprocated by squeezing mine. She said, "See you Wednesday." And then she got up and started towards the bat doors. At the entrance to the short hallway she turned to wave goodbye, just as Maude emerged from the kitchen with my food. As I waved back, it occurred to me that our brief coffee date might not remain a secret.

CHAPTER THIRTEEN

Any more, with all that had been going on in my life, I dreaded the night. It was like I was being held captive by the worry demons until the sun came up. Sunday night was no different. Betty Duke's request had caused me to conjure up a variety of scenarios, mostly not good, that I played over and over in my mind until I finally gave in and got up when it was barely light outside. Normally, I began each work day with a phone call to Grace to let her know my plans for the day. For some reason, I hadn't done that this morning. It may have been that I figured Grace would disagree with how I was intending to go about things. I was about half-way to the Duke place and still within radio range when she called. "Base to 604."

Reluctantly, I wrestled the mic from its holder on the dash and answered, "Mornin', Grace."

"Did you forget about me this morning?"

"I'm sorry, Grace, I guess so."

"Well, what are you up to today?"

I sighed and shook my head as I said to myself, *well here we go*. And then I keyed the mic, "I'm headed to the Duke ranch. Betty and Katie are moving out today. Betty asked that I be there to keep the peace."

"Did you happen to coordinate this with the highway patrol so one of them could be there too?"

"No, I figured if I showed up there like the seventh cavalry it would just make Sherm even madder. I'm hoping to appeal to his common sense."

"Right now, I'm wondering if you have any common sense. You know Duke's reputation."

"I know, Grace, but it's too late now. I've got to be there in about 20 minutes."

"Well, hopefully things will go ok. Highway patrol is tied up with a bad wreck south of town. There won't be anybody to come help you if this goes south."

"I'll keep that in mind."

"Well, watch yourself. You know, you barely dodged death just last week. I'm not sure how many of those passes God allows a person."

"Speaking of that, have you heard anything about the pickup that Sam Smith fella stole?"

"Not a word, but you should know, you're not the only one inquiring about it."

"How's that?"

"Roy Glover came by here. He said one of his constituents was wondering how it was you couldn't chase down a big old furniture truck in your pickup?"

Anger suddenly boiled up inside me to the point I had to purposely pause to push it out of my mind before answering. Finally, I said, "I figured he had too much head start. Besides, the highway patrol was waiting for him down on 29."

"Don't worry about it, Andy. You've got bigger fish to fry today."

"Alright, Grace, 604 clear."

"Be safe, Andy, Base clear."

I drove on, wondering how I'd gotten myself so thoroughly mixed up in the Duke family's affairs. Growing up in the valley, or at least until we moved away, I'd always heard adults talk about Sherm as being a mean, cold person. Few people liked him. And now here I was about to verify these rumors. As I turned onto the lane that led to the Duke ranch headquarters, everything looked peaceful. I drove slowly into the yard as if there was no urgency in my being there. Several orange colored chickens that were scratching and bugging just outside the weathered picket fence surrounding the Duke house scattered before my pickup. I'd just came to a stop and turned my engine off when I heard a scream from inside the house, followed by, "No, daddy, leave her alone."

I bailed out of my pickup, not bothering to close the door behind me, and ran to the Duke's front door. I immediately hammered on it while shouting, "Sheriff's Department, open up."

Inside I heard Sherm yell, "What the hell did you do?"

Betty sobbed, "It's the law, Sherm. You'll not stop us from leaving."

Sherm laughed. "You think I'm afraid of that Yarnell kid."

"You better pay heed to what he says or you'll wind up in jail."

I yelled again, "Sheriff's Department, open up."

"Dammit, Katie, don't open that door."

And then the door opened. Just beyond Katie, in the living room, I could see Sherm blocking Betty's path. To either side of her was a suitcase resting on the hardwood floor. She said, as she picked up the bags, "Let me by, Sherm."

"You ain't going anywhere."

I said in a stern voice, "Let her pass, Sherm. You can't keep her here against her will."

Sherm took several steps towards me and stopped, "You're on private property and uninvited, so I'm telling you to get out."

From behind Sherm, Betty called out, "You're wrong, Sherm, I asked Andy to come here. It's my house too."

Sherm snorted. "That may change if you abandon me. You're full of shit if you think you're gonna walk out and cause me to sell this place just to satisfy you."

Betty began to cry again. "Fine, Sherm, just give me the keys to the car."

"You wanna leave so bad, start walking."

Behind me, out the open door, I heard a vehicle drive up. I glanced around to see Bill Kyle, the game warden, park beside my pickup. Looking over my shoulder, Sherm said in his most sarcastic voice, "So you called your fish cop buddy to help you out, did ya?"

"Sherm, just let Betty and Katie out of the house."

Momentarily, Bill came along side of me, he said in a low voice, "Grace said you might like some company this morning."

Sherm came back, cocky and angry, "This is a fine *how do you do*, you two can't catch whoever it was that butchered my calves in Skinner Meadows, but you're *Johnny on the spot* when it comes to wantin' to throw my ass in jail."

Too quick to respond, I unknowingly stepped into Sherm's trap, "I did catch those fellows. One of 'em is going to court next week."

"Oh, that's right," said Sherm in a mocking tone while looking straight at me, "you caught the guys who butchered Milo Peterson's calves. Poor Milo, he only owns half the valley, but not to worry. I called the district attorney, he says your forest service buddy will have to pay for those calves but not mine, since he didn't confess to taking them. Too bad you let that other fella go, maybe he would've confessed to taking my calves. Yesirree, you're quite the lawman, mister Deputy Yarnell."

I was taken aback by the tongue lashing that Sherm had just given me. It was the one scenario I'd never envisioned. I kind of wished that'd he'd taken a swing at me instead of stomping all over my ego.

And then Bill stepped forward. "Mr. Duke, I know it ain't easy when you been wronged like you have, but give us a little time, we may catch this other fella yet."

Duke scoffed. "That don't mean I'll get paid for those calves he took."

Bill sighed and shook his head. "Probably not."

To the left of Sherm, I could see that Betty and Katie were anxious to leave. I said, "Sherm, we kinda got off track with what's going on here."

He looked at me in a contemptuous, defiant way and fired back, "That's right, mister do-gooder, you and your nosey mother. If it weren't for the likes of you two none of this would be happening. You should be real proud bustin' up my family like you are."

"Stop it, Sherm," cried Betty. "This has been a long time coming and you know it. Andy and his mother aren't doing anything that I haven't asked for. So, if you wanna be mad, be mad at me. I'm used to it."

Sherm went silent, his face radiating anger like a pot about to boil over. He looked at me and Bill, both of us bigger than him and both of us armed. Finally, he looked over at Betty and tossed his head slightly. "Fine, get your ass out."

"Give me the car keys."

Sherm snorted. "You two wanna go to town, start walkin'." And then he laughed at her as if he was genuinely funny, while everyone else in the room looked on in disgust.

Betty's face scrunched up into a look of exasperated anguish. She started to cry again, in between sobs she said, "Why do you have to be such a bastard, Sherm? Why is that?"

Sherm's eyes bugged out, like he'd been poked with a hot iron. "And you're some saint who never does anything wrong?"

"I've never claimed to be perfect, but I've never been cruel or physical with you, not ever."

Sherm scoffed like what she'd just said was stupid. "Well, you know where that would've got you."

"That's right, Sherm, maybe another black eye or a fat lip."

Seeing that things were only going to get worse if I allowed them to argue about the keys, I said, "You know, Sherm, I would think that what you do today might factor pretty heavy on down the road, if you have any hope of mending things between the two of you."

Sherm became quiet as if he were considering this. I glanced over at Betty, wondering if her pent up anger would cause her to blurt out something like, *there's not a snowball's chance in hell of that happening*, but she continued to quietly sob. The only sound in the room was her crying and the ticking of an old clock on the wall behind her. Its brass pendulum swung back and forth slowly advancing the black arrows from one Roman numeral to another. It seemed like Sherm was prepared to let the arrows go on and on because to surrender the keys would mean an end to life as he knew it. There'd be the nights, and the days too, when he'd be in this house and he'd hear that clock and know that he was alone, that he'd never hear Betty or Katie's voices ever again. But, if he was fearful of this happening, and hoping to avoid it by showing some decency, his actions didn't show it. A renewed expression of hate came back to his face as he looked at Betty and shook his head. He thrust his right hand into his pants pocket in an exaggerated motion and pulled the keys out. A devious smile came to his face as he held them out in front of him. "You want 'em, here they are."

Betty's lower lip began to tremble as she walked toward Sherm. Just as she closed the distance and reached for the keys, Sherm grabbed her by the wrist with his unoccupied hand. Betty shrieked, "No, Sherm."

It may have been because Bill was older and more experienced in dealing with angry people than I was, but he reached Sherm before I did. He stepped between them and gently pushed Sherm back, "Let her go."

Sherm scowled at Bill as he let go of Betty's wrist. "I guess I'm trying to understand what business this is of a damned fish cop or did you just come here to prop up the kid?"

I stepped up to Sherm's other side. I was hoping my voice wouldn't quiver, "Sherm, you're coming damned close to becoming a guest of the county. Now, not only will that take some money out of your pocket, there'll be nobody here to look after your place. So, think about what you're doing."

Sherm glared at me and then turned back to Bill. "Normally, I don't allow another man to put his hands on me, mister fish cop. So, consider yourself warned."

Bill laughed briefly. "Go ahead, dig that hole a little deeper."

"Sherm, don't make things any worse than they already are," pleaded Betty. "Please, just give me the keys."

Whether it was a spark of decency or common sense, Sherm reluctantly handed the keys to Betty. "Well, now you can high-tail it to town and get yourself some hotshot lawyer so you can take everything else."

Betty shook her head. "We'll talk, Sherm. I want to be fair."

Sherm laughed sarcastically. "I'll bet you do." He paused and then added, "Get the hell out and take your friends with you."

I made eye contact with Betty as if to say, *you should leave now*. She said, "I'm sorry, Sherm."

Sherm looked at her and shook his head in disgust as he walked past her allowing her a clear path to the front door.

I stood where I was until everyone had gone outside. It was just me and Sherm. He had taken a seat at the kitchen table. I could see him clearly from where I was. He appeared to be on the verge of crying. I couldn't help but feel a little sorry for him and, in that same fleeting moment, the image of Melvin lying dead up on Mink Creek came to mind. But then, in the next instant, it was no longer Melvin lying there with the back of his head blown away and his eyes plucked out by the ravens, it was Sherm. I was on the verge of saying something to console him when he sensed I was there. He looked up. "Unless you think you've got the moxie to arrest me for something, you need to get the hell out of my house."

I sighed, and allowing him to salvage some of his ego by ordering me out, I said simply, "Alright, Sherm." I closed the door behind me, wondering if one day I might be called back out here to investigate his death by his own hand. Just thinking about it made me cringe.

Betty was wasting no time in leaving now that she was out of the house. Her car, a black 38' Buick Coupe, was parked under a shed about 50 yards west of the house. Bill was carrying the bags with Betty and Katie walking along side. By the time I caught up, they were about to get in the car. Betty paused to give Bill a brief hug and then she did the same to me. "Thank you both, so much. I really appreciate your being here. He wouldn't have let me leave if you hadn't come. He wouldn't, he's that way."

For some reason, I turned and looked back at the house. Sherm was looking out the kitchen window. *This is probably rubbing salt in the wound*, I said to myself. To Betty, I said, "You had better go now. I'll follow you to Cedarville and then, if Sherm hasn't come after us, you can go on to town on your own. Tell my mother hello for me."

"Yes, of course. Thanks again, Andy. Both of you, thank you."

There was obvious relief in their faces as they shut the doors on the car and fired it up, knowing, I suppose, that we were there to stop Sherm from chasing after them. Bill and I drove out to where the road to the Duke's house intersected 29. We pulled over and parked. Bill had just lit a cigarette before he got out of his pickup. He had it tucked to the right side of his mouth, I suppose so he could still talk. "Do you think that crazy sonovabitch will try to chase them down?"

I stopped a few feet from Bill and glanced back at the Duke place. "I don't know. The man's life was pretty much ruined this morning. I guess you never know what a fella in that spot might do."

Bill gave a nervous, cautionary laugh, "You might want to watch yer back trail for a while."

"You probably ought to do the same."

He laughed again causing the cigarette in his mouth to bob up and down.

I said, "I appreciate your showing up this morning. I don't know that if you hadn't things might have gone south."

Bill took a long drag from his cigarette and then exhaled a good-sized blue cloud of smoke. "Well, refereeing domestic disputes ain't in the bold print on my job description, but I was glad to help out. I know you'd do the same for me."

"I would, Bill. I damned sure would."

We continued to shoot the breeze speculating on what Sherm might do and what would become of Betty and Katie and the possibility that Russell would be going to Deerlodge. And then Bill took the final draw on his cigarette and tossed the butt onto the dusty road. He said, as he ground the life out of it while exhaling the smoke, "Well, hell, if yer good with it, I believe I'm gonna vamonos. See if I can catch me some real criminals."

I extended my hand. "Thanks again."

Bill grinned and gave my hand a firm shake. "Boy, yer makin' me feel like this is deserving of a beer."

"Next time I catch you at the Antler, I'll stand you to one."

"All-right then, I'm gonna hold you to it."

And with that, Bill got in his pickup and headed north on 29, away from Cedarville. Before I got in my truck, I paused and looked down at the Duke place. It suddenly seemed lifeless. Even from where I stood, I felt as if Sherm's pain and anger had reached out to me. As far as I could tell he never came out of the house before I left, just sitting there, I supposed, listening to that clock tick.

I drove back to Cedarville. The owner of the store said that Betty and Katie had stopped for gas a little earlier and that they looked like they'd been crying a lot. He asked if I knew what that was about. I figured, since he gave me the information I wanted, it wouldn't be right to stonewall him. I said, *they're moving out from Sherm.* To which he replied, *it's about damned time.* But then he wanted to know where they were going to live. There was little doubt in my mind that it wouldn't be long before all of the details concerning Betty and Katie leaving, at least Sherm's version of it, would be common knowledge in the valley. I said, *I don't know.*

CHAPTER FOURTEEN

I was sitting on the stump in front of my cabin, leaning back against the wall reading the Hemingway book my mother had given me. It was almost too dark to read, but I was actually enjoying the book so I'd kept on, saying to myself, *I'll just finish this page,* about ten pages ago. I'd talked to my mother earlier in the day. She'd said that Betty and Katie had arrived there ok and were settled in her spare bedroom. She said too they were grilling hamburgers in the back yard and that she wished, they all did, I would come to supper. But I told her, with the gas situation being what it was, I didn't think I could afford it. I regretted, even before I ate my can of beef stew, not going. And so here I was sitting just outside my open door, listening to music from my radio inside and reading when I heard a vehicle coming down 29. It sounded like it was coming at a good clip, faster than the 35 miles per hour that the law allowed. I'd just lowered my book to listen when the vehicle slowed down, but not by too much. And then it was opposite the back side of my cabin. It's metallic squeaks and rattles were quick and loud when abruptly, they slowed and became faint. To my right, Willy Jones' old blue Chevy pickup suddenly came into view. A cloud of dust followed him as he came to a stop next to my truck. Grady got up from where he'd been laying next to me and barked a greeting. I, on the other hand, had the wheels of my mind spinning as this didn't appear to be a social call. The door of Willy's pickup flew open, almost before he was stopped, and out he came with the spryness of a twenty year old. By now, I had dropped my book on the ground beside the stump and gotten to my feet, waiting for what I knew wasn't going to be good. Willy looked upset, almost like he might be sick if he didn't rid himself of what it was that had made him this way. Then he shouted, "Bill Kyle's dead."

It was now my turn to feel sick. My legs felt weak and my heart felt like it could explode.   My response was spontaneous. I said, like it wasn't possible for a man to be so full of life in the morning and be robbed of it by dusk, "What? That can't be, I was just with him."

Willy started towards me. "He is, found him just a little bit ago floatin' in the river up near the Miller diversion. His pickup was parked right there at the headgate, but I didn't see him anywhere. I thought he might just be along the river checking fishermen, but I hadn't seen any other vehicles so I thought maybe I ought to look around and sure enough there he was about a hundred yards down the crik."

"He's still in the river?"

Willy paused, like some shame was due him for not fishing Bill out of the water, and then he said in an apologetic tone, "Well, yeah Andy, he's snagged on a tree the beavers chomped down that fell into the river. I don't think he 'll go anywhere."

I knew that none of this would be pleasant but to have to go into the river, to be the one to haul him out, was not going to make it any easier. For a brief moment, I was angry that Willy hadn't got Bill out of the water. But then my conscience jumped in, *You're the one who wanted to be a lawman. You expect a 70 year old man to do your job for you? What a turd you are. Besides, Bill showing up this morning likely prevented things from going haywire at the Duke place. This is the least you can do for him.* I said aloud, "That's alright, Willy, I'll tend to Bill. Gimme a few minutes and we'll go."

Willy took my spot on the stump while I went inside and changed into my deputy clothes and called the night dispatch. I told them that I needed the coroner to come out and somebody from the Game Department and gave them instructions on how to get to the Miller diversion. Within about 15 minutes I was ready to go. "I'll follow you, Willy."

Willy started north on 29, but not as fast as when he'd come down it a little while ago. It was almost dark. There was just enough light left in the day that a person, if they were hard pressed, could drive without their headlights on, but we did not. I knew where we were going so I stayed far enough behind Willy that I could have my windows down and not eat his dust. The cool night air rushing in felt good to me and I'm sure Grady as well, as he had his head out the passenger side window allowing the breeze to massage his floppy ears. But beyond this flicker, this smidgeon of feel-good, I felt tired. It wasn't so much a physical tired as it was mental. As much as I wanted to cleanse my mind of Melvin lying dead in the dirt, I could not. It seemed the harder I tried to not think about it the more I did. And now, the image of Sherm sitting alone at his kitchen table piled on with Melvin. But what bothered me most was that tonight, sitting there on my stump I had pushed Melvin and Sherm out of my mind. When I first heard Willy coming down 29, I was tagging along with Robert Jordan somewhere over in Spain. Now, there was no doubt about where I was at, and the fact I was about to add to the parade of unpleasant images in my mind.

From where we turned off of 29, it was a little over a mile to the Miller diversion which consisted of a weir that spanned the width of the river. Smaller headgates, just upstream from the weir, enabled specific amounts of water to be diverted into either of two canals that originated here. To get to the headgate and canal on the far, or east bank, a person had to walk across a plank, about a foot wide, that was suspended above the weir. Over the years, people parking next to the weir had worn away the vegetation and caused the dirt to become hardpacked in an area large enough for about three vehicles. Fortunately, Bill had parked in such a way that Willy and I were able to squeeze in next to him.

Willy paused near the front of his truck while I let Grady out. He said, "It'd probably work best if we was to go to the other side of the river and then go down to where he's at."

I shined my flashlight out over the water. It looked deep and swift upstream of the weir, which had created a mini-falls. The canal on our side of the river was dry, but the one on the other side was not. I said, "How deep do you figure the water to be where Bill's at?"

Willy tossed his head to the side. "I don't know, five feet maybe."

Short of stripping down to my birthday suit, it didn't sound like there was anyway I could avoid getting my clothes wet. But then I recalled that some ditch riders carried a long metal rod that was hooked on the end for pulling trash out of headgates. I came back, "You got one of them trash hooks, Willy?"

In the darkness I couldn't see his face, so I can only imagine why it was he hesitated to answer, but finally he did. "Yeah, I got one."

"Why don't ya bring it along? It might come in handy."

"Alright."

I went over to where the plank walkway started and shined the light on it so Grady knew to go across, which he did. Grady had just gotten on the other bank when Willy came with the hook. I shined my light on him. "You want me to carry that thing?"

He held the hook out to me. "That'd be fine with me. I don't see too good in the dark."

I took the hook. "I'll go across first and then shine the light back on the planks so you can see."

"Ok, just hold it steady. This plank is purty damned narrow."

I turned and started across the walkway, which was actually two planks. Each board was 16 feet long by a foot wide by two inches thick. Weather and time had turned them gray which caused me to wonder just how sturdy were they? The first plank extended from a cement wall to a slotted steel upright in the center of the spillway that was used to hold boards and back up the water so it could be diverted. A second plank ran from here to the cement footing on the other side. In total, I had 32 feet to cross in the dark. The fact I would be right above the splash pool and that the cascading water made a steady roar didn't help my confidence. I tried to not look anywhere but the plank. I told myself, *ain't no different than walking a straight line on dry ground*. By taking short, deliberate steps I made it to the midpoint with no problem. I paused and shined the light over the second plank. I could see Grady waiting for me just off the far end of it. I hollered, "Stay, Grady." He sat down. Reassured that I needed only to repeat what I'd just done I started onto the second plank, halfway across I could feel it sag slightly. The sensation froze me in my tracks. I hissed the word, "Shit." It was only then that I could see the plank had a fine, but deep, crack running from a knot on its right side diagonally for about three feet towards its opposite edge. Visions of the plank suddenly breaking flooded my mind. I took a deep breath to steady myself and then moved on, feeling it give again. Solid ground never felt so good. I turned and shined the light to the other side. It barely reached where the first plank began. I felt almost like a traitor for not shouting a warning to Willy about the second plank, but I reasoned, *hell, he comes here all the time, he knows how it is*. I hollered, "Ok, Willy."

He came across, careful, but quicker than me. He seemed un-phased. I said to him, "Did you feel that second plank give?"

He shook his head. "No, but you probably got 50 pounds on me."

Suddenly, the concern that had been brewing in my mind made itself known, *we can't carry Bill across this thing, it'll break for sure*. I sighed and then said to Willy, "So, he's downstream?"

"Yeah, it ain't too far."

I handed Willy the flashlight. "Lead the way."

We set off on a narrow winding trail that fishermen and cows had made from years of meandering through the willows and cottonwood trees and, occasionally, sagebrush that was nearly as tall as me until abruptly, Willy stopped. He turned to face me and gestured towards the river with the light. "He's over there."

189

I could see in the shaft of light that the beavers had been at work. There were several pointed stumps in front of us. I said, "Well, let's see if we can get Bill to shore."

Willy said nothing but started off towards the river, which was about 40 yards away. He was walking much slower now, scanning the area in front of him with the light, when all at once he stopped and pointed, "That's the tree he's caught up in."

I looked to where Willy was now shining the light. The beavers had gnawed around the base of a big cottonwood until it could no longer stand and had toppled over in the direction of the river. About 20 feet of it extended into the water. Willy tried to hone in on where he'd last seen Bill, but the light had now begun to dance. Embarrassed, he said, "Maybe you should take over."

I took the light and started toward the water, stepping over what branches remained. Behind me Willy shouted out, his voice nervous sounding, "Damned beavers, they never learn. Ain't nobody gonna let 'em dam the Gros Ventre."

In a few more steps I came to the edge of the water. It looked deep and cold. I suppose it must have been easier for the beavers to take the branches on land before the ones in the water, as that part of the tree was mostly intact. I started on the river bank and began to work the light along the partially submerged tree, trying to see into the branches.

"He's further out," said Willy, "or at least he was when I was here before."

And then I saw it, a hand, gently waving in the current. I followed with the light up the tan sleeve of Bill's shirt. Suddenly, there he was, staring back at me, his eyes wide open. Instantly, I felt sick and weak like I was going to collapse. My heart, as if it could deal with anymore adrenaline, struggled to beat faster.

From the darkness to my right, Willy said, his voice shaking, "The river must a moved him, honest, Andy, he was a lot farther out when I was here."

I felt sorry for Bill having to stay in the water this long, even if he was dead. Nonetheless, I said, "That's ok, the important thing is he didn't float on down the crik."

"Yeah, that wouldn't a been good."

I held the light out to Willy. "Hold this on him while I see if I can snag his belt with the trash hook."

Willy did as I asked putting the light on Bill's waist. I could see that the hook was too short for me to stand on dry ground and reach him, but not by much. I eased into the water up to my knees. My cowboy boots instantly filled, as they did, I kicked myself for not having taken them off, but in my defense, I was too fixated on getting Bill out of the river. I slowly began extending the hook towards him. However, the farther I reached with it the more off balance I became. I tried repeatedly to slip the hook under his gun belt or a loop in his Levis, but for the life of me, I couldn't get it done. It was slippery beneath my feet and I sensed the river bottom dropped off real quick, so I was hesitant to go much further as I still had my gun on.

Willy said, "I think yer fixin' to take a bath." His tone suggested he was more confident now of his earlier decision to not retrieve Bill.

I pulled the hook back part way and backed out of the water. Willy still had the light on Bill. It was clear to me I had no choice. I frowned and shook my head as I tossed the hook onto the bank. I then unbuckled my gun belt and laid it on a patch of grass. I dropped my hat on the ground next to it. No sooner had I done this than it suddenly occurred to me that I might be shooting myself in the foot to bring Bill out on this side of the river as I would still have to carry him over the rickety plank above the weir. I looked at Willy. "Can I have the light for a second?" He handed me the flashlight. I shined it out past the tree and across the river. Bill was in an oxbow, where the water was deepest. It looked like it got shallower beyond the end of the tree where he was hung up. I said to Willy, "I believe I'm just gonna haul Bill to the other side."

Willy came back quick. "I don't know if that's a good idea. It could be over your head out there."

"Just keep the light on me."

"I'll try, but I don't think it'll be much on the other side of the river."

"I guess we'll just have to make do. Once I get over there, bring Grady and my gun."

I slowly started into the water. I could feel the power of the current surging against my legs. It felt alive, like it was some evil thing trying to knock me off my feet. I moved my feet, not in deliberate steps but rather a cautious shuffle, skimming the river bottom so as to be able to feel what was before. The water was surprisingly cold for as hot as the day had been. It had just become thigh deep and I was thinking maybe I was moving too fast when I went under like I'd been clipped in football. I'd deviated just slightly from my shuffle routine with my right foot and it came down on nothing but deep water. My feet shot out from under me. Everything instantly went black. I frantically pawed my way to the surface only to find that I'd been carried into the branches of the tree and something else, Bill's leg. The realization of what it was caused me to abruptly let go of the tree and spring back in the water, but right away I sank below the surface. It was probably only a couple of feet before I was able to push off the bottom but, as far as I was concerned, it may as well have been ten. I felt afraid and regretted being there. Had it not been for Willy doing a good job of keeping the light on Bill and me, I may have allowed myself to show it. Maybe not actually cry, but whimper or swear or something to bleed off my fear. But here I was hanging onto the tree nestled next to Bill and trying to tread water with my damned boots on. How could I have been so stupid. I looked back at Willy and shouted, "Shine the light on across the river."

Willy did as I had asked, or at least he tried to. The batteries in my flashlight were getting weak. Its pale, yellow beam barely made it to the end of the tree, which was maybe another ten feet. I strained to see beyond where the light ended and then, it was as if Willy had read my mind, he hollered, "I'd guess you've got another 15 feet of deep water, after that you might be able to walk on the bottom."

I looked back at Bill. The current had wedged him into the branches in such a way that he didn't sink. I shook my head and said to myself, *If I pull him outta there he'll sink like a rock*. I took a deep breath to steady myself and then shouted at Willy, "I'm gonna head across. Keep the light on me as best you can."

"Alright, but if you get in trouble, let 'im go. We'll find him tomorrow."

Deep down, I knew that I would be hard pressed to do this to the man who saved me from a likely blowup at the Duke place. This was the man I'd promised to buy a drink at the Antler the next time I saw him there. I responded simply, "Ok."

I tried to not look Bill in the face as I decided how best to take hold of him. He was only the second dead person I'd ever touched. It was something I was certain that I'd never get used to. Finally, I reached beneath his head and got a fist full of shirt collar and the tee shirt beneath it and pulled. At first he didn't move, but then I jerked hard and all at once he broke free and bumped back into my chest. The feeling of him next to me caused me to want to recoil, but I couldn't without sinking and then suddenly I realized he was. Fortunately, I had the presence of mind to lunge toward the far shore. I held onto Bill with my left hand while laying on my side and pulling water with my right. At the same time, I was furiously kicking my feet, which were still encased in those damned boots. I made it about five feet before Bill went under taking me with him. To my credit, I did not let go in spite of the urge I was feeling to panic and save myself. The bottom didn't seem quite as far as it had been. I pushed off hard and burst out of the water. Bill came part way, but he was still mostly beneath the surface. Frantically, I started side-stroking before I went under. I made it another four or five feet and down I went again, except this time the top of my head was barely covered. I pushed off the bottom. My head barely cleared the water when I was pulled under as the lower half of Bill's body settled on the bottom. Fortunately, I'd taken a breath. Somehow, I had managed to hang onto Bill and in the darkness felt the current weakening and realized that I just needed to hold my breath and start walking. Towing Bill with his feet dragging on the bottom was not easy. Luckily for me, in a few more steps my head came out of the water. I stopped and gasped for air before moving on in the night, now mostly beyond Willy's light. The depth of the water and the effort needed to move Bill became less and less until, finally, I splashed through four or five feet of ankle deep water and up onto the river bank. I laid Bill on his back in a grassy area. From the other side of the river I heard Willy shout, "Andy, how ya fairin'?"

I looked toward the speck of light. "I made it across. Come on over."

"Alright, we'll be right there." The light then began darting here and there as Willy and Grady started up along the river and then it disappeared in the brush and trees. I sat down in the dirt next to Bill, like I would've had we just been hiking out in the mountains and were taking a breather and in the next little bit, he would be rolling a smoke. I was surprised by the fact that it was pitch black, except for the stars and a tiny sliver of moon, and I was sitting next to a dead man by myself and wasn't more disturbed by it than I was. I couldn't explain it, maybe it was because it was Bill and right now, I really couldn't make out much of his face. But then it occurred to me, if I was going to be a lawman, I had no choice but get used to this.

CHAPTER FIFTEEN

It was close to midnight before the coroner and Bill's boss found their way to the Miller diversion. Because of the darkness and the speculation offered by Willy early on that Bill had likely fell off the plank walkway above the weir maybe hitting his head and drowning in the splash pool, we went away thinking that's probably what happened. But that all changed after the coroner, Herman Cox, had a full day to look Bill over. On Wednesday, the day after the autopsy, he called me. It was a quarter past eleven in the morning. In spite of everything that had happened this week, my spirits were up today on account of my lunch date with Ellen over at the ranger station. I answered the phone.

"Hello, Andy, this is Herman."

My pulse picked up. "Mr. Cox, what can I do for you?"

"I haven't made it official yet, but I strongly suspect foul play was the cause of Bill Kyle's death. His nose was broken, which wasn't too suspicious in and of itself, but his windpipe was crushed and that does raise a red flag with me."

"You're thinking somebody hit him in the throat?"

"That's kinda what it looks like to me."

"It couldn't have been due to landing on a sharp rock or a log or something like that?"

"Well, I don't know. Something like that would've been more of a glancing blow, I think. The damage that was done to Mr. Kyle suggests to me that this was a powerful directed blow delivered just right beneath his chin. In nature, it would have taken a perfect set of circumstances."

"So, where do we stand?"

"I'm going to send Mr. Kyle up to Helena and let them take a look at him. If they concur with my findings, the ruling will be he died due to foul play." He paused and then asked, "Would you have any suspicions along those lines."

My mind instantly went back to Sherm Duke's living room and Bill pushing him away from Betty. I could think of no one else with an axe to grind against Bill except, maybe Russell, for Bill having brought to light his butchering beef. But then I said to myself, *Russell would be a damned fool to do this now. Nobody is that spiteful, except maybe Sherm Duke.* I said aloud, "I might have one possibility."

"Who would that be?"

"I'd rather not say just yet."

"Fine, it'll be a few days I suspect before I know what they think in Helena."

"Ok, just keep me posted."

Even before I hung up the phone my mind had gone to processing Sherm's reaction if, after having robbed him of his family, I was to now accuse him of murder. *He'll come un-hinged*, I said to myself. *If he did kill Bill, he probably won't hesitate to do the same to me.* And in the next instant, it suddenly made sense to me how Tom could walk away from being the sheriff. There'd be no more dead bodies or people wanting to kill you. Why wouldn't a person want to be shed of that?

It was a few minutes past noon when I parked in front of the ranger station. It was the second of September and the weather still hadn't cooled off. I brought the Cokes that I'd promised Ellen, and as a hedge against the heat, I'd filled two, pint size, Mason jars with ice cubes and screwed on the lids. I hoped to impress her by having cold drinks. I grabbed the paper bag containing all of this and started up the sidewalk with Grady following close behind. I'd barely opened the door when Ellen called out from her desk behind the counter, "Hi Andy, I'll be right there. I just need to finish typing this letter."

"Ok, take your time," I said as I shut the door behind me and Grady.

From an open doorway to her left came a voice. "Go have your lunch, Ellen. You can finish that later."

She looked up from her typewriter. "Are you sure?"

The opening suddenly filled. Clarence Hooper, the ranger for the Cedarville District, was standing there. "Yes, that letter won't go anywhere until tomorrow, so go eat." Looking at me, he said, "Andy here looks like he could use a good meal."

I grinned. "How are you, Mr. Hooper?"

The light-hearted look in his green eyes abruptly faded. From behind his salt and pepper walrus moustache, he said, "It's been a rocky few days here with having to give Russell and Gertie the boot." He paused and then added, "But, that's probably nothing compared to what you've been through lately."

Thinking of Melvin, I glanced over at Ellen. She looked away as if she had no interest in the conversation. Seeing this,

Clarence quickly added, "That's sure too bad about ole Bill Kyle drowning. It's been quite some time since anybody has drowned in the Gros Ventre. Whaddaya figure happened?"

I knew better than to share what the coroner had just told me, as that was speculation at this point. I verified what the gossip mill had likely already put out, "Our best guess is he fell off the walkway over the Miller diversion. Bill's boss said as far as he knew, Bill couldn't swim."

Clarence appeared as if he was about to probe deeper when Ellen slid her chair back. I looked at her. "I'll be right back, Andy. I'm gonna go get our lunch."

I seized the moment to withdraw from the conversation about Bill and me having to lie about what probably happened. "Well, should we just go eat?"

To his credit, Clarence said, "You two lovebirds go ahead. Don't let me stop you." He then turned and went back into his office.

Ellen's dark features mostly hid her blush, but for a few seconds I could see it in her eyes and then it went away, like she was comfortable with what her boss had said. After getting the lunch she'd made from the fridge in their break room we went behind the ranger station to a picnic table in the shade of a big ponderosa pine tree. For a time, we talked about the weather, new songs on the radio and the possibility of going to a movie in town.

Ellen said, "Charlie goes back this Sunday. Maybe after he's gone, we could try for a show."

"Your dad won't object?"

"Well, I am 20 years old. It's my life."

"But you live in his house."

Ellen smiled. "My mother isn't as meek and timid as she looks and she's on my side."

I laughed. "Oh, I wasn't sure where I stood with her."

Ellen became serious. "She just doesn't want me to be hurt. Since the war started and our family has been locked up, she has, we all have, felt like we don't belong."

"I'm sorry."

"Maybe when the war is over things will be better."

"I think they will."

"What about you? I heard Russell's partner wanted to kill you. Were you scared?"

I laughed incredulously.

Ellen came back, "That was a dumb question, huh?"

"No, but I was more scared than I've ever been in my life."

She reached across the table, obviously not caring who might see and report back to Charlie, and took hold of my hand. "I'm glad that nothing bad happened to you."

I wanted to kiss her and I sensed she wanted me to, but my instincts told me that would be pushing things. And then, suddenly, any doubt as to what I should do was erased as the Jenkins' black pickup came around the far end of the ranger station on the gravel road that led to the employee housing off to our right. Gertie, who was sitting on the passenger side, pointed out the window. Russell slowed the truck almost to a complete stop as they gawked at us, before shifting to a lower gear and driving on over to their house. I said, "How long before they have to be out?

"Day after tomorrow. What do you think they'll do to Russell?"

"I don't know. I'm going to put in a good word for him because he did save my life, but I still can't see him getting off with no jail time."

"Well, he did it to himself. It wasn't bad enough that he was starting fires, he had to steal cattle too."

I shook my head. "Sometimes, people just lose all their common sense."

"You think it was Gertie that drove him to do this?"

"She'd be a hard woman to keep up with."

"Clarence said she's going to work on Pete Wetzel's place cooking for his hired help. He said she's lucky to be getting any work at all in the valley, now that word has gotten around about Russell."

I scoffed, "Well, Pete is a widower."

"You really think Gertie's that way?"

I thought of sharing what I'd seen in the Antler, but I decided against it and just laughed.

Ellen smiled back. "I suppose I better get back to work."

"Maybe we can do this again sometime?"

"Yes, that would be nice, or maybe we could go to the show. Like I said, Charlie leaves on Sunday."

"It must be hard for your family to see him go back to the war."

For a few seconds Ellen remained silent, like she was afraid to answer. Finally, she said, "I hope I never regret saying this but, in a way, it will be nice to see him go."

"Why?"

"He's been drunk every night since he's been back. He drove down to Heart Mountain today to see my grandparents. My mother wanted to go but she made the excuse she had to work rather than be around his hate and bitterness. Going to Heart Mountain wouldn't help that."

"He must really hate white people."

Mild surprise came to Ellen's face. She was hesitant to answer and then she nodded. "He does."

201

I said, "I'm glad you don't."

Ellen's eyes had become moist, she said, "I can think of some in Fremont that I do."

"I don't blame you. Hopefully, I won't ever be part of that group."

She squeezed my hand. "I don't think you have to worry about that."

We held hands as we walked across the lawn to the back door of the ranger station. I looked down at her, still holding her hand, "Thanks for lunch."

"You're most welcome."

On impulse, I leaned down and kissed her softly on the lips. "Maybe I'll stop by later this week."

"Please do."

Grady and I went around the building to the front where I was parked. I had just started down the lane to 29. I was feeling euphoric after my lunch with Ellen when suddenly that feeling was vaporized. Driving by on his way into Cedarville was Sherm Duke. At some point, I knew I would have to ask him where he was on Monday afternoon and into the evening. It would be better here, I reasoned, than out at his ranch with no witnesses. I stepped down on the gas so as to catch up to him before he got out of his pickup and went in to wherever he was going. He appeared to be doing the speed limit, or a little less. Turning onto 29, I stayed about a hundred yards behind him. It looked as if he was oblivious to my following him until he was going by the Lumberjack and he checked his outside mirror. It caused him to twist around and briefly look out his rear window. I could only imagine what he was saying or thinking, probably none of it was good. I said to myself, *he'll likely be on the prod right from the git-go.* After a few seconds, he turned back and then his pickup slowed as he drifted to the right, coming to an abrupt halt in front of the store. He was out of his truck and coming towards me even before I had come to a complete stop.

He shouted, "Why are you following me? What the hell do you want now?"

I reached over and turned my engine off. The anger in his eyes was obvious. I said, out my window, "Settle yourself down. I just need to talk to you for a minute."

"Why are you hounding me? Haven't you nosed into my affairs enough?"

"I was asked to come to your place, with good reason, I believe."

"It wasn't me that asked you."

"Well, that should say something to you, Sherm."

The reality, I suppose, of knowing that I was right seemed to take some of the fight out of him. He came back, a little calmer, "So, what do you want now?"

From the corner of my right eye I could see that, Louie, the owner of the store, was standing in its open doorway. I knew, talking as loud as Sherm and I had been, that he'd heard everything. *Now is not the time*, I said to myself, *to jumpstart the rumor mill that Sherm murdered Bill*. I got out of my truck and stepped to within a few feet of Sherm. I said, in a low voice, "I need to know, after Bill Kyle and I left your place on Monday, where did you go?"

"Why do you need to know that?"

"I just do."

Sherm snorted. "Well, I figured since you can't hang onto these rustlers, if you do catch 'em, that I better go check on my cattle."

"So, you went up to the Skinner Meadows country?"

"Yeah, I did."

"Anybody see you up there?"

"Hell, I don't know. I didn't see anybody."

"What time did you get up there?"

"I don't know. I made myself a sandwich for lunch and then I went and changed a stream of water above the house and –" He paused. His eyes got a little watery before taking on a look of anger. "And then," he said as he jabbed the air in front of me with the index finger of his right hand, "I couldn't bring myself to go home because, thanks to you, there's not a damned thing there. No sir, you and your nosey damned mother have purty much ruined my life. I hope you can sleep good at night knowing that."

I had no need to plow this ground again with Sherm. I was confident that he had ruined his own life and would probably never be able to admit to himself that he had. I said, "I'm sorry for your troubles, Sherm, but I need to know, what time did you get to Skinner Meadows?"

Sherm shot me a dirty, exasperated look, like I'd worn him down. "Oh hell, I guess about 2:30."

"What time did you head home?"

"Well, I went horseback a fair amount of that country so, I don't know, about 6:30 I guess."

"So, it was after seven when you got home?"

Sherm paused and then spit the words at me, "What the hell is this about? You know, I ain't so stupid that I can't see you're working up to accusing me a something, so what is it?"

I glanced over at Louie and, from behind me, I could almost feel Oscar's eyes on my back as he peered around the OPEN sign in the Antler's window. I lowered my voice and looked straight at Sherm. "Herman Cox is leanin' towards Bill's death being a homicide."

Shock exploded in Sherm's face. "Why you simple shit. Somebody needs to take that badge away from you. This ain't recess, you know. You ain't playing cops and robbers. I'm half-tempted to take that tin star and shove it up yer ass."

"Settle down, Sherm. That ain't gonna happen and if you was to try, I'll be taking you to town, so get a handle on yourself."

Sherm looked away and took a deep breath. He shook his head, "I can't say I'm sorry that fish cop is dead, but I didn't kill him and I'd swear to that on a stack of bibles."

I didn't know if Sherm was a good liar or I was a poor judge of character, but I tended to believe he was telling the truth. Nonetheless, I said, "I had to ask, Sherm. Right now, you're the most likely suspect in all this."

He snorted and then laughed sarcastically. "I don't know if you think you're some kind of Dick Tracy or what, but you're barking up the wrong tree. I need to talk to somebody with some common sense. When's the sheriff coming back?"

As much as I wanted to appear confident, even smug, I resisted doing so as I knew if I provoked him, Sherm would go over my head. I said, respectfully, "The sheriff is going to resign. This is something you and I will have to work out. I promise you, though, I'll give you a fair shake." I was not quite done saying what I had when this feeling of awkwardness, brought on by the disparity in our ages, came over me. In the back of mind, the naysayer was shouting, *what are you doing? Accusing a man of murder, you're a kid, you're a snot-nosed kid.*

Sherm spit, not tobacco juice, just plain spit, on the ground between us. He looked at me more cold and disgusted than anybody ever has, and said, "Are we done?"

"For now, we are."

He snorted and walked off towards the store. For a few seconds I watched him go. I wondered how he would explain himself inside, or if Louie would dare ask. If what he had said was true, he would have a pretty strong alibi. If he was lying, I'd have to prove that he was and then prove that he had caved in Bill's windpipe. Somehow, him doing this just didn't play well in my mind. It was one thing to beat up women, but a grown man your own size?

I was just turning into my cabin when Grace came over the radio. I parked where I usually did before keying the mic. "Go ahead, Grace."

"Hi, Andy. Just thought I'd let you know the highway patrol caught up to the fella that wanted to kill you. He was over around Glendive somewhere."

"Well, I'm sure Victor Hodgson will be glad to get his pickup back."

"I don't know about that, Andy. The state boys had to chase this guy down. Apparently, he missed a curve and rolled down a steep embankment four or five times. He was killed and, according to the state boys, the truck was totaled."

I shook my head and whispered, "Hodgson is gonna be mad as hell." Into the mic, I said, "Alright, Grace, thanks for the update. I'll let the owner of the truck know."

"Oh, Andy, and another thing, not that its news, but Tom made it official. The county commissioners got his letter of resignation yesterday."

"When does it take effect?"

"September 14th is what Mr. Glover told me."

"Did he say what the commission intends to do?"

"Not to me, he didn't. For some reason, he seemed to want to hold those cards close to his vest."

I snorted and tossed my head back slightly saying to myself, *that turd knows exactly what he intends to do.* To Grace, I said, "Do you have any more good news?"

She came back, beginning deliberately with that pitchy laugh of hers before saying, "No, that's it." The radio went silent for a few seconds and then the speaker below the dash sounded again, "Don't worry, Andy. Things will turn out, you'll see."

I grinned. Some days Grace was like my second mother. "Thanks, Grace. Andy clear."

It was slightly over an hour's drive to the Hodgson place. Things went about like I figured they would. Victor was mad as hell. He was mad at me for not just catching Sam Smith up on the forest so none of this would have happened. And he was mad at the highway patrol for not easing up on the guy when he was parked somewhere in town and thereby keeping his truck from being destroyed. And he was mad at the insurance company. He made that point real clear to me. *I've paid my premiums all these years and now these sonsabitches are saying I ain't covered if somebody steals my truck. I'll tell you if I wasn't an old man, I'd drive into town and whip that Ted Phillips' ass. He's the sonovabitch that sold me this policy.* And then, before I could caution him against doing this, he came back to me and said, like I wasn't standing there, *the county needs to get somebody other than a pecker neck kid to enforce the law.* Shortly after this, he said right to my face, *you need to get the hell off of my place. All you cops are worthless.* And with that he turned and went into his house. At this point, I was glad to leave.

On the drive back to Cedarville, I tried to occupy my mind with something other than police business by listening to the radio and thinking about Ellen. For a time it seemed to work, but then the worrisome things crept back in, mainly, the fact that I'd accused Sherm of murder and he too was mad as hell at me. And to think, on Friday I had to go to court with Russell and put in a good word for him, the guy who was the root cause of Victor having just chewed me out. I couldn't help but laugh out loud at the seemingly hopeless-ness of it all. I looked over at Grady who had his head out the window. "We're in a fine fix now, ain't we Grady?"

He looked back at me as if to say, *Well, I'm on your side.* And then he put his face into the wind.

CHAPTER SIXTEEN

If there was anything positive that occurred on my drive back from Hodgson's, it was that I may have come up with a way to verify Sherm's alibi of him being around Skinner Meadows about the time Bill would have been killed. From where Bill had found Sherm's butchered calves and the elk, it was about three miles, as the crow flies, to the Bald Peak lookout. Any lookout worth their salt would definitely spot a smoke at this distance and a vehicle too. The smoke would require they report it, but a vehicle, they might not give it a second thought. In any event, I thought it was worth a try. Besides, it would give me an excuse to stop by the ranger station tomorrow morning and ask Ellen to call the lookout.

I'd barely stepped in the door of my cabin when the phone began to ring. By the time I picked it up it was on its fourth ring. "Gros Ventre Sheriff's office, Deputy Yarnell speaking."

"Deputy Yarnell, this is Caleb Bolander, Bill's boss. We met the other night on the river."

"Oh yes, how are you?"

"I've done better."

"What can I do for you?"

"We can't locate Bill's citation book. We've gone all through his pickup and checked with the coroner and it's nowhere to be found. I was just wondering if by chance you might have picked it up when you pulled him out of the river and just forgot to mention it?"

"No sir, I didn't."

"I guess you know the coroner think's Bill might have met with foul play."

"Yeah, he told me that."

"Well, today I got a call from the court clerk in Fremont. She told me a guy came in and paid a fine for a ticket that Bill gave him on the day he died. It was for fishing without a license at 1:20 p.m. at the confluence of Antelope Creek and the Gros Ventre river."

I cut in, "That's a couple of miles north of the Miller Diversion."

"I know, I looked it up on a map. What I'm wondering though is if Bill wrote any tickets at the Diversion. If he did, one of them might be our culprit or maybe they saw something suspicious."

Hearing this caused my gut to churn. I said to myself, *And here I've gone and accused Sherm. Shit.* I said aloud, "That makes some sense." I paused not really wanting to admit my confrontation with Sherm but then I said, "Bill and I had a bit of a run-in on the day he died with a fella named Duke over a domestic dispute. He has an alibi that sounds solid, but I hope to know for sure tomorrow."

"Well, let me know how that turns out. I'd sure hate to see whoever did this get away with it."

"Yeah, me too. Bill was a good guy."

"All right then, Deputy, we'll talk to you later."

In the morning there was a touch of fall in the air. It being the 3rd of September, the night had cooled a little more from what it had been a week ago. I felt justified in firing up my wood stove and cooking myself some bacon and eggs and brewing a pot of coffee. I was in no hurry to go to the ranger station as the lookout didn't come on duty until 10:00 a.m., even though he could never escape the radio unless he left the tower. In a way, he was kind of like me. I got paid for eight hours a day, but my location and phone number were common knowledge to most everybody, so unless I took off my deputy shirt and went somewhere in my personal truck, I could be on the clock 24 hours a day, if there was a need. I respected the fact the lookout was in the same situation, right now was his personal time.

At ten o'clock, Grady and I drove over to the ranger station. Grady found some shade just outside the front door and I went inside. Ellen looked pleasantly surprised but glad to see me. She stood up from her desk and came to the counter. She smiled. "You're a little early for lunch."

"City folks would call this brunch."

She laughed politely as she reached over to touch my hand, which was resting on the counter. "I'm glad you stopped by."

Suddenly, to my right the District Ranger's voice boomed, "Mornin', Andy, what brings you by?"

Ellen abruptly pulled her hand back. It caused the ranger to grin.

I said, "Well sir, I need to ask your Bald Mountain look-out a question."

The ranger's face became business like. "And what would that be?"

I'd been hoping to keep my request to just Ellen and I. Obviously, that wasn't going to be possible now. Sherm's reputation, deserved or not, was about to get dinged again. There'd be no stone-walling Clarence. I said, "I'm trying to determine if a particular fella was up around Skinner Meadows on Monday afternoon."

"Well, who's that?"

And so, the dominoes of gossip began to fall. "Sherm Duke."

"Sherm, he's a crusty guy. You looking at him for something?"

"I'm not sure, maybe."

"Whaddaya think he did?"

"Well, I –"

"You think he had something to do with the game warden drowning?"

I started to play dumb. "The game warden?"

Clarence grinned. "You can tell me. My wife is friends with Nadine Cox. She said Herman ran Kyle's body over to Helena for a second opinion on account of he suspects foul play."

Suddenly, it seemed as if I had nothing to hide. I came back. "There was some hard feelings between Sherm and Bill, but that doesn't necessarily mean he did anything to Bill. Heck, lots a people don't like the game warden."

"Well, maybe we should just call Bald Mountain and see what he's got to say? Ellen, get Eddy on the radio."

Ellen went to the radio, which was sitting on a counter above some cupboards behind her desk, and leaned over to key the mic. "Bald Mountain Lookout, this is Gros Ventre Ranger Station."

Within a few seconds, the response came, "Bald Mountain, go ahead."

Ellen glanced over at me. "Do you want to ask him?"

Clarence chimed in, "Go ahead, Andy."

I started around the end of the counter for the radio but, before I could get there, it sounded again. "This is Bald Mountain, go ahead Gros Ventre."

I keyed the mic, "Eddy, this is Deputy Sheriff Andy Yarnell. I was wondering if you recall seeing any vehicles or riders in the Skinner Meadows area this past Monday, probably late afternoon."

I'd barely finished speaking, when Eddy came back, "I did. There was a black pickup towing a horse trailer that went in on the south side of the meadows. He unloaded a buckskin horse at the Fish Lake trailhead."

"Do you remember what time that was?"

"1512."

In my mind, I made the time conversion, *3:12*, "You sound pretty certain of that."

"Got it wrote down right here in my log. This fella loaded up and left at 1755."

"Thanks, Eddy, appreciate the information. Gros Ventre clear."

In turn, Eddy was quick to clear himself. "Bald Mountain."

"Eddy's one of our better lookouts," said Clarence with some pride in his voice, "Not much gets by him."

I nodded as I struggled to suppress the obvious question in my mind of, *with Eddy being this detailed in his observations, how was it he didn't see Russell butchering Sherm's calves and the elk in Skinner Meadows*? I glanced at Ellen. I suspected, based on our past conversations concerning

Russell, that she was thinking the same thing. Clarence, on the other hand, was basking in the satisfaction that his man had answered my question so thoroughly. With Sam Smith dead, and Russell likely going to prison, I said to Clarence, "Yes sir, that Eddy is Johnny-on-the-spot when it comes to spottin' things and keepin' records."

Had it not been for Ellen having to answer a phone call I might have stayed a little longer, but as it was, I was now left with Clarence who would likely try and get me to speculate on who else might have killed Bill. In that regard, I had no idea. I said, "Well, I guess I better get on down the road."

Ellen cut in, "This call is for you, Mr. Hooper."

"We'll see ya, Andy," said Clarence as he wheeled around towards his office.

Ellen listened just briefly until she was certain that Clarence had picked up and then set the phone on its receiver. She smiled. "I'm glad you stopped by even if it wasn't just to see me."

We both laughed. I said, "Maybe next week we can go on a real date."

"That would be swell. After Sunday, Charlie will be gone. I don't think my father will have any objections to you coming to the house to pick me up. My mother won't let him."

I glanced in the direction of Clarence's office. He was out of sight, talking loudly on the phone. Ellen met me at the end of the counter. We kissed and hugged briefly. Stepping back, I said, "See ya later," and then I went out the door.

CHAPTER SEVENTEEN

On Friday morning I went to the Antler early to shower and shave. I was to appear in court with Russell at one o'clock. Amazingly, or maybe not so amazingly given the valley's thirst for gossip, Oscar knew that Sherm was a suspect in Bill's death. It required me sticking around for a cup of coffee to set him straight. However, by 11:45 a.m. I had made it to town. At lunch, I learned from my mother that Betty had gotten a job at the grocery store as a checker and that Katie was starting back to school next week. She said too, that Sherm had called the house three times. The first time, he started out hateful and threatening until Betty finally hung up on him. He called back a little while later. Betty said it took him some time before he could bring himself to say he was sorry, but eventually he did. She said it sounded like he was crying. It was the first time, according to her, that he'd done either in 18 years of marriage. The third time that he'd called was just last night. This time, Betty cried. My mother was afraid she might go back to him.

When I walked into the court room it was quiet. What few people that were there were whispering or not talking at all. I felt as if I'd walked in late to a funeral. For Russell, I suppose this emotion had more meaning. And then the judge came in. We all stood up and then, seconds later, sat back down. Determining Russell's fate was all so routine, so casual, almost like deciding, *do I want cheese on my hamburger or not*? I was allowed to say my piece, which took about a minute. The judge appeared as if I was boring him. I said to myself, *he's already made up his mind*. When I turned to go sit down, I could see it in Russell's eyes. The hope that had been there when I first came in, was gone. It had been replaced by the not too well disguised emotions of fear and anger. Had his eyes been able to speak, I suspect they would have said, *this sonovabitch is going to send me to Deerlodge*. And then he did it. He took three years of Russell's life, fined him $200 and ordered him to pay another $200 restitution for Milo Peterson's calves. He said to Russell, as if to shame him further, "I find it despicable, that you as a federal official charged with enforcing the grazing laws would use your position to steal from the very people who pay your salary." In my mind, I laughed sarcastically, *it's a good thing this guy doesn't know that Russell also used his position to set the woods on fire*. Suddenly, I began to feel guilty as my sympathy for Russell went away. Even though he'd saved my life, the best I could do now was pity him for being so stupid. Gertie, who was directly behind Russell, began to silently cry. He turned to comfort her but then the judge said he was to be remanded to custody pending his transport to the penitentiary tomorrow morning. This made Gertie cry out loud. The judge seemed oblivious to her sorrow as he banged his gavel and left the room, barely giving the rest of us time to stand. A city cop, who had been standing at the side of the proceedings, came for Russell with his handcuffs out.

Russell pleaded, "Can I kiss my wife goodbye?"

The cop appeared indifferent but nodded, "Be quick about it."

I thought, *and so begins Russell's loss of freedom. The damned fool could've been riding these mountains for a long time to come. He ain't gonna do well at Deerlodge.* It occurred to me, while he was being cuffed, to tell him good luck, but I did not. I don't know why, maybe it was because Gertie gave me a hateful look, but I just walked out, feeling like I'd just added another helping of guilt to my plate.

I'd no sooner started my pickup when Grace came on the radio asking me to drop by the office before I left town.

I was ready to be shed of Fremont, but I told her, "Be right there."

The Sheriff's Office was housed in a small red brick building on the north side of town. It was bounded by lush green grass on the south and east sides and gravel for parking to the west and around back. Tom's pickup and Grace's personal car were the only vehicles on the gravel. Even with having to stop at several intersections, I was there within a couple of minutes. I parked nose-in to the curb. Grady followed me up the cement walk that ran through the grass to the front door. As soon as we stepped inside, I was greeted by a breeze coming from an oscillating fan sitting on the front counter.

From her desk behind the counter, Grace called out, "How was court?"

"The judge gave 'im three years."

"Serves him right, having a good government job like he did and then going and stealing. I'll tell ya, Andy, people are like a bruised apple. At first, it's no big deal, but then it turns bad and by and by it just ruins the whole apple."

I nodded. "So, what was it you needed?"

"That fella with the game department over in Helena called. He said another guy paid a ticket that Bill Kyle gave him on the day that he died." Grace paused and picked up a piece of paper from the clutter on her desk. She held it up before her. The liver spots on the backs of her bony hands seemed to justify the need for the glasses perched on the end of her nose. She scanned the paper for a few seconds and then went on, "He said this ticket was issued at 3:10 p.m. approximately one-tenth mile north of the Miller Diversion on the east side of the river. I guess the guy who got it lives in Bozeman. This game department fella said he's gonna go look him up and ask him if he saw anything peculiar that day."

"Well, that's good to know. Maybe this fella in Bozeman can shed some light on what happened out there."

Grace stood and came to the counter with the paper in her hand. "Here, I may as well give you this."

I took the paper and looked over it. There were numbers beside each time that a citation had been issued. The one that Grace had just told me about that was written at 3:10 was number 43-00213 while the one that Caleb had told me about over the phone that was written at 1:20 was number 43-00211. I said to Grace, "There's still an outstanding ticket that hasn't been paid."

She said, like she'd already told me that, "Well, yeah, I think that's what this game department fella was wondering about, why these two men was quick to settle up and this other guy, whoever he is, hasn't."

I sighed and shook my head. "Bill's ticket book is missing so we don't have any way of finding out who this is, unless we can locate somebody that might have seen something."

"Well, maybe this guy in Bozeman will be able to help."

"I certainly hope so."

From out of the blue, Grace asked, "So whaddaya think about Tom quittin'?"

Since he'd first told me, I'd had time to think about things. I said, "I suspect he'll sleep better at night."

Grace snickered slightly like she agreed as she took a tissue from a side pocket in the dress she was wearing. She dabbed at her nose before saying, "I just wonder if he won't regret not having a regular check every month."

"Well, the county is a regular paycheck but, I promise you, there are some parts of this job that you damned sure are not paid enough to do."

Grace knew what I was talking about as she said simply, "I know."

Switching gears, I asked, "And Glover, has he been around lately?"

Grace shook her head. "That guy is always coming in here. You'd think he was the sheriff."

I laughed. "Maybe when he gets his new man in that job he'll be happy and won't come around so much."

"That would be nice."

Just then the phone rang, and since our conversation had pretty much deteriorated to gossip, I waved goodbye to Grace and headed home. *Tonight*, I said to myself, *would be a good night for a beer at the Antler.*

Grady and I went on home. In a way it felt strange calling the county's cabin home but, for now, it's all I had. Lately, I'd fantasized of what it would be like if Ellen and I had a home together. These were mostly pleasant thoughts unless Charlie found his way into them. But then, I was quick to remind myself that day after tomorrow, he would be going back to the Marines. Maybe next week I could take Ellen to the show. Tonight, however, I was on my own. It had been some time since I'd been to the Antler for anything other than a shower. For supper, I made myself a peanut butter and jam sandwich along with chips and a glass of milk. I'd become more mindful of how I spent my money so that I could treat Ellen in the event we could go out. Still, I reasoned, one or two beers while listening to the Antler's juke box would be okay.

It was a little past seven when Grady and I reached the Antler. There were three vehicles parked out front. One belonged to Jim Meadows, the other two, I didn't know. Dusk had made the light from the neon signs in the windows seem brighter. I could hear voices and laughter and the smack of pool balls and, above it all, "In The Mood" was playing on the juke box. It was a snappy tune, one of my favorites. In a way, I wished that it was playing elsewhere and that Ellen was with me. I knew from high school that she was a good dancer, but tonight was what it was. I looked down at Grady and ruffled his ears, "Hound dog, take yourself a nap. I won't be too long." And then here come Jim Meadows' dog, Buster, his tail wagging. I laughed, "Alright, Grady, you two stay out of trouble."

I opened the door and went inside just as the younger of two men at the pool table yelled out to his friend, "Well, that's some shithouse luck if I ever saw it."

The shooter, a middle-aged man wearing Levis, a green checkered shirt and a gray Stetson came back, "You just don't know talent when you see it." And then they both laughed, probably longer than the comment deserved but, looking at the number of empties on the little table beneath the cue stick rack, it made sense. I sat down on the stool nearest the window with the OPEN sign so I could look out occasionally to see what Grady was up to. Three stools to my left was Jim Meadows and next to him on his left was a stranger. Oscar broke away from them and came my way. "Whaddaya drinkin', Andy?"

"Pabst."

Oscar retrieved my beer from the big cooler behind the bar, opened it and set it in front of me. "So, whatcha been up to?"

"Oh, I went to town today. Had to go to court with Russell."

"Yeah, I heard you was gonna put in a good word for 'im."

"Well, I don't know that it helped."

"What did he get?"

"Three years."

Oscar snorted. "Fifty or 60 years ago they wudda just hung his ass."

I nodded, "Probably so," and then I took a long drink of my beer.

Oscar went on, "I'll tell ya, there ain't no one in this valley, except maybe Gertie, that's gonna shed a tear over him going to prison."

"You're probably right, but three years seems like a long time considering I'd be worm food right now if he hadn't stopped that other fella from shootin' me."

Oscar shook his head. "I don't know, Andy. I guess it's all in how you look at it. I mean he had a job. He didn't need to steal."

I looked away from Oscar, lest my eyes give away what my mind had loaded onto my tongue, *hell, probably a lot of his ill-gotten gain ended up here via Gertie, or him and Gertie together, drinkin' and eatin' steaks that Maude cooked up for 'em.* Fortunately, my common sense intervened, I said simply, "You're probably right."

"Well, yeah, Andy, I think most everybody in the valley looks at it that way."

It occurred to me that the value of my life hadn't really factored into Oscar's reasoning. I said nothing and took another swig of my beer.

Suddenly, Oscar's expression became sour as the door behind me opened. In the mirror above the back bar I could see why. Gertie came up to the side of me. I twisted around on my stool to face her. She appeared to be drunk. A thin column of smoke was drifting up between us from a lit cigarette that she was holding in her right hand, just down from her face, like she wanted it at the ready in case she needed another drag from it. She looked hatefully at me and said sarcastically, "Whaddaya doin', celebratin'?"

"You know that ain't true."

"The hell it ain't."

"How do you figure, Gertie?"

"Today didn't need to happen."

"It didn't?"

She poked the cigarette hand towards me. "No, you cudda just let Russell go after he stopped Sam from shootin' yer ass you ungrateful sonovabitch."

To my left, I could see that the cowboys had stopped playing pool and were staring at me and Gertie. In fact, everybody in the room was looking at us. I wanted badly to say to her, *Yeah, Gertie, today wouldn't have happened if you'd stayed out of the bars.* But that, I knew, would be pouring gas on the fire. I said, "Gertie, you need to let this rest and just go on home."

"Home, why you simple shit, did you forget I ain't got a home thanks to you?"

"Russell broke the law and you and I both know what happened on Bell Mountain wasn't the first time."

Gertie scoffed, "You ain't got no proof of anything else."

The anger within me was about to overtake my patience. I shook my head. "Is that what you want, Gertie? You want me to dig into who butchered Sherm Duke's calves and, I guess while I'm at it, maybe how some of these suspicious fires we've had got started. Is that what you want?"

With no warning, Gertie's left hand came up to slap me. Had she not been drunk I probably wouldn't have been able to deflect it. From across the room, the middle-aged cowboy started towards us intent on, it appeared, defending Gertie's honor. Seeing that he meant trouble, I stood up. He was just about to me when Oscar hollered, "You better hold up Mister, this fella's the law."

The cowboy stopped and looked at me. I was wearing faded Levis, high top white tennis shoes, a blue tee shirt and my baseball cap. A smile slowly came to his face as he sized me up and then he out right laughed. "This guy's the law around here?"

Oscar, nor anyone else, said anything. I could feel my face turning red. Peripherally, I could see that Gertie was smiling, enjoying every second of my embarrassment. Finally, I said to the cowboy, "This is none of your concern."

From the other side of the pool table, the younger cowboy said, "You better butt out, Jake. Can't you see how she is?"

Gertie shot the guy a dirty look and then swiveled her attention back to me. She stared at me for a few seconds before snorting, as if I disgusted her and wasn't worthy of talking to. She then walked away through the bat doors to the café. About this time, "Moonlight Serenade" came on the jukebox. Any other time, it would've been soothing, relaxing, but not tonight. All eyes seemed to be watching me. I stood up, left my half full beer on the bar, and walked out. Nobody said a word, not a single word.

CHAPTER EIGHTEEN

The leaves on the cottonwoods along the Gros Ventre had turned yellow and had begun to fall. Their intense color defined where the river ran. From high up in the mountains, if a person looked down on the valley, it looked like a long, crooked snake. In the mostly brown fields to either side of it were red and black specks as all the cattle were now off of their summer range. They say, whoever they are, that time heals all. This may be true but Thanksgiving was two weeks away, and I still hadn't gone back to the Antler. My run-in with Gertie and the response, or lack of, from the local people there had created a slow burning anger within me. I told myself, *as long as you're the deputy sheriff, you'll never be able to go in there and be just Andy Yarnell.* Boycotting the Antler was not an easy decision. I suspect I would have gone back on it had the forest service not been so accommodating in letting me shower in the fire crew bunkhouse. Fire season was over and I had the facilities all to myself. My decision to stay out of the Antler looked even better when I started noticing Pete Wentzel's pickup parked there a couple of nights a week. Drinking with the hired help when you're the boss was never a good idea. The rumor mill amongst the coffee drinkers over at the Lumberjack was speculating hot and heavy how this union between Pete and Gertie would turn out. None of them saw it ending good for Pete. Mostly, however, my will power to steer clear of the Antler, the valley's social outlet for those wanting a beer, a game of pool and a hamburger while listening to good tunes was due to Ellen. We were seeing one another just about every day, if not for lunch at the forest service she would stop by my cabin before she went home. She had even invited me, with her parents' blessing, out to their place for Sunday dinner on several occasions. And too, our relationship had gone where Charlie had warned me not to go. It was a new untested experience for the both of us, but one that we savored.

Compared to the flurry of activity over the summer things had gotten really quiet, which was ok with me. The medical examiner in Helena had agreed with Herman Cox that Bill's death had been the result of foul play. Somebody had meant to hurt him bad, if not kill him. Beyond this, I didn't know anything new. The ticket recipient from Bozeman who'd been fishing at the diversion that day, hadn't seen anyone else or any other vehicles, except Bill's. The only person who might have seen something was ticket recipient number 43-00212. The fact that he hadn't paid his fine made me all the more suspicious of him, but without the carbon copy from Bill's ticket book I was at a dead end.

It was mid-morning. I was about ten miles north of Cedarville on 29. The sky was completely covered over with dark ashen clouds and there was a stiff wind out of the northeast. Needless to say, I had the windows up and the heater on. I'd gotten several complaints from ranchers about deer hunters trespassing on their property, throwing out empty

SECRETS OF THE GROS VENTRE

beer bottles and leaving gates open that allowed cattle to escape. Naturally, of course, no one caught them in the act. I doubted that I would be lucky enough to find anything that incriminated any of these guys, but I had an obligation to check it out. So, here I was about to turn off onto a two-track when Grace came over my radio.

I keyed the mic, "Mornin', Grace."

"Good morning, Andy, I'm afraid I've got some bad news for you."

A surge of fear shot through me as an explosion of possibilities flooded my mind. I came back, not wanting to hear what she had to say, "For me?"

"Well, I guess what makes it bad for you is you're the one that's gonna have to deliver the message."

Slightly relieved, I still wanted to yell into the mic but I said, trying to keep the frustration from my voice, "So, what's the message?"

"You need to get word to Gertie Jenkins that Russell hung himself last night."

I was stunned but not surprised. "That's too bad."

"Apparently, Russell had just gotten a letter from Gertie wanting a divorce. I guess that, on top of being in prison, was just too much."

I couldn't help but feel sorry for Russell. To have sacrificed his career with the forest service because of Gertie and now this, I said, "Yeah, I suppose it was."

"The prison people want to know where Gertie wants the body shipped to. Sheriff Burns would like you to find that out today by two o'clock so he can let them know. Do you suppose you can do that?"

I shook my head. My new boss seldom ever talked to me directly which, in a way was ok, but at the same time, we weren't building the kind of relationship that I'd had with Tom. I said, "If Gertie's home I'll try to get an answer from her, but if she's not there, I guess the people in Deerlodge will just have to wait."

"Alright, Andy, do what you can. Base clear."

I turned around and headed south on 29. The Wentzel place was east of Cedarville. It would take me about a half hour to get there. I could only imagine the reception I would get from Gertie, as the last time I talked to her was in the Antler when she tried to slap me.

Light fluffy snowflakes had begun to fall by the time I pulled into Pete Wentzel's yard. His place, like so many others in the valley, was located next to the Gros Ventre. Off to my right was a big red barn that was badly in need of paint. It had a hayloft that appeared to be only partially full. Next to this was a corral complex that emptied out into a large pasture adjacent to the river. To my left was a small bunkhouse and a shop. Directly in front of me, beneath several huge cottonwood trees, was the house. It was made of logs that were weathered and gray, as were all of the buildings except for the barn, which was built with milled boards. Two rocking chairs sat on the covered front porch of the house. I envisioned Pete and Gertie sitting out here in the evening. A waist high fence made of wood posts and hog wire with a wooden top rail surrounded the yard. The grass looked to be mostly dead. I stopped my truck in front of the house and got out. Blue smoke was coming from a rusted stovepipe protruding from its dirt roof. The wind was stiff, swirling snowflakes around my face and cottonwood leaves at my feet. As I was going through the gate I saw the white curtains in the window to the left of the door part, just slightly, so the person looking out could see me but I couldn't them. Within a few seconds the hand holding the curtains open went away. I'd not made it off the bare, hard-packed dirt path that lead to the porch when the front door opened. It was not Pete, as I had expected, but Gertie. She was dressed like a man in Levis, a solid brown flannel shirt and cowboy boots. Her hair, long and straight, hung down her back. She said, "What the hell do you want?"

From the look in her eyes and the tone of her voice I could tell that nothing had changed from that night at the Antler. I thought, *well fine, I'll not sugar coat it.* I said, allowing my eyes to hate too, "Russell's dead. He hung himself." And then I stood still, peering through the snow which was heavier now, looking for the effects of my words, kind of like a hunter does his bullet after shooting at an animal. It appeared that I had missed.

There were no tears. It was more like I was bothering her. Finally, she said, "I'm sorry he's dead."

"The prison folks want to know where to ship his body?"

There was no thinking about it. She came back as quick as a rattlesnake strikes. "Ship? I can't afford to bury him. I'm still making payments to the court, or have you forgotten that? I don't know what to tell you. The state took him away, I guess they can bury him."

Gertie's cold indifference made me want to fire back at her hard and mean. My mind, and I suppose my eyes did too, went there, *Why, you worthless bitch, after all you've put him through, you won't even bring him home.* I allowed some time for her to absorb this before saying, "Alright, Gertie, if that's what you want me to tell them, I will."

In the biting cold, she folded her arms across her chest and frowned at me for having judged her, "Money don't grow on trees, you know. Hell, if it was up to Russell, he'd be ok if they was to just haul him up in the mountains and leave him for the critters."

I nodded, as I could hear Russell saying something like that and mean it, but I said, "You know the state won't do that."

"Well then, quit badgering me about it. They can just do what they're gonna do."

"Ok, Gertie, I'll tell them." I started to go but then added, "Is this where you get your mail these days? The prison will likely send you a copy of Russell's death certificate and any personal effects he might have had."

She nodded and, right away, went inside. I wasn't certain, but I thought I heard her crying.

On the drive back to Cedarville, I couldn't get my mind off of the fact that Russell would never leave the prison grounds, that they would put him in a simple pine box and bury him in the prison cemetery. Shortly before two o'clock, I called the sheriff and told him that's what they should do.

CHAPTER NINETEEN

One of the good things about fall and the cold weather was that it put an end to the flies. And too, if I was at the cabin, I had a legitimate need to keep a fire going in the stove. Lying in bed at night it was soothing, listening to it snap and pop along with music on the radio. I fantasized about the day when Ellen could be there with me. But the nights also gave me time to ponder the things that had carried over from the summer. About two weeks ago, Betty Duke went back to Sherm. Katie, on the other hand, stayed with my mother. So far, Sherm had been on his best behavior. However, the Lumberjack coffee drinkers were making bets that this wouldn't last till spring. As for me, I fully expected to have to go back out to the Duke place one day. I just hoped that Betty would be ok when that day came as I also believed, that deep down, Sherm wasn't right in the head. And then there was the matter of Bill Kyle's death. By now everybody in the valley had an opinion as to what had happened. The consensus of the Lumberjack crew was that Bill had given somebody a ticket who got mad and decided to give him a whipping and it just got out of hand. The speculation as to who might have done this was as varied as rocks in the river but the one thing that most agreed upon, after Sherm's alibi proved out, was that it had to be somebody from outside the valley. *Likely some city fella with a few beers under his belt*, they'd said. *Probably come over from Billings. There is some rough characters over there, don't you know.*

Sometime past midnight fatigue finally turned off my mind, but not for long, as at 5:17 I was awake thinking about Bill's ticket book. I got up and walked across the cold wood floor with my bare feet to let Grady out for a nature call. I stuck my head outside. There was about an inch of snow on the ground. I could see my breath in the air. Overhead, the stars were bright suggesting the day would warm up. *This snow will probably be gone by ten o'clock*, I said to myself. And then my mind went right back to the depths of last night, *today might be your last chance till spring to search for that book.* And so, when the sun was well above the horizon and I'd had hotcakes and eggs and all the coffee I could stand, I headed for the Miller Diversion. In the past, I'd scoured the east side of the river to the point I could easily recreate every tree stump, cow trail and bush in my mind. The book just wasn't there, but then I was quick to recall why the game department people and I had quit looking. Common sense told us that the book came out of Bill's pocket and floated downstream to who knows where, or number 43-00212 took it and probably burned it. Nonetheless, Grady and I started off from the Diversion parking area down through the frost laden brush beneath the cottonwoods. My breath pulsed out in front of me, momentarily hanging in the air before dying away. The day was not warming as quickly as I had hoped, but on we went staying close to the river bank. We came to and passed by the place where I'd hauled

Bill out of the water. About 50 yards beyond this, the willows got really thick causing me to jog inland a good way to get around them. I'd just said to Grady, "Hound dog, I think we're wastin' our time this far from the river," when my eye spotted a cream-colored piece of what looked like paper lodged against the base of a sagebrush plant. I quickly went over and picked it up. My heart rate jumped. It was no more than an inch across but printed on it in black were the letters, Mont. The edges of the paper were tattered like it'd been chewed on. And then, like this shred of evidence had been purposely offered up, I saw over to my right a wood rat midden. It was a pile of tightly compacted sticks about four feet high and maybe five feet wide at the base. I walked over to it. I shook my head and smiled. Like the proverbial trail of bread crumbs, scattered bits of yellow paper lay near the entrance to the midden. I picked up one of the larger pieces. It had part of a person's signature. Another piece had a date written on it. I had found, or so I hoped, Bill's ticket book. I was consumed with excitement as I hunted for a big stick to tear open the midden. Finally, after locating a piece of a dead cottonwood limb about five feet long, I went to work on the rat's house. At first it was resistant to my probes, but then it started to come apart and with it their treasures. There were pieces of cans, a spoon, a black button, a nickle, part of a leather glove, a red bead and then the jackpot, a nest area lined with shredded yellow paper, leaves and grass. I quickly bent over and scooped up this tangled mass and carried it to a large flat cottonwood stump that was nearby and set it down. I then started to pick through it. Parts of names, dates, locations, violations, times – it was like a pile of jigsaw puzzle pieces, I just needed to put it together. It looked like this would take some time but then, suddenly, I happened to brush through a part of the pile and there it was, intact, like it was meant to be, *Charlie Lujack*. The impact of seeing Charlie's signature suddenly made me weak. I dropped down on my knees in the snow and mud next to the stump. I read the name again, foolishly hoping that I'd made a mistake, but it was still the same. Closing my eyes, I sighed and briefly shook my head, I whispered, "Damn you, Charlie." My mind's eye went to the obvious. Images of Ellen and what we had become in Charlie's absence stood out all bright and good, but then reality abruptly took me away as a wisp of wind rolled another shred of paper on the stump. Like I needed more convincing, fate or God or Bill Kyle's ghost or whoever is in charge of making things right offered up the numbers, 0212. My thoughts raced ahead to when I would have to tell Ellen and her parents and Phil Lujack yelling at me, *All this means is he got a ticket that he didn't pay. It don't mean he killed that game warden.* He had me there, or so I wanted in the worst way to believe. I knew we'd be alone in this faulty belief. It'd never pass muster with the Lumberjack patrons, nor for that matter, probably most everyone in the valley. The same would hold true for Bill's boss, and mine too. I could make the new sheriff, and myself, look good by solving Bill's murder. And too, Roy Glover's constant sniping at my abilities would likely hold less water. But then, suddenly, this one-sided pep talk vanished as I saw what pursuing Charlie might do to my relationship with Ellen. The sadness was overwhelming. It caused me to lean against the stump. Hot tears came to my eyes, within seconds they began to trickle down my cheeks. Sensing my emotion, Grady nuzzled in under my left arm and began licking my chin. I looked down at him and smiled. "Oh, hound dog, what would I do without you?" Grady looked up at me and pawed my chest a couple of times. "All right," I said, "maybe we should go."

After taking a few minutes to sort the paper scraps from the grass and leaves, I put all 27 of them in my coat pocket and started back to my pickup. What I was going to do with them was still a coin toss in my mind. As I drove back down 29, I was now dreading having to face Ellen. She was coming to my cabin for lunch today. Her folks had invited my mother and I to Thanksgiving dinner. My mother, of course, was insistent that she bring something. Ellen was to have consulted with her mother last night and let me know today. And what was I to say, *Oh, yes, my mother would be happy to bring pumpkin pie. And oh, by the way, did you know Charlie killed the game warden? Won't that make for great Thanksgiving dinner conversation?*

Suddenly, my bath of sarcasm was interrupted by the radio. I had to make a conscience effort to glean it from my voice. "Good morning, Grace."

"Mornin' Andy, just thought I'd remind you that today is timesheet day."

"Ok, I'll drop it in the mail after lunch."

"Thank-you. Anything else going on out there?"

The words slipped off my tongue like there was never any doubt they would. "No, it's pretty quiet." And, in the next instant, guilt and shame set in.

"All right, Andy, base clear."

I said to myself, *Well, there was the first lie.* I sighed and drove on.

It was about a quarter till twelve when I got to my cabin. I had 15 minutes to decide if I was going to tell another lie. I was stoking the fire when I heard Ellen pull up out front and then her car door slam. Grady barked. And then her voice, happy and cheerful, "Oh, I see you, Grady. How's my favorite dog in the whole world? Huh? Are you having a good day?" And then she laughed, the sound of her voice getting closer and then the door opened. She was smiling, her eyes bright and seemingly unaware of any of the bad things that had happened over the summer. She came to me and kissed me on the mouth and then drew back slightly. "And how's my favorite deputy sheriff in the whole wide world?"

I made myself smile. She didn't deserve anything less. I said, as I wrapped her into a tight hug, "I'm doing good." Over her shoulder and across the room where my coat was hanging on the wall, I could see that the button on the pocket containing the pieces of paper was securely fastened.

EPILOGUE

It was the 19th of June, 1945 when the messenger from Fremont stopped at the store and asked for directions to the Lujack place. Niko happened to be working that day. She suspected right away why the guy was there, but what else was she to do but tell him who she was, and what else was he to do but give her the telegram. She collapsed behind the counter and somehow Louie, the store owner, was summoned and he called up to the county's cabin where I happened to be doing paperwork. I went right away and helped Niko to my pickup and drove her to the little house just outside of Cedarville where Ellen and our new baby boy lived.

Charlie never came home. They buried him in a nice cemetery right there on Okinawa. I never told Ellen, nor anyone, what I'd found along the Gros Ventre. I always had my suspicions as to what they, as a family, knew about Charlie's activities the day Bill Kyle was killed, but I never went there, not even once. A few days after we received the telegram, I took the sealed envelope that contained the pieces of paper with me to the county's cabin. And even though it was a hot day, I built a fire in the stove on the pretext of making myself a pot of coffee and I burned them, one or two at a time until they were gone.

ABOUT THE AUTHOR

Secrets of the Gros Ventre is the ninth book by award winning author, John Hansen. For information concerning all of his books please visit his website at https://johnhansen.net/. John and his wife Debi live in Western Montana.